TH

**Return this item by
the last date shown.**

Items may be renewed
by telephone or at
www.eastrenfrewshire.gov.uk/libraries

E. V. Thompson was born in London. After spending nine years in the Royal Navy, he served as a Vice Squad policeman in Bristol, became an investigator for British Overseas Airways (during which time he was seconded to the Hong Kong Police Narcotics Bureau), then headed Rhodesia's Department of Civil Aviation Security Section. While in Rhodesia, he published over 200 short stories before moving back to England to become a full-time award-winning writer. His first novel, *Chase the Wind*, the opening book in the Retallick saga, won the Best Historical Novel Award, and since then more than thirty novels have won him thousands of admirers around the world. In 2011 E. V. Thompson was awarded an MBE for services to literature and to the Cornish community. He died peacefully at his Launceston home in 2012; *The Bonds of Earth* was his last book.

THE BONDS OF EARTH

1837. When rich deposits of copper ore are discovered near Bodmin Moor, a huge influx of out-of-work miners flock to the area from Cornwall's far west, bringing with them problems alien to the hard-working but easy-going countrymen. Young Goran Trebartha, whose working life is divided between two farms, finds himself caught between the seemingly incompatible cultures when he meets and gets to know the daughters of a mine captain who settles nearby. Avarice and intrigue, the vicissitudes of farming life and the sheer desperation of hungry miners all add to the bewildering changes that will irrevocably alter the course of Goran's life.

E. V. THOMPSON

THE BONDS
OF EARTH

Complete and Unabridged

CHARNWOOD
Leicester

First published in Great Britain in 2012 by
Robert Hale Limited
London

First Charnwood Edition
published 2013
by arrangement with
Robert Hale Limited
London

A catalogue record for this book is available
from the British Library.

ISBN 978–1–4448–1775–1

Published by
F. A. Thorpe (Publishing)
Anstey, Leicestershire

Set by Words & Graphics Ltd.
Anstey, Leicestershire
Printed and bound in Great Britain by
T. J. International Ltd., Padstow, Cornwall

1

1837

Making his way back to Roach Farm after a fruitless search on the high moor for Agnes Roach's missing milk-cow, Goran Trebartha decided to take a short cut through a strip of land that extended like a warning finger from the vast Spurre Estate, barring access from a large part of Agnes's farm to the wide upland expanse of Bodmin Moor.

Although there was a proliferation of 'Private' and 'Trespassers will be prosecuted' notices posted around this small outreach of the estate there was little reason for anyone to want to trespass here. The steep granite-strewn slope had not supported a profitable crop for many years and gorse and ferns proliferated. There was also woodland of sorts here, a number of trees having been planted by long forgotten members of the Spurre family.

The gorse, dense in places, hid many springs from which a skein of streams tumbled down the hillside to add zest to the otherwise lethargic River Lynher on its meandering course through Cornwall from the heights of Bodmin Moor to feed the tidal River Tamar on the south coast of the county.

It was as he skirted one of these springs that Goran heard a sound so alien to his surroundings that it brought him to an immediate and disbelieving halt. It was the sound of laughter — the laughter of young girls — and was coming from within an extensive clump of gorse bushes.

The area was familiar to him, his cottage home being on an adjacent farm, and he knew there were no girls living in the immediate vicinity. Indeed, there were very few dwellings. The moor which towered above the surrounding countryside on this side of the river was an inhospitable place and communities had tended to choose the comparative shelter of Cornish valleys. Only an occasional remote farm like those worked by Agnes Roach and her brother Elworthy clung tenaciously to the slopes of the moor, its occupants eking out a meagre yet fiercely independent existence.

Pushing his way through the needle-sharp foliage of the gorse, Goran suddenly emerged into a small clearing. Here, the bubbling waters of the spring had carved out a crystal clear pool of water bordered by tiny island clumps of both soft and compact rushes.

In the pool was the source of the merriment he had heard. A young girl of about three or four years of age was seated in the water, splashing two others. One, aged about sixteen, was also sitting in the water. The third, possibly a year or two older, was standing in the pool laughingly protesting at the young child's antics.

All were stark naked.

The youngest of the trio had her back to him and, unaware of his sudden unexpected arrival, continued splashing happily. The others saw him immediately, but their reactions differed.

The second girl screamed and hunched forward in the water, arms crossed in a vain attempt to cover newly matured breasts. The oldest girl was also startled, but only for a few moments. Aware she could not cover herself with any real degree of modesty, she dropped her hands to her side and lifted her chin arrogantly. 'If you've seen all you want and have finished gawking you can make yourself useful and throw me one of those towels you're almost standing on.'

Startled though he was at coming across three naked girls so unexpectedly, he was relieved when he heard her speak. His first thought had been that he had stumbled upon some young residents of the estate on which he was trespassing enjoying a private bathe. Had that been so he would have been in serious trouble, but this girl's accent was decidedly working-class Cornish. He doubted whether she and the others had more entitlement to be here than had he.

Recovering his senses, he picked up the largest of three threadbare lengths of towelling lying at his feet. Trying not to look directly at the girl standing so boldly before him, he screwed it into a loose bundle and threw it in her direction.

Deftly catching it, she wrapped it about her body with a relieved haste which belied her brazen attempt at nonchalance. Now feeling less vulnerable, she demanded, 'What do you mean by coming here and frightening the life out of us . . . have you been peeping at us through the bushes?'

'I haven't been peeping at anyone. I've been

up on the moor searching for Agnes Roach's milk-cow which broke its way out of her field and I was on my way back to her farm when I heard you all laughing. I've never seen any girls up around here before so I came to find out what was going on.'

'Well, now you've seen more of us than anyone else ever has you can go on your way again.'

At that moment the girl who was crouching low over the surface of the shallow pool in a vain attempt to hide her nakedness, pleaded, 'Morwenna, will you give me *my* towel, I'm *freezing* in here?'

Stepping clear of the pool, Morwenna picked up a towel and took it to the shivering girl at the same time saying to the youngest one, 'Do you want a towel too?'

Instead of replying to the question, the young girl asked, 'Do we have to go now?' Looking at Goran accusingly, she added, 'We were having fun before you came.'

Stepping out of the pool once more, Morwenna said to Goran, 'I thought I told you to go. We haven't seen anything of any old cow, so you can go and look for her somewhere else. Who are you, anyway?'

'Goran Trebartha, from the cottage at Elworthy Farm. I work for widow Agnes Roach . . . at least, I do in the afternoon. Mornings I work for Elworthy Coumbe, Agnes's brother, on the farm next to hers.' He turned his head away as he spoke, to avoid watching the girls as they dressed.

'You might as well be talking of places on the

4

moon for all I know about 'em, but I *do* know we were all enjoying a bathe before you came along,' Morwenna commented.

'You are lucky it was me and not Marcus Grimble, Sir John Spurre's head gamekeeper. He'd not have bothered to come through the gorse to find out who was in here. He'd have put a blast of bird-shot into the bushes and ordered whoever it was in here to come out before he fired something heavier.'

'He wouldn't do that . . . it might well kill someone!'

'That wouldn't worry him, he likes boasting about the number of Frenchies he killed in the war against Napoleon. If he shot you he'd make up some story about why he did it — and Sir John would back him up. There's more than one miner who's gone home with his backside peppered with buckshot after poaching on the Spurre Estate.'

'Our dad's a mine *captain*,' the small girl spoke again, more cheerfully than before. Pulling on her dress without drying herself properly, she had encountered problems pulling it down over her wet body. Now, the task satisfactorily completed she wriggled herself into the dress more comfortably and, smiling innocently at Goran, added, 'I'm Jennifer, Jennifer Pyne.'

She had an infectious smile, but at that moment Goran heard the baying of a hound somewhere in the near-distance — and the sound alarmed him.

'That's probably Grimble now, walking a young hound. We'd all better get off Spurre land

5

before the hound gets our scent. Quick, follow me!'

For a moment it seemed Morwenna would argue with him, but, as Goran pushed his way through the gorse, returning the way he had come, the second of the three sisters snatched up Jennifer. When she followed him, Morwenna hurriedly picked up the towels and hurried after them.

Goran led the three girls between trees and gorse bushes until they reached a free-stone granite wall which marked the boundary of the estate. Choosing a spot where a number of pieces of stone had been dislodged, he shinned over then turned to take Jennifer from her sister. Lifting her over the wall he deposited her in the field which was part of Agnes Roach's farm, before helping the sister over. He would have done the same for Morwenna but she ignored his proffered hand and jumped heavily to the ground.

Their escape had only just been achieved when a young foxhound came into view. Seeing Goran and the girls beyond the low part of the wall it bounded towards them baying enthusiastically, the sound carrying high notes of immaturity.

When the animal reached the wall it scrambled over clumsily and, arriving among the small party greeted them with tail-wagging enthusiasm.

Tentatively at first, but with increasing delight, the girls returned the affection of their new-found canine friend, much to the displeasure of the red-faced, breathless gamekeeper who appeared at the wall some moments later.

'Leave that hound alone, it's a working animal not a pet. If it gets too friendly with people it'll need to be put down.'

'It may be a working dog when it's on your side of the wall, Mr Grimble, but over here on Mrs Roach's land it seems to like making friends.'

'It's a nice dog . . . it just licked my face!' Jennifer Pyne's words were accompanied by an expression of distaste, swiftly belied by a delighted giggle.

'It's not supposed to be friendly,' Marcus Grimble scowled, adding a loud-voiced 'Come here!' to the hound.

'Does it have a name?' The question came from the middle sister.

'I'll give it more than a name if it doesn't come here when I call it . . . Come here, damn you!'

Recognizing the authority in Grimble's shouted command, the young foxhound abandoned its new found friends. Leaping at the wall it made a splay-legged attempt to make it to the other side, giving a yelp of pain when it was helped none-too-gently by the gamekeeper.

In response to the murmured protests from the three girls, Grimble said, 'Unless I'm very much mistaken you've been trespassing on the estate . . . and there's no good trying to deny it. The hound may be disobedient but there's nothing wrong with its nose. It followed your scent straight here.'

'It probably had nothing to do with the dog's

nose,' Goran retorted. 'The girls were larking about and making a noise. You wouldn't have been able to hear them but the dog could.'

The explanation was feasible enough to give Grimble pause but, reluctant to accept it, he said, 'That might be so, or it might not. Whichever, you make certain you stay off the estate . . . all of you. If I catch you trespassing you'll be taken straight before the magistrate.'

'Then be sure you keep your hounds on Spurre land and don't let 'em come over here,' Goran replied, ' . . . another thing, the hunt damaged Mrs Roach's hedges last season and no one's been around to fix 'em yet. As a result her milk-cow got out today. Should anything have happened to it Sir John will be getting a bill from her, and if I know Sir John he'll be deducting it from someone's pay.'

Goran was aware that in addition to his game-keeper's duties Marcus Grimble was responsible for the foxhounds and would be expected to right any damage caused during hunting.

'You have far too much to say for yourself, young Trebartha. It'll land you in trouble one day. You and your friends would do well to keep out of my way.'

With this the gamekeeper stooped down behind the wall to slip a loop of rope around the fox-hound's neck before brutally tugging the animal around in order to return the way they had come.

2

'What a horrid man!'

The remark was made by the second of the three girls, who Goran had heard called 'Nessa' by her younger sister.

'He's not particularly nice,' Goran agreed, 'but what he says is quite true. Anyone caught trespassing on the Spurre Estate is taken before a magistrate who always points out that there are a great many signs around the estate giving warning that it's private land.'

'You must have been trespassing or you wouldn't have found us there,' Nessa pointed out.

'I *was* trespassing,' Goran admitted, 'but only because it was a short cut back to the farm where I work, I was keeping a sharp look-out for anyone belonging to the estate — and wasn't contaminating the water from one of their springs by bathing in it! What made you choose to bathe there anyway? Where do you come from? I haven't seen you around this way before.'

'Where we come from is none of your business,' Morwenna said sharply, feeling she had been left out of the conversation for long enough.

'True enough,' Goran shrugged, 'but if I knew where you lived I could tell you the best way to get back there without going on Sir John's land. I could also probably tell you of a better place to

9

bathe than in water from a spring on the estate
. . . You were stupid to be there in the first place.
As I've said, there are plenty of signs telling you
it's private.'

'That's all very well if you can read. I've never
bothered to learn and don't see any reason to.'

'Nessa can read,' Jennifer said seriously. 'She
reads stories to me sometimes. She's going to
teach *me* to read too.'

When Goran looked at Nessa questioningly,
she said, 'I saw the signs telling people to keep
out but Morwenna wouldn't listen to me.'

'I don't take any notice of such things,'
Morwenna said defiantly, 'I'll go wherever I like.'

Aware Morwenna was being deliberately
confrontational, Nessa said placatingly to Goran,
'It was just as well you came along when you
did, Pa wouldn't have been very happy if we'd
got into trouble. We've just moved here from
West Cornwall because he's been asked to open
up a mine a little way along the edge of the moor
from here.'

Startled by her news, Goran queried, 'Whereabouts?'

There *were* mines around the fringes of
the moor, many mines, but they were well to the
south of the Spurre Estate and the farms of
Agnes Roach and Elworthy Coumbe. He knew
little about any of them even though his father
had been a miner who died in a mining accident.
The mining and farming communities chose not
to mix with each other.

Observing the sudden tightening of Morwenna's
expression and trying to avoid another bad-tempered

outburst from her, Goran added quickly, 'I know the area around here as well as anyone and could probably point out a spring that's closer to your home and more private than the one you were using today. There are quite a few of them coming off the moor, although some are no more than a trickle when there hasn't been much rain up there.'

'What you mean is you'll show us a place where you'll be able to watch us bathing without us seeing you,' Morwenna suggested spitefully.

'Please yourself. You can find your own place . . . find your own way home too, as far as I'm concerned, I'm just trying to be helpful.'

'Take no notice of Morwenna: she's been an old misery-guts ever since we arrived here,' Nessa said, adding in explanation, 'She had a sweetheart down west and was hoping he'd ask her to marry him before we left.'

'He would have done,' Morwenna said, heatedly. 'I don't know why we had to leave there at all!'

'Pa explained that to us — and even promised to give Alan work if he wanted to come with us.'

Addressing Goran once more, Nessa explained, 'Alan was Morwenna's sweetheart, but we had to leave because the mine Pa was managing was almost played out and Alan didn't want to come with us. Mr Williams, the man who owned our mine, told Pa they'd found copper around this way and he'd bought mining rights for some parts of the moor. When Pa came to look around here a few weeks ago he found somewhere that looks promising this side of Hawkswood. A few

11

of the miners Pa brought with him have put up a house for us nearby. It's not much of a place at the moment but Ma says she's lived in worse. If the mine comes good Pa's promised to have a really big house built for us, one where we can all have our own bedrooms.'

'You don't have to tell our life story to every stranger we meet up with,' Morwenna said, peevishly. 'We hardly know the first thing about *him*.'

Jennifer had been following the conversation and now she said unhappily, 'I don't want to sleep in a room on my own. I like us all sleeping in a bed together.'

'Well we won't have to worry about it for a long time yet,' Nessa said comfortingly. Turning back to Goran she said, 'Now you know where we live can you think of a place where we can bathe without being spied on?'

'I think so. It'll take me out of my way but I'll show it to you now. It's quite a good spot. Although it's on Agnes Roach's land it's right at the top end where it borders her brother's farm. It's moorland really, and far from both farmhouses. Agnes is getting too old to toil all the way up there even if she did have objections and Elworthy wouldn't bother you. He never bothers anyone and is far too busy doing things around his own farm to notice what's going on elsewhere. It's pretty well hidden from view too. I sometimes put one or two sheep up there, although more usually it's the milk-cow . . . and that reminds me, I'm supposed to be looking for her! I need to find her before dark because she'll need milking and we have to make butter for market day in Launceston. Come on, I'll show you where the spring is.'

'If we do decide to use it for bathing you can be sure we'll have a good look around each time, in case you're hiding anywhere to watch us!'

Nessa began to apologize to Goran at her sister's words but stopped when he smiled at her. He had only just met the three girls but he felt it might be pleasant having them around . . . especially Nessa.

★ ★ ★

Agnes Roach was not amused when Goran told her of his encounter with the girls — omitting their state of undress when he had first discovered them. 'There's me thinking you'd come to grief on the moor and all the while you were passing the time of day with some girls! As for the milking-cow, it's as well she went off in the direction of the village and not up on the moor. At least there was someone down there with sense enough to recognize her and bring her back, even though I had to give him threepence for doing it. I ought to dock it off your wages.'

'Would you rather I'd have left the girls where they were so they could get caught by Marcus Grimble?'

Goran was not too concerned by Agnes's threats. She was basically a kind and generous woman and he was aware she liked neither Grimble nor his employer.

Capitulating, Agnes said, 'You know the

13

answer to that. They were lucky you got to them before Grimble did . . . but where's this house of theirs and the mine their father's supposed to be captain of? I've heard no mention of it from anyone hereabouts?'

'I never actually saw the cottage, but it sounds as though the mine's going to be up on the moor, just beyond our high grazing lands.'

'Is it, now? Well they're not driving any road through my farm to get at it.'

'I shouldn't think they'll need to. As they're already up there and built their cottage it must mean they've found another way to reach the spot — probably by coming across the moor.'

'You're probably right, but it makes me uneasy. When miners start working in an area they're not particular who they upset and have no consideration for anyone or anything but themselves and their mining. All they're interested in is making a profit for them as are backing them — 'adventurers' I think they're called. For the most part these adventurers are men like Sir John Spurre, paying little attention to the rights of others.'

Her mood changed suddenly and, looking at Goran speculatively, Agnes said, 'But you might not have wasted all your time today after all, young Goran. Now you've met with this mine captain's daughters we might be able to make some use of it if you get to know him and can find out what it is he expects to find and how far the mine is likely to extend. I'd like to know how deep and in which direction they're going to be tunnelling. We can't have land collapsing under our sheep or cows, or us when we're driving a loaded wagon. Besides, if he's coming beneath our farm there are dues to be paid. You might be able to find out what it is they're up to. When you do, be sure you let me know about it.'

'I don't think they are likely to affect us too much and we might be able to sell milk, butter and eggs to them . . . wheat too if you'd let me till a couple of the fields down by the river.'

For almost as long as he had been working for Agnes, Goran had wanted to sow wheat on the farm, but she had always dismissed the idea — unreasonably, in his opinion. He felt it would be profitable, especially during the times when it was in short supply — as it was at the moment — but Agnes Roach was in no mood to change her mind on the subject.

'If you think you have time to do all the work involved in growing and harvesting wheat then it's obvious I'm not giving you enough to do about the farm. Now, the cow's in the shed waiting to be milked and there's butter to be made; you'd best be getting on with it if you want to be home before nightfall.'

★   ★   ★

When Goran returned home to the Trebarthas' small cottage on Elworthy Farm that evening and told his mother about the events of the day, he found her no more enthusiastic about the new mine than Agnes had been.

A small, tidy woman, Mabel Trebartha had not had the easiest of lives. Married to a

15

tin-miner and widowed when Goran was seven years old she had needed to work hard to bring him up 'properly', despite suffering from debilitating asthma. When Goran reached the age of ten she had been fortunate enough to find work in the house of Elworthy Coumbe, the simple-minded brother of Agnes Roach, and she and Goran moved into a small cottage that was part of the Elworthy Farm complex.

Her work involved running the house for Elworthy and carrying out light work about the farm, but it was not long before Goran began working for both Elworthy and Agnes on their adjacent farms. With the income he brought in, although it was by no means generous, she was able to take things easier than at any time in her adult life. Goran's news of the opening of a mine near the farm troubled her.

'I don't like the thought of having a mine as close to us as this one,' she said, ladling out a thick potato and ham-bone stew from a pot suspended by a hook above the open fire. Carrying the brimming plate to the table and placing it carefully in front of him, she added, 'Miners bring trouble with them. If the mine doesn't produce as well as it should there'll be hungry families scouring the countryside for anything they can lay their hands on to keep from starving and nothing will be safe. If they strike it rich the miners will spend much of their earnings on drink and causing mayhem as a result. I'd sooner they all stayed up Caradon way where they belong. That's plenty close enough.'

'I thought you'd be understanding, Ma,

especially as Pa was a miner.'

'It's *because* he was a miner that I know what we can expect from them! Your pa was a good man, but he was as wild as any of them before I married him. Mind you, my mother used to tell me that was the reason I married him in the first place. Perhaps she was right, but she never really approved of him, even though he was as good to her as he was to me. Mind you, things weren't easy for us and living among miners and their families was very different to the life I'd known as the daughter of a farm worker.'

Intrigued by what she had revealed to him, Goran said, 'You've never talked very much about your life before you married, Ma. How did you and Pa come to meet each other?'

'Hard times are best forgotten, but the way you found those miner's girls today has brought back memories. Your pa and me met up in a very similar manner. It was harvest time on the farm and rain was threatening, so everyone who could be rounded up was working hard to gather the crop in before the weather broke. Then someone noticed that a couple of old ewes being fattened up for the winter had got out of their field. As I couldn't work as hard as the others I was sent off to fetch 'em back. They led me a merry dance right up to the moor but your pa happened to be up there. He'd hurt a hand and was off work. When he saw what was happening he headed off the ewes and turned 'em back. Then he helped me drive 'em back to the farm.'

Giving the fire an unnecessary poke with the iron rod that was used as a poker, her mind took

17

her back many years. Gazing into the red ashes that had been stirred into flickering life, she continued, 'I was just seventeen at the time and don't think I'd ever spoken to a miner before, but we got to talking about his work and how he'd come to hurt his hand and I thought it must be very exciting to be working far underground doing something so dangerous. Well, when we got the sheep back to where they belonged he helped me build up the wall where they'd got out, then he went back to the place where he lived, close to the mine.

'I thought that was the last I'd ever see of him and was very disappointed, but the very next day he came back to the farm asking if we had any butter and eggs we could sell him. I knew he must have really come back to see *me* because while we were bringing the sheep back he'd told me his family kept chickens up at the mine. I was thrilled to bits because he seemed so much more exciting than the boys I'd met around the farm.

'He came back a few times after that and I began walking out with him. Ma never approved but Pa was relieved I'd found someone. Because of my asthma I couldn't work as hard as other girls and I think he believed he'd need to look after me for the rest of his life!

'Well, we got married and had you and although life was never easy we were happy enough. Then, when times became really hard, he took a job on a mine that had a bad record for accidents. I didn't want him to and had we not been so desperate for money he'd never have gone there. But he did . . . and only a couple of weeks later part of one of the tunnels collapsed killing him and three other miners.'

Recalling her husband's death distressed Mabel and bringing herself back to the present with a visible effort, she said, 'But there's no sense dwelling on such things. Your pa's been gone a long time now and so have my ma and pa too. All that's in the past, but I'd be much happier if mines and everything to do with them stayed well away from us.'

Aware how upset his mother was, Goran said, 'Don't let it worry you overmuch, Ma, I don't suppose I'll ever meet up with the girls again. Agnes wants me to find out in which direction their pa thinks he'll be tunnelling, but he and his miners will have plenty of work to do up on the moor so I doubt if they'll be any bother to us down here.'

3

In spite of the assurances he had made to his mother, Goran nursed a secret hope that he *might* meet the Pyne girls again. The life he led coupled with the long hours he worked meant he had come into contact with very few girls — and his encounter with Morwenna, Nessa and Jennifer had been revealing in every sense of the word.

Because of this, the freestone wall that formed a boundary between open moorland and the two farms of Elworthy Coumbe and Agnes Roach received more attention from him than ever before and every loose granite stone was carefully — and slowly — replaced, in the hope that while he was working he might catch sight of one or more of the Pyne girls exploring the moor on which the family had made its home.

Engaged in this self-imposed activity a few days later, his mind far away, he was startled to suddenly see a young boy of about thirteen years of age scramble untidily over the wall from the Spurre Estate, at the spot where he and the Pyne girls had made their escape from gamekeeper Grimble.

The boy jumped to the ground heavily and fell to his knees, but, scrambling quickly to his feet, ran in Goran's direction and was momentarily lost behind one of the clumps of gorse scattered about the field.

Leaving what he was doing, Goran ran to intercept him and the two met when the boy appeared from behind the gorse. He was in such a blind panic, an expression of sheer terror on his face, that he never even noticed Goran until he was almost upon him.

Changing direction immediately the boy tried to bypass him but Goran was too quick, grabbing first the threadbare, collarless shirt he was wearing, then one of the boy's arms.

He fought desperately to free himself but Goran only tightened his grip.

'Hey . . . Hey . . . What's the matter . . . ? What's your hurry?'

'Let me go . . . '

Catching the free arm that was flailing around in the boy's desperate bid to break free, Goran said, 'Calm down! If you're in trouble tell me, I might be able to help.'

The frantic efforts gradually subsided, more a result of exhaustion than from Goran's attempts to calm him and, breathing heavily, the boy demanded, 'Who are you . . . do you work for the big estate?'

'No, I work here, on the farm . . . but what's happened in there to frighten you so much?'

Still breathless, the boy looked at Goran uncertainly and he saw tears springing up in his eyes.

'Look, I'm nothing at all to do with the estate and am not particularly friendly with anyone there, so you can tell me what's happened.'

The boy held back for as long as he could but then, shoulders sagging, he said tearfully, 'It's Pa

21

. . . he's caught his leg in a trap in there and is bleeding . . . bleeding bad.'

'He's caught in a mantrap?'

Goran was horrified, mantraps were a fearful form of deterrent used for many years by landowners to trap poachers. Made of iron and powerfully sprung, their sharp teeth were intended to trap a man's leg and hold him until he was found by a gamekeeper . . . or until he bled to death. Such 'deterrents' had been banned by law some years before but Goran had seen one hanging on the wall of the local blacksmith's shop and it was rumoured such barbaric instruments were still being laid in the woods on the Spurre Estate, a rumour deliberately perpetuated by the gamekeepers.

'Where's your pa now?'

'Still in the trap, I couldn't free him and there's blood everywhere!' The tears were flowing unheeded now.

'Show me where.' Releasing the boy's arms, Goran picked up an iron bar he had been carrying when he ran to intercept the boy. He had been using it to either prise loose stones from the wall or hammer them back into place. 'Do you think you'll be able to find him again quickly?'

The boy nodded vigorously, 'Yes.'

'Come on then, there's no time to lose.'

★   ★   ★

The boy's father was some distance inside the estate but his groans could be heard long before

22

they reached him. Along the way Goran had learned the boy's name was Jenken Bolitho and that his father, Albert, was a miner.

They had little time, or breath, for more talk, but Goran would later learn that the family had come from West Cornwall hoping Albert might find work with Captain Pyne. Unfortunately, although the mine captain had promised to take Bolitho on eventually, it would be to make use of his mining skills and not until the main shaft and the mine workings were in place. In the meantime, Albert Bolitho had a family to feed. With no money and his family suffering from hunger, he had turned to poaching.

When Goran and Jenken reached him, Albert Bolitho was lying on his back, exhausted by loss of blood and the vain efforts to free himself. The jagged teeth of the mantrap were firmly clamped about the lower calf of his left leg, his torn trousers heavily soaked with blood.

On the ground beside him two rabbits protruded from a satchel, one with a wire suture about its neck, incriminating evidence of Bolitho's activities at the time he trod on the mantrap.

However, in his present situation the miner was beyond caring about the legal consequences of being caught poaching. His face contorted with agony, he looked up at Goran and pleaded, 'Get me out of here . . . my leg!'

Wasting no time on a reply and trying to remember the blacksmith's explanation of how a mantrap worked, Goran said to Jenken, 'He's going to need your help. I'll prise the jaws open and hold them apart with the bar but you'll need to free his leg then help drag him clear. Do you think you can do that?'

Wide-eyed, Jenken nodded.

'Good, then here we go!'

There was a bar on the trap so shaped that when the trap was sprung it held the serrated jaws clamped tightly shut on the unfortunate victim's leg. Goran needed to stand on this bar and bounce up and down upon it before it moved sufficiently to allow him to place the iron bar low down between the jaws and force them apart.

It was a painful process and although one of the jaws sprung free of Bolitho's leg almost immediately the other remained embedded in the flesh of his calf muscle. Speaking to the boy, Goran said, 'You'll need to free your pa's leg before you can pull him clear, but hurry, I can't hold the jaws apart for very long.'

After only a moment's hesitation, the young boy did as he was instructed, sobbing intermittently as he pulled the mutilated leg clear of the embedded metal jaws.

'Good boy, that's it! Now take hold of your pa beneath his armpits and pull for all you're worth. Ignore his cries of pain, *just do it — quickly*!' Striving with all his strength to keep the jaws of the trap open, Goran spoke with an urgency that spurred the boy on.

Goran needed to make an extra effort to force the jaws even farther apart when the miner's boot became caught in them — but suddenly Albert Bolitho was free!

24

Pulling the iron bar free from the closed jaws of the trap with difficulty, Goran dropped to his knees to inspect the miner's injured leg — and saw exposed yellow bone.

'Do you think you'll be able to get to your feet?'

By way of a reply the miner struggled to make the attempt but failed. However, with Jenken's aid Goran succeeded in raising him and even managed to take a couple of steps with his arm about him for support, but it was going to take a long time to reach safety . . . too long.

'Jenken, I want you to run to the mine as quickly as you can and tell Captain Pyne, or some of the men who know your pa, what's happened. Tell them we need help urgently with as many men as can be spared — and get them to bring something we can carry him on . . . No, don't bother about that, there are a couple of sheep hurdles in the top corner of the field where you found me. One of those can be used when the men get here — but you need to be quick. Run as you've never run before. Your pa must be off Spurre land before anyone from the estate finds him, otherwise we'll all be in trouble. Deep trouble!'

4

Goran's progress with the injured man was slow. Frighteningly so. He had picked up the satchel with its snares and dead rabbits so they would not be discovered, but was aware that if he met Grimble — or any of the other gamekeepers — with these in his possession Albert Bolitho could look forward to transportation and if Goran did not receive a similar sentence he would face a lengthy spell in prison as an accomplice.

It was a grim prospect but it was impossible to hurry the injured man. Albert Bolitho was so weak he twice collapsed in a faint and Goran could only stagger a few erratic paces with him before needing to stop and support the miner while he gathered strength again.

However, he could not afford to allow Bolitho to lie down and rest as he frequently pleaded to be allowed to do. If he did, Goran knew he would not be able to lift him to his feet again. Struggling on, he hoped Jenken would soon return with help.

Goran was less than halfway to the boundary wall with his burden when he heard a sound that struck dread into him, causing his stomach to contract in fear. It was the sound of a hound baying in the woods, an indication that a gamekeeper — most probably Marcus Grimble — was on his rounds.

Although the sound was still some distance away, if the gamekeeper was heading in his direction Goran knew there was no way he could reach the boundary wall with the injured man before the hound picked up their scent.

Then, to Goran's great relief he heard the sound of men running towards him from the direction of the estate's boundary wall. Minutes later young Jenken, accompanied by a number of men in miners' garb put in an appearance.

Explanations could wait for later. Breathlessly, Goran said, 'Quick! Carry Bolitho back to the wall and get him off Spurre land; there's a gamekeeper heading this way with a foxhound that'll pick up our scent in no time. If we're caught we'll all be in serious trouble.'

The miners wasted no time and when two men lifted Albert Bolitho bodily between them the party hurried him towards the boundary wall.

The sound of the hound was much closer now, its excited baying suggesting it had picked up their scent. It was with great relief that the miners lifted their injured colleague over the wall into Agnes Roach's field before the animal and its keeper came into view.

For a moment Goran was taken aback to find the three Pyne girls there. They had been with their father when Jenken reached the mine with his dramatic news and had followed the res-cue party at a slower pace, arriving at the scene just as the miners lifted their injured colleague over the wall.

However, this was not the moment to question

the reason for their presence, the hound was dangerously close and Goran took it upon himself to give orders to the miners carrying Albert Bolitho.

'Take Bolitho to that second clump of gorse, there's room to hide him there. Take the haversack with you — and keep him quiet. If it's gamekeeper Grimble with the hound, he'll be carrying a gun and won't hesitate to use it.'

'Tom, Arthur . . . go with Albert and do as the boy says. Gag him if you think it's necessary.' The man issuing the order spoke with authority and Goran realized this must be Captain Pyne.

Within minutes the gorse bushes had closed around the miners and the injured man, but they were only just in time. The branches had hardly ceased trembling when a foxhound came over the wall from the estate and Goran recognized the same young hound he and the girls had met with before. It seemed the hound recognized the girls too. It bounded towards them, tail flailing the air in pleasure and the miners looked on in momentary amusement at Jennifer's feigned protestations when she was singled out for special attention.

Their amusement was short-lived. Appearing on the far side of the wall, gamekeeper Grimble took in the scene and, reaching over, placed his gun against the wall on the field side. Climbing over after it, he called in vain for the frisky young hound to come to him.

'Your dog is too pleased at making new friends to hear you.' The comment was made by Captain Pyne.

Retrieving his gun, Grimble growled angrily, 'It's a hound, not a dog, and he's bred to hunt foxes, not to make friends.'

'It would appear his training is not yet complete,' Captain Pyne said, 'but we haven't been introduced. I'm Piran Pyne, captain of the Wheal Hope mine we're opening up a little way along the edge of the moor.'

Ignoring the hand held out to him, Gamekeeper Grimble said, 'In my experience mines and miners bring nothing but trouble in their wake and unless I'm mistaken it's already arrived. Someone's been trespassing on Spurre land after rabbits. I've been aware of the snares for a day or two and today I found a lot of blood close to a warren. Whoever hurt himself would have needed help to get away. Nobody I can see looks to be hurt but it's more than coincidence you all being here. What have you done with the poacher?'

'I really don't know what you're talking about, but this so-called poacher ... how was he injured? Did he have a gun and accidentally shoot himself, or was the injury caused in some other way? Perhaps you'd like to take me to the place where this 'accident' happened, so I'll have some idea how badly he's been hurt, then I can check to make sure none of my miners is involved.'

'You'll keep off the Spurre Estate — you and your men, or you'll find yourself in serious trouble.'

'I don't think so. In fact, I intend coming on Sir John's estate very soon. He's been to see me

29

about the dues he can expect if we follow a lode beneath his land and has said I can go anywhere I like on Spurre land in order to locate worthwhile lodes. While I'm about it I'd like to see where this accident took place, then I'll be able to pursue the matter further.'

Captain Pyne had called Marcus Grimble's bluff and the gamekeeper knew it. He also knew that if the mantrap was found there would be serious consequences for him and his employer. He would need to remove the trap — and others like it — before the mine captain ventured onto the estate.

'If Sir John has given you permission to go on his land there's nothing I can do about it, but while you're there you'd better remember what it is you're supposed to be doing and not get up to anything else . . . neither you nor any of your men.'

'Of course not, laws are made to be obeyed, aren't they? We should all be fully aware of the punishments that will be dealt out to those who break any of them.'

Grimble glared uncertainly at Captain Pyne for a few moments before turning and heading back towards the tumbledown section of the boundary wall.

'Don't forget your hound, gamekeeper. You don't want him to become too attached to my girls.'

Turning back, the gamekeeper called the hound to him in a voice that brooked no disobedience. Knowing it was in trouble, the hound leapt to obey the furious command but

30

when it neared the gamekeeper, aware of the aura of fury emanating from him, it dropped to its belly and crawled towards him obsequiously. Reaching him the hound looked up fearfully. It had seriously overstepped the mark and anticipated certain chastisement.

Before anyone realized what was about to happen, Grimble lowered the gun he was holding and, with the end of the barrel against the hound's head, pulled the trigger.

The sudden loud report startled the watching miners and terrified the young girls. As the hound fell on its side, dead, Morwenna and Nessa screamed and Jennifer burst into tears.

Angrily, Captain Pyne demanded, 'Was that really necessary — and in front of the children?'

'If it wasn't for them it would still be alive. A foxhound's bred to hunt foxes, not get friendly with every child it meets. The hound was no good for the job it was bred for.'

With this Grimble turned to walk away, but Goran, who was upset at the callousness of the gamekeeper, called after him, 'What about the hound?'

'It's no good to me, feed it to your pigs.'

He had reached the wall when Goran said, 'You leave a dead hound on Mrs Roach's land and Sir John Spurre will find it lying across his doorstep in the morning with a note tied to it telling him to ask you for an explanation.'

Grimble turned back angrily with the apparent intent to take issue with him about his remarks, but two of the miners, who had been as appalled as Goran at the gamekeeper's callous action,

31

moved to stand alongside him.

Coming no closer, Grimble said, 'You're growing too big for your boots, young Trebartha, you'd do well to stay out of my way.'

With this, he reached down and taking hold of the dead young foxhound, heaved it over the wall before climbing after it.

★　★　★

The two oldest Pyne girls were tearful and Jennifer was sobbing bitterly when her father picked her up. Comforting her he gave instructions for his men to carry Albert Bolitho to Wheal Hope on one of the sheep hurdles. A doctor had been sent for when they set out to rescue him and the miner would be treated there.

This done, the mine captain turned to Goran. 'Are all the estate gamekeepers like that one?'

'They all do a job I wouldn't care for, but most are reasonable men. Marcus Grimble isn't. He goes out of his way to upset people and enjoys doing it.'

'He's upset my girls and my men too, so word will get around about the type of man he is. He'd do well to steer well clear of Wheal Hope miners, they're hard on men like Grimble. But you stood up to him . . . and I understand you did the same for my girls the other day. Now you've saved Albert Bolitho from transportation — and saved his life too, probably. None of us will forget that, so if Grimble gives you trouble let me know, we have ways of dealing with men like him.'

Embarrassed by the nods of approval from the

remaining miners and the way the two oldest Pyne girls were looking at him, Goran said, 'Thanks. I hope I never need to call for your help but it's good to know it's there. You mentioned that Sir John has given you permission to make checks on his land. Do you expect the underground work of the mine to extend this far?'

'Probably. We've started work on a copper find that will likely go down deep where we are at the moment, but I've also come across another lode that seems to be running in this direction, and in my opinion it's likely to be a rich one.'

Knowing the position of the mine, the extent of the Spurre Estate and Agnes's words when he had told her of his first meeting with the Pyne girls, Goran pursued his questioning. 'That means you'll be working beneath the farms of both Agnes Roach and her brother, Elworthy Coumbe. I work on both, and we're standing on Agnes's land right now. Their lands extend up to the ridge and along it for six or seven fields to where the moor dips into a valley. I think she's interested in mining rights.'

Captain Pyne frowned, 'When I met Sir John we discussed the direction the lode was likely to take and he told me all mining rights on the edge of the moor around here were his. We even discussed the percentages of dues he wants for working beneath his lands.'

'Well, nothing has been said about it to Agnes. She didn't even know you'd begun mining up this way until I told her . . . and that wasn't until after I'd met your girls.'

33

'I don't like the sound of this. I hope Sir John isn't trying to get more than he's entitled to. If the lodes are as rich as I believe them to be there could be a lot of money involved — and disputed dues and mining rights have resulted in more than one good mine failing. Will you tell your two employers I'd like to come down and speak to them as soon as I can find time? But I need to get back to the mine, there's a lot of work going on there right now. Thank you once more for all you did for Albert Bolitho, he's got enough troubles without this. I'll make certain he and his family don't starve but, much as I'd like to, I can't afford to support every out of work miner and regrettably there are far too many of them.'

Captain Pyne left with his remaining miners and the three girls, the still sobbing Jennifer being carried in his arms. After the unwelcome confrontation with Marcus Grimble and what Captain Pyne had said about mining rights and dues, Goran had been left with a great deal to think about.

He felt a little better when, before the party from the mine passed out of sight, Jennifer waved to him over her father's shoulder and Nessa turned and did the same. However, she turned back so quickly he was not sure whether she saw him raise his arm in acknowledgement.

5

When Goran returned to the farmhouse and told Agnes Roach of the latest incident involving Grimble and the miners from Wheal Hope, she expressed her disapproval.

'When I first heard about the mine I said there'd be trouble. It follows miners as surely as night follows day. Mining and farming don't sit comfortably with each other. We look after the land, putting as much back into it as we take out, knowing that if we take care of it the land will always be here for those who come after. The miner takes what he wants and puts nothing back. When there's no more to take he moves on to do the same somewhere else. We're like oil and water. Mind you, that doesn't mean I hold with these mantraps. They might just as easily have caught one of those young girls you found on Spurre land. When I was a young girl a little lad belonging to a washerwoman at the Hall trod on one of them. It took the poor little soul's leg clean off and he was dead before they could get help to him. I thought they weren't allowed to put them down any more. Not that a ban would stop Sir John using them if he wanted to, he believes he's above the law — and I doubt there's anyone in Cornwall would argue with that.'

'Talking about the law and Sir John, Captain Pyne who's in charge of the Wheal Hope says he's had a meeting with Sir John who told him he owns mining rights to all the land hereabouts. They even talked about the amount of money he would be given for the ore they took out.'

'Sir John said that? If this mine captain comes down here to see me I'll soon tell him different. If there's any mining done beneath either farm then the dues come to us, not to anyone else!'

'That's more-or-less what I told him. He said he'll come down and see you when he's not quite so busy and he'd like me to show him where the boundaries are for the two farms so he'll have a better idea about it when he talks to Sir John again.'

'Good. When he comes here I'll prove that whatever Sir John may own doesn't include any rights for our land. None at all.'

Goran was aware Agnes disliked the land-owner intensely. He hoped she knew what she was talking about when it came to mining rights . . . but she was still speaking.

'This miner who was caught in the mantrap, you say he was poaching on the Spurre estate?'

'That's right, he knew he was doing wrong but it sounds as though his family are close to starving. He was desperate to get them something to eat.'

'We've got two fields almost ready to be cut for hay and Elworthy will have the same, as well you know. Old George Yates as good as said last year it would be the last time he'd be able to help us bring it in and I know he was bad for most of the winter, so we're going to have to take

36

someone else on. Will this miner be fit enough to help?'

Goran shook his head, 'He'll be lucky if he's ever able to walk properly again — but he's got a son of about thirteen. He's a sturdy lad and fit enough. He ran all the way from the Spurre estate to the mine to fetch help for his pa, then ran back again with Captain Pyne and the miners. I think you'd find he'll work twice as hard as anyone else to prove he can do a man's job and help his family.'

'He might *try* but he's *not* a man and couldn't expect to pick up a man's pay, but if you think he can do the job . . . Anyway, it's you who'll need to work all the harder if he can't. Do you know where he lives?'

'No, but they'll know up at the mine.'

Goran realized Agnes was working something out in her head and now she said, 'You've got work to catch up on tonight, but if you work a bit faster and finish your chores early enough tomorrow afternoon you can take a few eggs up to the mine for this miner and find out whether his son would like to help in the haymaking with you. I'll give him a shilling for half a day's work and see that Elworthy does the same. He'll have a meal here before he goes home and no doubt your ma will find some breakfast for him when he's working over there with you. That'll make things a little easier for the family, but you can tell him he'll need to work hard for it — and while you're up at the mine speak to this Captain Pyne. Tell him he's to take no notice of what Sir John's told him and that he'd better come and

37

see me before he thinks of going beneath any of our farmland.'

★   ★   ★

Goran enjoyed the unaccustomed luxury of having a task to perform on a fine summer's evening that consisted of nothing more than carrying a basket of eggs, two loaves of farm-baked bread and a pound of butter from Agnes's farm to the Wheal Hope. Agnes was a good-hearted woman, despite the impression she chose to give to others, and the plight of Albert Bolitho and his family had moved her.

When he arrived on the site of the new mine, Goran was impressed by the way work had progressed in a short time. The main shaft was well advanced and a number of buildings, including a solid granite engine house, were under construction, but he could see none of the miners who had been involved in the rescue of Albert Bolitho and enquiries for Captain Pyne revealed the mine captain was underground with a team of miners. Goran guessed the men he had met on that occasion were probably with him.

However, when he asked after the injured miner the attitude of the men he was speaking to became openly hostile and Goran realized the cause of Albert Bolitho's injuries was no secret here and his colleagues were suspicious of anyone who came asking about him.

Fortunately, when he explained it was he who had found Albert Bolitho when he was 'hurt' and that he was bringing food for his family, the miners' attitude changed immediately. One of them said, 'Albert and his family put together a place up among the rocks on the moor. I'm not exactly sure whereabouts it is but if you go ask at Captain Pyne's house they'll know there.'

Goran was directed to a newly erected cottage hidden from the mine workings by a clump of trees immediately beneath the rim of the moor. When he arrived there he saw a woman taking in washing from a line slung between two trees at the rear of the cottage, where it would have been dried by the afternoon sun. The woman's features were so similar to those of Morwenna that Goran realized she must be the mother of the three Pyne girls.

When he introduced himself, her face broke into an amused smile, 'Then you must be the young man who has seen more of my daughters than any young man should?'

Deeply embarrassed, Goran stuttered, 'I'm sorry . . . but I didn't know they were going to be . . . like they were. I heard their voices in among the gorse and wondered who they were . . . what they were doing.'

Taking pity on him, Annie Pyne said, 'From all the girls told me, they were very lucky it was you who found them and not that gamekeeper. Poor Jennifer had a nightmare about that poor dog of his last night and woke us all up with her screaming. She was very upset. The man must be some kind of monster, what with that and poor Albert Bolitho.'

'It's actually Mr Bolitho and his family I've come up here to find. Agnes Roach, the farmer I work for, has sent a couple of things for them.'

'That's very kind of her, very kind indeed. I sent the girls up to them earlier today with a couple of things I'd baked, but they can do with anything they can get hold of to eat. Unfortunately, Albert is one of those foolishly proud men who feels that accepting things from others is almost as bad as workhouse charity.'

'Thanks for warning me, but I think I can get over that problem. I mentioned Jenken to Agnes and she's said she'll take him on to help me with the haymaking. I'll tell Mr Bolitho we're so desperate for help that she's sent me with this basket as a sort of bribe.'

Annie Pyne nodded her approval, 'That should work, and having Jenken bringing money into the home will be a godsend for them all. Your employer must be a very kind woman.'

It was Goran's turn to smile now. 'She wouldn't thank you for saying that. She tries to convince everyone she's a hard-headed, no-nonsense farmer, and in some ways she is, but she *is* a kindly woman and let me leave work early today to bring these things up here . . . but that reminds me, the reason I've called on you is that no one at the mine could tell me where Mr Bolitho and his family live. They said you might know.'

'I've been there only once and doubt if I would be able to find it again, but Nessa will, she's in the house doing some school work. You'd never be able to find it on your own. Wait here while I take this washing in and I'll send her out to you.'

Inside the cottage Nessa was seated at a table, utilizing the light streaming through a south-facing window by which to copy words from a large, leather-bound dictionary.

'There's someone outside wanting directions to where the Bolithos live. I said you would show him.'

'Oh, Ma! I'm trying to finish this before the light goes.'

'Of course, I forgot you were doing something important. I'll go out and tell him you're busy when I've put this washing down.' Then, in an off-hand manner, Annie Pyne added, 'It's that young man you met when you, Morwenna and Jennifer were trespassing on the Spurre estate.'

'It's Goran?' Nessa's sudden change of attitude was startling, even though her mother had been expecting her to become more interested when she knew who was outside.

The heavy book was closed hurriedly and Nessa rose to her feet so swiftly that her mother's eyebrows were raised in unfeigned surprise as, all interest in her bookwork forgotten, Nessa demanded, 'Where is he . . . ?'

Without waiting for a reply, she darted to the door saying, 'I won't be long, Ma. I'll just show him to the Bolithos' house.'

Behind her, Annie Pyne was left with a great deal to think about.

Outside the cottage Nessa had a moment of panic when there was no immediate sign of Goran, then she remembered her mother had been outside taking washing off the line behind the cottage.

She had recovered much of her composure by the time she found him waiting by the back door, back towards her, holding the basket.

'Hello, what are you doing here?'

It was not as casual as she would have liked it to appear but, turning, Goran returned her smile and lifted the basket. 'Agnes Roach has sent this for the Bolitho family but I don't know where they live. I just spoke to your mother and she said you would know.'

'I do, but it's out on the moor and you'll never find it on your own. I'll take you there.'

'Thanks, but I also want to speak to your pa, Agnes says she wants him to call on her at the farm. I've been to the mine but they said he was below ground with some of the miners.'

'He should be home by the time we get back from the Bolithos'. You can tell me what it's about on the way and why she's sent things for Albert and his family . . . they'll certainly be welcome. The family are desperately poor.'

6

Walking away from the cottage, Nessa struck out across the open moor with Goran by her side heading in the general direction of a ragged ridge of fractured granite that rose in impressive dominance above the surrounding moorland.

'I love it up here,' Nessa said, happily. 'It's so different from where we lived down west. There it was impossible to escape from the noise and clatter of the mines all around us, but here it's so quiet sometimes you can imagine you're the only person in the world.'

'I know what you mean, but you can hear the noise from the mines around Caradon when the wind's in the wrong direction — and Wheal Hope will be closer than any of *them*.'

Looking at him questioningly, Nessa asked, 'Don't you like mines, or mining?'

'I don't know enough about them to say whether I really like them or not,' Goran replied honestly, 'but my pa was killed working on a mine when I was small and Ma has always been very bitter about it, so I suppose that's bound to have had some effect on how I think about them.'

'Oh! I'm sorry, I didn't know.'

He shrugged, 'How could you? Neither of us knows very much about the other. We've only met a couple of times . . . '

Even as he was speaking Goran was thinking of their first meeting, when he saw more of the

43

Pyne sisters than most men viewed of any woman, even those to whom they were married. He wondered whether Nessa was remembering it too! Dismissing the thought immediately, he hastily changed the subject.

'Your ma said you were in the house doing school work when I arrived.'

'That's right, I was learning new words and writing them down, with their meanings. One of Ma's brothers teaches in his own school in London and he sends books and sets work for me. It's something I want to do when I'm older.'

She thought of asking Goran how well he could read or write, but changed her mind. If he could do neither well it might cause him embarrassment and she had no wish to do that.

However, Goran himself pursued the matter. 'I can read and write a bit. One of my pa's sisters teaches school too and she was teaching me until Pa died and we moved away. She'd sometimes come visiting and leave me books and things to work on, but not long afterwards she went to America and there are so many words in the books I don't understand that I got fed up trying to read them. But I'm not bad at sums. I work mornings for Elworthy Coumbe, Agnes's brother, who has the farm next to hers and because he can't read or write I keep a tally of what money's spent and what comes in. Agnes checks everything because she has a good mind for money but she says I'm pretty good too and it's not often she finds anything wrong.'

'Don't you have a dictionary?'

'A what?'

'A dictionary, a book that tells you what every word means. It's what I was using when you came to the house. It's fun, you find all sorts of words there you've never heard of.' Having a sudden idea, she added, 'My uncle sent a couple of dictionaries, one for me and another for Morwenna, but she's never bothered to learn to read and doesn't use it. When we go back home I'll ask Ma if you can borrow it. You'll enjoy using it and be surprised how useful it is. If you only learn two new words a day, by the end of a year you'll know more than seven hundred new words — as well as all those you'll have learned from the books you've been able to read.'

Her enthusiasm was such that Goran said, 'You obviously really *do* enjoy learning, you'll be a good teacher one day. I'm surprised Morwenna doesn't feel the same way.'

With a hint of remorse, Nessa explained, 'I don't think our uncle helped very much when he used to come to see us. He would keep on about how clever *I* was and never say anything kind about Morwenna at all. I think she was so upset she decided that if she couldn't be better than me at learning she wasn't even going to try. It's a pity because she's quite clever, really, but I suppose it doesn't matter too much, all she wants to do is get married and have a home and family of her own.'

'And that's not something you want?'

'I want to get married and have a family too . . . eventually. But before even thinking about that I want to *do* something. Teaching, if I can.'

Goran was impressed. He had met few girls in

45

his young life and certainly none with Nessa's learning or ambition. The few he had come across thought as did Morwenna, looking forward to marriage and a family as their ultimate aim in life.

'Where's Morwenna now, back at the cottage?'

Nessa looked at him sharply. 'No, she's taken Jennifer for a walk to North Hill village. It seems there's a shop there and Ma wanted to know what they sell as it's probably our nearest. Why do you ask?'

'No particular reason. She won't find very much in the shop although they can usually get anything you ask for . . . but they do sell sweets, so they might help Jennifer forget the nightmare your ma said she had last night.'

'Yes, it was about that gamekeeper shooting that nice young hound,' she explained. 'It was a horrid thing to do. I'm surprised they keep such a man on at the big estate.'

'Marcus Grimble can do no wrong in Sir John Spurre's eyes. He served as his personal orderly in the Napoleonic wars and Sir John will not hear anything said against him.'

'I don't think I'd like this Sir John Spurre, although I doubt whether I'll ever meet him so what I think won't matter to either of us . . . but we're almost at the place where Albert Bolitho lives: it's over there, in among those large rocks.'

★   ★   ★

The Bolitho 'home' was no more than a piece of ground about the size of the living-room in

46

Goran's cottage and was surrounded on three sides by man-high granite boulders. Tree branches had been laid across the top of the space, on which there rested an untidy 'thatch' of gorse, coarse grass and turf.

The open front of the primitive shelter was hung with a frayed and holed tarpaulin sheet which failed to quite reach the ground. A corner had been folded back to reveal a number of flat stones which had apparently been manhandled inside to serve as makeshift seats.

Almost half the floor area was covered by a thick layer of fern on which was strewn three or four frayed blankets. Two scantily clad young boys, scarcely more than babies, were sharing this improvised bed with their injured father while another two, not much older and with only a little more ragged clothing, were outside in the company of a skin-and-bone woman who, a defeated expression on her pinched face, squatted, snapping twigs with which to feed a low-burning fire.

Beside the lack-lustre fire was a smoke-blackened pot containing what Goran thought was probably the remains of a stew made from the rabbits obtained at such a great cost by the head of the Bolitho family.

The state of the hovel and its occupants came as a shock to Goran. He and his mother were by no means well off and he had seen many farm labourers with even less than they possessed, but he had never before witnessed such abject poverty as this.

The woman eagerly seized the basket of food he brought but she had hardly begun to thank

47

him for it when her husband's tremulous voice called from inside the improvised home.

'Who is it? Who's out there?'

The miner's wife looked at Goran questioningly and he called, 'It's Goran Trebartha — I'm the one who found you yesterday.'

There was a pause as Albert Bolitho digested this information before calling, 'What are you doing here? Come inside where I can see you.'

Stooping in order to pass through the triangular opening, Goran entered the primitive dwelling. Albert Bolitho did not appear to have strength enough to rise up from his fern bed but he raised an arm towards Goran, 'I'd like to shake your hand, son. The doctor says I owe my life to you — and my freedom too. I won't ever forget it. But what are you doing here . . . and who's that with you? Has someone found out what I was doing?'

He asked the question when he heard his wife say something to Nessa and there was fear in his voice as the possibility occurred to him.

'No, and no one will. Your wife is talking to Nessa Pyne, she brought me here. I'm here because I mentioned Jenken to Agnes Roach, the farmer I work for, and told her he seemed a sturdy lad. We've got haymaking coming up on the farm very soon and are desperate for someone to help us out. Agnes wants to take him on to work with me getting the hay cut and dried. She asked me to come here and speak to him and has sent a couple of things for the family. You'd be doing us a great favour by allowing him to come and work with me.'

'He'll do it, of course. To be honest, it would be a lifeline for the family, me being laid up the way I am. Have you spoken to him yet?'

'No, your wife says he's gone off to the doctor at Rilla Mill to get something that's being made up to put on your leg . . . how is it feeling now?'

'The only feeling right now is pain, but the doctor reckons I'm lucky to have that. He believes if I'd been ten minutes later getting to him I'd have lost my leg and should have been grateful had that been all. He says he's seen men die from far less.'

'Well, you're still here and going to get better. Hopefully by the time you are fit again there will be work for you at the Wheal Hope, they seem to be getting on well with things there.'

'Captain Pyne has some good men working for him and once I'm well again I'll be more than happy to take any work he can offer me, but I won't forget who I have to thank for being able to do it. God bless you, boy. I'm not much good to man or beast at the moment but when I'm up and about again you'll never need to ask twice for my help in anything, it'll be there for you.'

7

Walking back with Nessa from the Bolithos' hovel, Goran was still haunted by the poverty of the injured miner and his family but when he voiced his thoughts to Nessa, her response was philosophical.

'It's possibly the worst conditions I've seen a *family* in but it's something a great many miners accept as part of their way of life. There are always far more miners in Cornwall than there is work for them and when news of a rich find goes around they flock to the area in the hope of being taken on. Sometimes they're lucky and enough mines start up to give them all work, but not all mines succeed. When they close there can be hundreds of miners, thousands even, desperately searching for work and they make their homes where they can, with whatever is at hand.'

'I don't think I'd like that sort of life.' The mere thought of living in the same conditions as the Bolithos caused Goran to shudder.

'I doubt very much whether they do, but they say that once you're a miner, you're *always* a miner and if that's what it takes . . . ' The gesture that ended her statement indicated an acceptance of the facts but, changing the subject abruptly, she asked, 'Where exactly is it *you* live?'

'In a cottage on Elworthy Coumbe's farm, close to the farm-house. If you aren't in too much of a hurry to get back to the mine I'll show you. We won't need to go far out of your way; you'll be able to see it from the edge of the moor.'

'I'd like that.'

There was a natural ease in their new-found relationship that they both recognized, even though neither had experienced it before with anyone other than family. Goran was an only child, brought up for many years on a fairly isolated farm and although Nessa had been brought up in a family environment in the midst of a bustling mining community, she had always lived in the shadow of her older and more outgoing sister.

'That's the farm down there.' They had reached the edge of the moor and Goran pointed to where a cluster of farm buildings huddled in a shallow hollow surrounded by fields that extended down the slope of the moor's edge to the River Lynher which formed a natural eastern boundary of the farm. 'Our cottage is the building with smoke coming from the chimney, just to the right of the farmhouse.'

Shifting his gaze further to the left, he said, 'That hedge over there, running up to the wall of the field where the sheep are, is the boundary between Elworthy's farm and that of his sister, Agnes Roach. I work on his farm from dawn to noon, and hers from one o'clock until dusk.'

Nessa gave him a sympathetic look, 'Don't you ever have time off to do things *you* want to do?'

'Not very often. Agnes isn't the healthiest of women — and although Elworthy is capable

51

of working as hard as any two men, he doesn't always think about things and needs to be watched in case he does something stupid. But it isn't as bad as it sounds. Whenever I take animals to market, or things to sell on fair days in Launceston and Liskeard, I often have time to wander around and see things, although if Elworthy is with me I need to look after him. He's as good a farmer as anyone when he's doing what's familiar but he gets confused when he's away from the farm, especially if there are a lot of people around him.'

'Is that Elworthy down there by the river, talking to a man with a horse?'

Nessa pointed to where two men were talking by a narrow bridge which spanned the river in the far corner of the farm. One of the men was wearing a smock, an article of clothing adopted by many of those who worked the land, but it was sight of the other man which caused Goran to start in surprise. Holding the reins of a thorough-bred horse as he talked to his companion, he was dressed in the manner of a gentleman . . . and Goran recognized him immediately.

'Yes, that's Elworthy, but what's Sir John Spurre doing down there talking to him? As far as I'm aware it's the first time he's ever come to either of the two farms.'

As they watched, Elworthy began pointing in various directions and Goran pulled a startled Nessa behind a clump of gorse before the two talking men looked in their direction.

'I'd rather Sir John didn't see us,' he explained. 'He's up to something or he wouldn't be down there talking to Elworthy and it certainly won't be a social visit. Sir John despises small independent farmers like Elworthy and Agnes. I'll need to tell her about this.'

'Why, what could he be saying that's likely to cause any trouble?'

'I don't know, but Elworthy is so much in awe of anyone in authority he would agree to anything they said, even if he had no idea what they were talking about — and Elworthy seldom understands what strangers say to him. I'm going to have to go right away to tell Agnes what we're seeing, Nessa, I think it could be important. I was meant to speak to your pa while I was up here on the moor, but will you do it for me? Tell him Agnes would like to speak to him about something they need to discuss. If Sir John Spurre is planning something it will be to *his* benefit and nobody else's and I suspect it has to do with your pa's mine opening up here.'

Nessa was disappointed that her meeting with Goran was coming to such an abrupt end but she accepted it was due to a matter of some importance.

'I'll be certain to tell Pa tonight, but will I be seeing you again soon?'

'I hope so . . . I've enjoyed being with you today.' Struggling to think of a reason why they *should* meet, he said, 'Why don't you come down to the cottage sometime? A Sunday evening would be best. Agnes goes to the chapel down the road then and sends me home early. One of Elworthy's sows has just had thirteen piglets and you could bring Jennifer to see them.'

Both Nessa and Goran went their different ways happy in the knowledge they would meet again soon, but, as he neared Agnes's farm, Goran put thoughts of Nessa out of his mind for the moment. He had an uneasy feeling Sir John's visit to Elworthy's farm spelled trouble.

★   ★   ★

'Are you certain it was Sir John you saw talking to Elworthy? I don't doubt you might have seen him on the farm. Although he's quick enough to jump on anyone who trespasses on *his* land he doesn't believe the same laws apply to him. Even so, I can't think what he and Elworthy would have to say to each other.' Agnes Roach shook her head in disbelief.

'It was Sir John right enough, and Elworthy had his hat off, holding it in both hands as though he was nervous. At least, that was the impression I got although I was too far away to see his expression.'

'It has to be something to do with the mine and the rights they want, but Sir John would have got no sense out of Elworthy, he's been getting worse lately and wouldn't have understood what Sir John was talking about. That reminds me, did you tell that mine captain I want to speak to him?'

'He was underground all the time I was up at the mine but I left word with one of his daughters, the one who showed me where the Bolithos were living. She promised to tell him when he came home.'

'I hope she does! Young girls are so empty-headed these days all they seem to think about are young men and enjoying themselves.'

'I think her older sister might be like that, but not Nessa, she can read and write and knows a lot about all sorts of things. She hopes to be a schoolteacher one day.'

Agnes looked at him questioningly, 'So, Nessa, is it? You seem to know a great deal about a girl who hasn't been in the area for more than five minutes and whom you've hardly met.'

'I had to go to Captain Pyne's house to find out where Albert Bolitho and his family are living,' Goran said defensively. 'Mrs Pyne asked Nessa to take me to them. If she hadn't I'd have never found it.'

Memories of the family's home flooded back and he said, 'You should have seen their place, it was *awful*, our pigs are better housed! He's got a wife and five young boys living in a gap between rocks that's covered over with bracken and with only the one bracken bed for all of them. Instead of chairs and tables they're using rocks. There can't be anyone in the whole world with less!'

Aware that Goran was truly upset by the plight of the injured miner and his family, Agnes said, 'Then the things you took up there for them won't be wasted. Did you see the boy about helping us with the haymaking?'

'No, he'd gone to Rilla Mill to collect ointment from the doctor for his pa's leg, but Albert Bolitho said Jenken would do it and I'm sure he will, the family is absolutely desperate for anything that comes their way.'

55

'Well, I hope he'll earn what I'll be paying him . . . but I'm still curious about the mine captain's daughter you seem to know so well . . . '

'I'm sorry, Agnes, but I must go now, Ma will have a meal ready for me and be wondering where I've got to . . . '

Watching him hurrying away from the farm, Agnes thought Goran was reaching an age when most young men were thinking of finding a girl and settling down. Intelligent and hardworking, he would be a catch for any young woman.

Not until he passed out of sight did her thoughts turn to the news he had brought about Elworthy and Sir John Spurre being seen together. She would need to pay a visit to her brother and discover what was going on. He was far too simple to recognize the wiles of a man as unscrupulous as the titled landowner and she did not want him landing himself in trouble.

8

The following morning when Goran began working with Elworthy he tackled him about the meeting with Sir John Spurre the previous evening but Elworthy refused to reveal what they had been discussing.

'We was talking business, man-to-man, and when two men talk between themselves it ain't nothing to do with anyone else.'

Goran realized that Elworthy's words did not reflect his own thinking — such as it was — but were words that would have been used by the owner of the Spurre estate. He wondered what had been said that Sir John wanted kept secret. However, he knew if he continued questioning his employer about it he would only become increasingly stubborn. He decided to get on with his work and leave Agnes to learn the reason for Sir John's unprecedented visit to the farm, as she most certainly would!

But that afternoon when Goran reached the neighbouring farm to begin his half-day's work there he found to his surprise that Agnes was far less concerned about her brother's meeting with the owner of the Spurre estate than the fact that Captain Pyne had not yet called on her.

When he asked her what it was that was of such importance she was no more forthcoming than her brother had been earlier that day.

'What we have to discuss will be between him

and me. All I'll say is that if he's a straightforward and honest man, the sort of person I can do business with, it will be to the advantage of all of us should his mine workings extend beneath either this farm or Elworthy's.'

'But what about Sir John, where does he come into all this? He wouldn't have been talking to Elworthy unless it was about something that is going to be to his advantage — and I don't doubt it has something to do with the working of the mine.'

'You let *me* worry about Sir John Spurre, I'll deal with him if and when the need arises . . . but don't you have work to do? From all you had to say last evening about the mine-captain's daughter you didn't hurry yourselves finding this injured miner and giving him and his family the victuals I sent to them out of the goodness of my heart. There'll be some catching up to do about the farm, so you'd best be getting on with it.'

* * *

The words of Agnes were reassuring, but Goran's confidence in the woman farmer received a severe jolt the following evening. He returned home to the cottage on Elworthy Farm to find his mother so upset she had not even prepared the evening meal.

It seemed Sir John had paid another unexpected visit to the farm that afternoon and after spending some time talking to Elworthy in the farmhouse had taken a walk about the farm in his company, inspecting the outbuildings

58

— and even the cottage where Goran and his mother lived.

Visibly very upset, Mabel Trebartha said, 'He walked in without so much as a 'by your leave' and behaved as though I wasn't here. After looking around him he turned up his nose and walked back out again without having said a single word to me.'

'What was Elworthy doing? Didn't he explain what the visit was all about?'

'He never said a word the whole time the pair of them were in here. Just followed Sir John around like some cowed dog and there wasn't anything I could say to him while they were both here together. I looked for him after Sir John rode off, but he wasn't to be found anywhere, and he still isn't around. It's quite obvious he intends selling up but is too embarrassed about it to tell me.'

'I'll go and look for him now and find out exactly what's going on, but I'll build up the fire first so you can have something cooking for us when I've found him.'

★　★　★

Locating Elworthy was not as easy as Goran had anticipated. He was nowhere to be found in the farmhouse or in the farm complex and during his search Goran discovered that neither the chickens nor the pigs had been shut up for the night. The cow had been milked by his mother but the milk was still in the bucket into which it had been drawn and Elworthy had not

59

performed his usual task of taking it to the wooden churn at the gate by the river, from where it would be collected by customers from the village using their own vessels.

After taking the milk down to the farm entrance himself, Goran walked slowly back to the farm. He was beginning to worry about Elworthy. The simple farmer could not always be relied upon to make a rational decision when one was necessary, but Goran had never known him fail to perform any of the many routine tasks about the farm. Something was wrong, *very* wrong, and the fact that Sir John Spurre was somehow involved made it all the more serious.

Having visited all the places where the farmer might possibly have been working, Goran was about to return to the cottage to tell his mother his search had been unsuccessful, when he remembered something that had occurred a few years before.

One of the mares on the farm had produced a foal to which Elworthy had become deeply attached. It was the first animal to receive his attention each morning, coming to him when it heard his voice, and he was often to be seen leaning on the field gate as the young animal frisked in the field it shared with its mother.

One evening, after paying a final visit to the foal Elworthy must have failed to properly secure the gate to the field and it blew open during the night. As a result both mare and foal wandered out of the field and were not to be seen the next morning.

After a frantic search involving men and

women from the nearby village, the disconsolate mare was spotted standing dangerously close to a long abandoned exploratory mine shaft on the moor. The foal was discovered lying at the bottom of the shaft, its neck broken by the fall.

Inconsolable, Elworthy had disappeared in the same manner as today. Goran had eventually located him in the hayloft above the stable, but he could not be persuaded to leave his hiding-place until Agnes had been fetched from the neighbouring farm. She had then spent more than an hour consoling her distraught brother and convincing him it was not entirely his fault the foal had died.

Making his way to the hayloft now, Goran climbed the steep, wide-stepped ladder from the stable and entered the loft. There was a strong aroma of musty hay here and it was too dark to distinguish anything very clearly. Gingerly making his way across the ancient, woodworm-infested boards, Goran opened the door through which newly mown hay would soon be forked from hay-wagons, and late evening light flooded into the loft.

Turning back from the open door, he heard a scuffling from a far corner where the remainder of last season's hay was piled and saw the legs of Elworthy extended across the dusty boards, much of his upper body concealed behind a cross-beam which was supporting a roof truss.

'Close the door, I don't want no light.'

The words were muffled and indistinct and the simple farmer sounded desperately unhappy.

'What's the matter, Elworthy, what are you

61

doing hiding away up here?'

'Go away, I don't want to talk about it.'

'You *have* to talk about it, Elworthy. Unless you tell me what it is that's making you so unhappy I won't be able to do anything to make it better. You can't stay up here for ever.'

'You can't do anything to help me, I've been silly. Very silly.'

Goran's eyes were becoming accustomed to the poor light in the loft and he could make out Elworthy's face now. It was evident he had been crying.

Crouching down with the beam between them, Goran said sympathetically, 'We all do silly things sometimes, Elworthy, and I'm sure that whatever you've done is nothing to be so upset about. Come down with me and have some supper. Ma's cooking it now. While we're eating you can tell us what you think you've done wrong.'

'I don't want any supper — and you can't help me, nobody can, not now.'

'That's probably not true, but we can't help until we know what it is you've done. Does Sir John Spurre have something to do with it?'

The silence that greeted the question was an answer in itself and Goran said, 'You mustn't take any notice of anything Sir John says to you, Elworthy, he's not a nice man and if ever he tries to bully you you're fully entitled to order him off your land. He may think he's a great man because everyone on the Spurre estate bows and scrapes to him, but on this farm it's *you* who's in charge, *you* who gives the orders and *you* who decides who's allowed here.'

Instead of reassuring him, Goran's words seemed to upset Elworthy even more and, suddenly, he blurted out, 'I can't tell *anyone* what to do here, Goran, because I don't own the farm any more. I've told Sir John he can buy it. He's coming here in the morning with papers for me to sign selling it to him.'

Looking up at Goran, bottom lip pushed out and his chin trembling, Elworthy added, tearfully, 'Agnes is going to be very cross with me, isn't she? I don't know what I can do . . . '

In spite of the deep dismay he felt at Elworthy's admission, Goran could not help feeling sorry for the simple farmer. He had seldom seen anyone quite this unhappy, and Elworthy did not have the mental capability to deal with it.

'Yes, Agnes is going to be cross, and it's something that will affect us all, but she'll be even more angry with Sir John than with you and it might be something she can sort out. Come on down now, have some supper and go to bed. We'll talk about it in the morning.'

★ ★ ★

When Goran followed Elworthy into the cottage, Mabel Trebartha took one look at the distraught farmer and exclaimed, 'Look at you! What on earth is the matter?'

Behind Elworthy's back Goran signalled frantically but silently for his mother not to ask any questions. It seemed for some moments she would ignore him but, eventually accepting that her son would tell her later what had been happening, she clamped her mouth shut and turned her attention back to the pots and pans which had been waiting alongside the fire for the arrival of her son and his employer.

The meal was eaten in an uncomfortable silence, Elworthy too unhappy to speak, Mabel barely concealing her impatience to learn what was happening and Goran wondering how he was going to break the devastating news to her of the imminent sale of the farm and their home.

When Elworthy left the cottage and returned to the farm-house, Goran told Mabel what had happened and she was as upset as he had anticipated. He tried unsuccessfully to reassure her by saying they must not accept the accuracy of what the simple farmer had said until he had spoken to Agnes, but he too was very concerned about both their futures.

9

Goran was of necessity an early riser in order to fit work on the two adjacent farms into the day, but the following morning he rose even earlier than usual and after letting out the animals and domestic birds housed within the farmyard complex, he left for Roach farm before Elworthy put in an appearance.

Agnes had not yet risen from her bed and, although the front door of the farmhouse was never locked, Goran dared not enter the house before she was up and about.

It was some time before a window was thrown open in response to his persistent hammering on the door and when Agnes showed herself at the window, her nightcap was awry and she appeared bleary-eyed and not fully awake.

'What on earth are you doing here at this time of the morning? Why aren't you at Elworthy's farm? Is something wrong with him? Is he ill?'

'He's not ill, but he's very unhappy. Yesterday evening he hid himself away in the hayloft, just as he did that time his foal was killed.'

'Why, what's happened this time?' Irritably exhaling a deep and noisy breath, Agnes added, 'Whatever did I do so wrong that I deserve a brother like Elworthy?'

'He's sold the farm to Sir John and is desperately unhappy about it, as am I and Ma. Sir John must have bullied him into it and he's coming to the farm this morning with the papers for Elworthy to sign.'

'He's *what*!' Irritability disappeared with all remnants of sleepiness and, suddenly decisive, Agnes said, 'Catch the pony and harness it to the light cart. By the time you've done that I'll be dressed and you can take me to Elworthy. Once I've sorted *him* out we'll wait for Sir John — and you can tell your ma she has nothing to worry about. Sell Elworthy indeed . . . '

★   ★   ★

On the way to her brother's farm in the light cart, Agnes muttered darkly about the threatened purchase of Elworthy Farm. 'It's the thought of mineral rights that's brought this about, you mark my words, but Sir John Spurre is going to have to think again about his plans because he's not having the farm. As for Elworthy, I despair of him, I really do!'

Goran thought it wise to say as little as possible on the short journey between the two farms lest Agnes should vent her simmering anger upon him. Instead he allowed Agnes to do all the talking.

'Do you know that Elworthy got his name from the farm where he was born? It's as well he wasn't born on Roach Farm. It was called Caspar Farm in those days — and Caspar is supposed to have been one of the three wise men who visited the stable in Bethlehem when Our Lord was born. Can you imagine Elworthy being named after a wise man? Our father would have been a laughing stock!'

'I don't suppose there are many folk around here who remember your farm when it had that name. It's been Roach Farm for the whole of my lifetime.'

'Elworthy, Casper or Roach Farms, they'll never be part of the Spurre estate as long as I'm alive. Why, my father would turn in his grave at the very thought of it!'

It was only a short distance to the farm and as they approached the buildings Elworthy came out of the farmhouse.

When the simple farmer saw his sister, Goran thought he was about to run back into the house, but Agnes called, 'Elworthy! I want to speak to you.'

Her voice would have caused a braver man than Elworthy to quail. He stopped and, ill-at-ease, took off his soft hat and twisted it nervously in his hands as he stood staring down at the ground, awaiting the inevitable confrontation with his sister.

Walking stiffly towards him, a result of the uncomfortable ride she had endured in the utilitarian farm wagon, Agnes reached him and stood looking at him for a full minute, taking in his unshaven and untidy appearance before asking, in a surprisingly gentle voice, 'What am I going to do with you, Elworthy? What would our ma say if she was alive to see you today?'

Looking up at her, his lower lip trembling, Elworthy said dejectedly, 'I'm sorry, our Agnes, I've done something bad, haven't I?'

'Well, you have never been the brightest button in the box, but let's go inside and you can tell me about it.' Taking his arm, she led her unhappy brother to the farmhouse.

At the doorway she turned and called to Goran, 'Let the pony have a drink and give it a nose-bag, then you can do whatever needs doing around the farmhouse, but don't go out to the fields, I want you here when Sir John arrives, although I suspect he won't be here until much later in the day. But before you do anything else ask your mother to cook a good breakfast for all of us. I have a feeling we're going to need all the sustenance we can get today.'

★   ★   ★

The large breakfast produced by Mabel Trebartha in her cottage no more than half-an-hour later was eaten in silence, Agnes being in a thoughtful state of mind, Elworthy subdued and neither Goran nor his mother wanting to be the first to broach the subject that was dominating the thoughts of each one of them.

It was not until the meal came to an end and Agnes was ushering Elworthy from the cottage that the woman farmer said, 'There will be no need to extend the usual courtesies to Sir John when he arrives, Mabel. He's not welcome here and I want him to be fully aware of it — and you can stop worrying about what's going to happen. When he rides away the only thing he'll be taking with him will be a flea in his ear.'

'What do you think she meant?' Mabel asked Goran when the brother and sister had left the cottage.

'I don't know, Ma, but Agnes isn't in the habit of talking for the sake of it. If she says things are going to be all right she'll have something planned to stop Sir John having his way.'

'Well, you know her better than I do, but I won't breathe easy until after he's been and gone.'

★ ★ ★

Sir John Spurre arrived at Elworthy Farm shortly before noon accompanied by a soberly dressed man whom Goran had never seen before, but who his mother said was Simeon Quainton, Spurre's solicitor from Launceston. This was confirmed shortly afterwards when Elworthy came to tell Goran that Agnes wanted him in the farmhouse. He added, 'She's told me I'm to stay out here and carry on with your work.'

The party were in the farmhouse's 'best room'. To Goran's knowledge it had never been used during the whole of the time he had been working at Elworthy and there was a damp smell about it that emphasized its lack of use.

Goran was known by sight to the landowner but when he entered the room neither he nor Agnes bothered to introduce him to the solicitor. Instead, Agnes said, 'I've called you in here to witness what's said, Goran. One day you may be called upon to repeat in a court of law what is said here, so be certain you listen and remember.'

Sir John said angrily, 'I have told you, there is no need to involve anyone else. This is a private

69

business affair between me and your brother. It is nothing to do with you and involving an employee is utterly intolerable.'

'That's where you're wrong,' Agnes retorted. 'I want an honest witness present to hear everything that's said. One who won't be afraid to tell the truth if the need arises.'

'Let us not become heated about this matter, Mrs Roach,' the solicitor said soothingly, 'but I am in full agreement with Sir John. I see no reason at all why you are even involved in what is a perfectly straightforward business transaction. Sir John has made an offer for Elworthy Farm and your brother has accepted the offer. All that is now required are the signatures of the two interested parties on the deed of sale and an agreed date for your brother and any tenants to quit the premises. I will then arrange for the sum involved to be paid over and the interests of all parties will be satisfied.'

'No, Mr Quainton, the only interested party to be satisfied *if* such a sale was to go through would be Sir John. He'd be satisfied because he'd successfully bullied a simple soul into parting with something for less than a third of its value and be rubbing his hands with glee because he'd be expecting more from mining rights than he's offering for the farm. If it was anyone else doing it they'd be taken to court for trying to swindle a simple man, but *trying* to swindle Elworthy is all it will be because it's not going to happen.'

'Really, Mrs Roach! I find your remarks most offensive, to both Sir John and myself. Now, as the sale is between Sir John and Mr Coumbe and has nothing at all to do with you I suggest you leave the property immediately.'

Turning to Goran, the solicitor said imperiously, 'Young man, please find Mr Coumbe and ask him to return here to sign the deed of sale. Sir John is a busy man with more to occupy his time than listening to the virulence of an embittered old woman.'

'Goran! Stay where you are.'

Agnes's fierce glance rested briefly upon Goran before returning to the solicitor and his client who was nodding smugly at Quainton's words.

'I said I wanted him to stay here to be a witness to what is said, and that's exactly what he's going to do. Besides, even if Elworthy came in here and signed a hundred such deeds, they'd all be just as worthless as the words of you and Sir John.'

'Mr Coumbe made a firm commitment to sell the farm to me at the price I offered him, and it was a fair price. I suggest you do as Mr Quainton has suggested and go away before we send for the constable and have you removed from what will be my land very soon.'

'Elworthy Farm will *never* be yours . . . any more than it's Elworthy's.'

The bold statement took everyone in the room by surprise, but Agnes had more to say.

'My father was fully aware of my brother's feeble mind and before he died he made a will leaving both this and Roach Farm to *me*, the only condition being that I allow Elworthy to live

71

here for as long as his mental state poses no problem, either to himself or to anyone else. I think we may have reached the time now where poor Elworthy has become a problem to himself, thanks in no small measure to you, but, whether he has or not, the fact remains that the farm is not Elworthy's to sell. It belongs to me and even if I were inclined to sell — which I'm not — you'd be the last person on this earth I would sell it to, even if you were to offer me *twice* its real value — which is probably about six times what you thought you were going to pay to my brother. So, I think it's now my turn to say you'd both better get off my farm before I call the constable to remove *you*.'

'You can prove the farm belongs to you and not to your brother, of course?' This from a tight-lipped Solicitor Quainton.

'I can, but I've no intention of doing it here and now. If you want proof you can pay a call on *my* solicitor, Fletcher Pascoe of Liskeard. While you're there and before you try to swindle anyone else, I suggest you also ask him about the mineral rights that were passed on to me by my father.'

★ ★ ★

Outside the farmhouse a furious Sir John Spurre turned on his solicitor, 'I will never forgive you for this, Quainton, I have never been so humiliated in all my life! If all that damned woman says is true you should have known the facts before I made a fool of myself.'

72

'With all due respect, Sir John, it was *you* who insisted I draw up the documents for the purchase of Elworthy Farm in such a hasty manner, despite my warning that I deemed it extremely unwise. I told you it took time to look into a great many matters before making such a purchase. Your instructions to me were that I should forego all such — I think you called them 'pettifogging' — details. I was extremely concerned about such a course of action but you were insistent. You are, of course, a valued client and in your capacity as a Justice of the Peace not unfamiliar with the law so I carried out your instructions. In view of what has happened, as a result I will make full enquiries concerning this whole unfortunate situation and inform you of my findings at the earliest opportunity, but I have no doubt you are aware of what the outcome is likely to be.'

The two men had reached their horses now and, swinging himself up into the saddle, the still angry landowner looked down at the solicitor and said. 'While you are about it check on what that damned woman said about mineral rights. I want no repeat of what has happened here today.'

10

'Is it true what you told Sir John? The farm belongs to you and not to Elworthy?' Agnes's revelation had severely shaken Goran, not least because of her hint that Elworthy was no longer capable of taking care of himself. It could be that his own future was in jeopardy.

'I'm not in the habit of telling lies about things that really matter. Yes, it's perfectly true.'

'You also said Elworthy might not be able to take care of himself in the future: where does that leave Ma and me?'

'We'll talk about that later, but you and Mabel have nothing to worry about, you'll still have a home here. For now, go and find Elworthy, I need to have a long and serious talk to him. While I'm doing that you can be getting on with whatever it is you do about the place on a normal working day.'

Goran went on his way thinking that this was far from being a 'normal' working day. He found Elworthy cleaning out the pigsties with a vigour fed by his nervousness about what was happening in the farmhouse. When he saw Goran, he said anxiously, 'I saw Sir John and the other man leave. When are they coming back? Am I going to have to leave the farm?'

'He won't be coming back, Elworthy, and he won't be buying the farm either so you can stop worrying about him now. But Agnes wants to speak to you so I'll carry on here.'

'Is she angry? What's she going to say to me?'

'She's angry with Sir John, not with you. All she said to me was that she wants to speak to you. She didn't tell me what it would be about, so you'd better go to her now and find out for yourself.'

★ ★ ★

Cleaning out the pigsties was not the easiest of tasks. In addition to the sow with her many piglets there were fourteen huge pigs currently being fattened up, each more than twice the weight of Goran. A Launceston butcher would soon be coming to take all but one of them off to his abattoir. The reprieve for the remaining pig would be merely temporary, it being earmarked to provide winter meat for both farms.

Despite the difficulties posed by the lumbering but lively animals, by the time Elworthy returned Goran had finished the task and was wondering what Agnes had to say to her brother that was taking so long.

Elworthy seemed bemused but was no longer unhappy. Beaming at Goran, he declared, 'Agnes says I'm a good worker and because of that she wants me to go and help her run Roach Farm.'

His words jolted Goran. 'You work at Roach Farm? What about me?'

'I don't know. She said I'm to tell you to bring Mabel to the house 'cos she wants to talk to you both.'

Perturbed at the thought of what Agnes might

have to say to him and his mother about their futures, Goran went into the cottage deep in thought.

His mother was equally apprehensive. She had been brought up to consider landowners — even those she knew well, like Agnes Roach — omnipotent. As they walked the short distance from cottage to farm, she said, 'First Sir John walks into our cottage yesterday as though he owned the place and now Agnes is here and wants to speak to us both. Do you think Elworthy Farm is being sold and she's going to warn us that we'll need to move out?'

'I don't think so, Ma, she's already promised me we won't be turned off the farm and Agnes doesn't go back on her word. I wouldn't be surprised if she were to put the farm up for sale, but it certainly won't go to Sir John and she'll make sure we are kept on.'

'Once the place is sold whatever goes on here will be out of her hands.'

'Well, we'll know soon enough,' Goran said philosophically, hoping he sounded more confident than he felt about Agnes's plans for Elworthy Farm and its tenants.

Agnes was still in the musty-smelling sitting-room when they entered the farmhouse and she greeted Mabel with a reassuring warmth, 'Hello, Mabel, take a seat; you don't need to stand on ceremony with me, we've known each other for far too long. It's been a long time since I was last here but I'm delighted to see that both the house and the farm itself have been well looked after. I doubt whether Elworthy can be thanked for that.'

'Elworthy's no trouble and doesn't make much mess about the house. As for the farm, that's Goran's doing, he takes a pride in his work. It would be criminal if it passed to Sir John Spurre and Goran were to be dismissed.'

Goran gave his mother a warning look, but Agnes had been anticipating some such comment.

'I agree, Mabel. Fortunately Sir John will never get his hands on either Elworthy or Roach Farm as long as I'm alive and I'll do my best to make sure it doesn't happen when I'm gone, either.'

Mabel sagged in relief, but although Goran accepted what Agnes had told them he was not entirely convinced the crisis was over.

'Elworthy told me you want him to help you work Roach Farm. There's not enough work up there for two except at haymaking time, does that mean I won't be needed?'

'Not very often, I trust.'

The reply dismayed both Goran and Mabel, losing half of their income would prove a very real hardship . . . but Agnes had more to say about the situation.

'You'll not be coming to Roach Farm because you'll be needed here full-time if you agree with what I suggest.'

Trying unsuccessfully to outguess what Agnes had in mind for him, Goran gave up and Agnes continued, 'I've known for some time by things Elworthy has said to me that his mind is getting worse and realized that one day I'd need to have him living with me in order to keep an eye on him. I've put off doing anything about it because I've got used to living my life in my own way, not needing to concern myself about anyone else, but this business with Sir John means it's time to make good the promise I made to both my mother and father before they died, to take care of Elworthy. For me to do that he's going to have to move to Roach Farm. I've spoken to him about it and managed to convince him I need him there to take care of *me* and he likes that idea. He says it makes him feel important, poor soul.'

'I think you're quite right about him,' Mabel said. 'I've noticed in recent months that he's getting worse at remembering things and even knowing what he's supposed to be doing at times, but what's going to happen to this farm — and Goran — if Elworthy moves in with you?'

'That's what I want to talk to you about. If you agree to what I have in mind, it will mean a major change in everyone's life.'

Switching her attention to Goran, Agnes said, 'I'd like you and Mabel to move into the farmhouse here, and for you to run Elworthy Farm.'

Stunned, Goran said, 'You mean work here full time, drawing a full day's pay?'

'No. That *was* my original plan, but since coming here today I've come up with another idea that might be better for both of us. I really don't want the responsibility of running two farms. At my age one is more than enough, so why don't you *rent* Elworthy Farm from me? You've been virtually managing it on your own anyway, but this would mean you'd be your own master and could try out some of those new-fangled ideas of yours that I'm too set in my ways to even think about.'

The thought of becoming a tenant farmer and his own master excited Goran greatly but, forcing himself to come down to earth, he spoke more cautiously, 'It's a wonderful idea, Agnes, it really is, but there's an obvious problem — and a very big one. I've no money to pay you rent or spend what's needed to set myself up in farming.'

'I've thought of that. You've worked hard for me ever since you were a young lad and I've appreciated it, even though I have probably never put my feelings into so many words. If Mabel is prepared to come and help me with house and dairy work three times a week and you come to Roach once or twice a week to make certain Elworthy is doing things properly there, I'll forego the first year's rent. It will be hard work for you — even harder than now — and you'll need money to keep Elworthy Farm running for that year as well as putting some by for the following year's expenses, but I believe there are a good many pigs here ready for market right now. Sell them off and the money you make should help keep things going. You'll also have money coming in from the milk and eggs sold in the village. No doubt you'll be able to sell produce to the mine too once it gets working and there's a hay crop coming in which will help with winter feeding.'

Goran was silent for a long time. The prospect

of being a farmer and not merely a farm labourer excited him so much he could hardly think straight but he forced himself to face practicalities.

'Your offer is very generous, Agnes, so generous that I am itching to shout 'Yes!', but I'm trying to be sensible about it. All the things you have mentioned will keep things running as they are now for a year, at least, but it leaves nothing left over for me to plan for the future of the farm. Next year I would need to pay you rent and I doubt I'll have made enough in the first year to afford that.'

'I'm sure we'll find a way, Goran.'

Mabel had been completely won over by the thought of her son becoming a farmer. In all the hopes she had entertained for his future she had never set her sights this high and she did not want him putting obstacles in the way of such an unexpected opportunity.

Aware of the thoughts that prompted his mother's optimistic plea, Goran chose to ignore it. Still questioning Agnes, he asked, 'And what will happen about mining rights if a lode from Captain Pyne's mine is found to run beneath Elworthy land?'

'Goran!' Dismayed that Goran had not seized on Agnes's offer immediately, Mabel pleaded, 'Agnes is being incredibly generous, don't spoil everything by being greedy.'

'He's not being greedy,' Agnes's reply was unexpected. 'I'm glad he's giving my offer some sensible thought and not just grabbing it because of the idea of having people look up to him in the future. There is a lot more to farming than that. Plenty of hard work, for a start, and a successful farmer needs to plan well ahead and have something put by to cope with unexpected happenings — and there are no shortages of those on any farm.'

Turning back to Goran, she asked, 'What do you have in mind for these mining dues — if they should happen?'

'I would think that as it's not money you've been expecting to come your way you might give me something from them — for perhaps a couple of years or so, anyway — so I can make improvements to Elworthy. It will increase the value of the farm for you and mean I'll be able to cope with any of the unexpected happenings you've mentioned.'

Agnes looked at him thoughtfully for some time before saying, 'There are improvements that need to be made at Roach too and *I'll* need money for them . . . but, all right, I'll give you half what I get from the mine for Elworthy's rights for the first two years and we'll look at the situation again then. We'll set a date of the first of next month for you to take over here and I'll have my solicitor draw up a tenancy agreement. We'll tie up any loose ends then.'

Struggling up from the sagging armchair in which she had been sitting, she nodded approvingly at Goran and said, 'The day has turned out much better than I thought it was going to be when we set out from Roach Farm this morning, but we're done here now so you can take me back home again.'

Turning to Mabel who had not dared say a word for at least two minutes, Agnes said, 'Collect together all the things Elworthy is likely to need when he comes to live with me and be firm with him. I haven't room in my home for all the useless things he's collected over the years. Don't allow him to procrastinate, either, it's not long to the end of the month and he'll need to be out of here by then.'

Making her way heavily towards the door, she returned her attention to Goran. 'When you come back from Roach I want you to go up to the mine and find Captain Pyne. Tell him to come and see me before the day is out as a matter of urgency. I want to speak to him and show him the documents I hold concerning mineral rights. Tell him I think he'll find them very interesting.'

11

After taking Agnes home Goran returned to Elworthy Farm to find his mother unsettled and in a state of nervous excitement. She had been planning what furniture she would take from their cottage to the much larger farmhouse and where she would place it.

'We won't know ourselves,' she said happily, 'Our furniture's going to be lost in a house that size.'

'On the way back to her farm Agnes said she'll only let Elworthy take a few of the bits and pieces he's particularly fond of. We can either keep the remainder, or throw it out. She says the choice is ours.'

'She said that? There's some good stuff in the farmhouse, Goran, her parents must have been worth a bit of money in their time and they didn't stint on what they spent making themselves comfortable. I can hardly believe this is happening to us, you a tenant farmer and us living in a farmhouse that's nigh as big as a mansion! Your pa would have been so proud of you, as I am.'

'Don't get too carried away, Ma, I'm going to have to work hard to make a success of it, and you, too. Agnes expects you to work for her over at Roach as well as helping here and I've got so many ideas about what I want to do with the farm that I feel my head's likely to burst!'

'Ideas are all right as long as you don't get carried away by 'em and try to do too much too soon. If you work yourself too hard and become ill that'll be the end of everything. We won't be able to take anyone on to help you for a while.'

'Ah! That's something I want to talk about to you. I've already mentioned it to Agnes and she's quite agreeable, but said I should discuss it with you first as it will probably affect you more than me.'

'What's likely to affect me?' Mabel asked, guardedly.

'It concerns this cottage, Ma. When we move into the farm we won't want it to remain empty. Agnes has already agreed to take on young Jenken Bolitho, the son of the man caught in Sir John's mantrap, to help out with the haymaking. He and his family are living in abject poverty up on the moor. Jenken has four brothers, two are still babies and although the other two aren't much more than that, they are old enough to put in a couple of hours a day weeding or chasing birds away from the crops I'm hoping to put in, and it wouldn't cost us more than a few pence.'

Aware of his mother's uncertainty about the idea, Goran said hurriedly, 'Agnes has never let me sow any kind of crop, Ma, but I'm convinced it would bring us in a good deal of money and I'd like to prove it.'

'You know more about farming than I do, but I'm not sure about having someone living so close to us on the farm, especially a woman with an invalid husband and five young boys. They could prove more of a nuisance than a help and

84

I don't think Agnes would approve of that any more than I would.'

'I don't think they'd bother us too much, but when I mentioned it to Agnes she said that once I take over Elworthy Farm I can do whatever I want with it, but she also said I should be sure you agree, for the very reason you've just mentioned, that of having a family of boys living so close to us. Mind you, I think the cottage is far enough away not to prove a nuisance to us.'

'I'm not so sure,' Mabel said, dubiously. 'It depends very much on the family — and I've never even met any of them.'

'I'll tell you what, Agnes wants me to go up to the mine right away and ask Captain Pyne to go to Roach Farm and talk to her about mining rights. Why don't you come with me? We can take a few eggs and some of that bread you baked yesterday to the Bolithos, then you can see the family for yourself and decide whether or not you could live with them as our neighbours. I wouldn't want them living on Elworthy if you weren't going to get along . . . but they *could* be a help.'

Mabel thought about his suggestion for a long while before eventually saying, 'All right, I'll come up there with you to meet them, but don't expect me to make up my mind right away. It's a big decision, one likely to affect us for a very long time.'

'True,' Goran nodded agreement, 'but it's fairly certain Albert Bolitho will want to get back to mining as soon as he's fit again and he's likely to have his own plans for his family.'

'It seems a very long time since I last came up here. I'd forgotten just how beautiful and open it all is.'

Mabel made the observation when she and Goran paused for a brief rest after passing through a gate from the highest field on Elworthy Farm and came out onto open moorland. Above them a buzzard glided in a wide circle, its plaintive call vying with the distant thud of a mine stamp engine, carried on the wind from the mine complex at Caradon, out of sight beyond the near horizon of the moor.

'We have grazing rights up here,' Goran commented, 'Elworthy never made much use of it but I intend to, especially when I have crops in some of the lower fields.'

Unlike his mother, Goran was viewing the moor through a farmer's eyes and it made her feel very proud of him, but she voiced a cautionary warning.

'Just as long as you don't try to run before you've learned to walk. But where's this mine, I'm not used to all this exercise?'

They continued on their way in silence until the incomplete Wheal Hope engine-house came into view. It had only been a few days since Goran was last here but the building was almost ready for the massively heavy iron rocking beam to be lifted into place on the stout granite wall needed to support its considerable weight.

★ ★ ★

In answer to Goran's knock on the closed door of the office, a voice called, 'Come in,' and Goran and his mother entered the room. Two men were seated at the desk on which a number of papers were spread out. One of the men was Captain Pyne, the other's style of dress was that of a townsman and not a mining man.

Both men stood when they saw Mabel and, apologizing for the interruption, Goran explained the purpose of his visit and said he was being accompanied by Mabel because she had a few things to take to Harriet Bolitho.

Nodding approvingly, Captain Pyne said, 'The Bolithos will be pleased to accept anything you have to give them. My wife said she was going up there some time today, so if we go to the cottage now she'll take you up there with her. But why does Mrs Roach want to see me so urgently?'

'It's to do with mining rights and dues. She thinks Sir John Spurre may have given you wrong information about them — and matters have come to a head. He was down at Elworthy Farm with his solicitor yesterday, expecting to buy the farm and all the dues that go with it. Agnes Roach put a stop to the sale and Sir John was very angry.'

Nodding in the direction of the man who had been seated at the desk with him, Captain Pyne said, 'You've arrived at an opportune time, this is Mr Foster, the lawyer employed by the Wheal Hope adventurers. We have just been discussing the various rights that need to be taken into consideration when we begin bringing ore to surface. He and I will go together to see Mrs

Roach, but we'll go to the cottage first and introduce your mother to my wife. I have no doubt you would appreciate a cup of tea, Mrs Trebartha, it's a warm day to be climbing up here to the mine.'

Accompanied by the solicitor, Captain Pyne led Mabel and Goran to the cottage. On the way he said, 'Do I take it that Sir John Spurre and Mrs Roach had a falling out when they met yesterday?'

'Yes. Sir John thought he'd succeeded in bullying Elworthy Coumbe into selling the farm to him and all the rights that go with it, but it turns out that Agnes — who is Elworthy's sister — is the actual owner of the farm. Her father left both farms to her because Elworthy is a simple soul and not capable of thinking things out for himself.'

'Do you believe Sir John is aware of Elworthy Coumbe's condition?' The question came from the solicitor.

'Oh yes, everyone knows.'

'I see.'

There was an exchange of glances between the solicitor and Captain Pyne and although no words were spoken both had grasped the situation.

When the mine-captain's cottage was reached they were met by Annie Pyne. After cursory introductions and a brief explanation of why they had all come to the house, the mine captain and solicitor set off for Roach Farm leaving Goran and his mother with Annie Pyne and young Jennifer.

'Nessa will be very disappointed to have missed you,' Annie said to Goran, 'She and Morwenna have both gone to Caradon where the father of friends of theirs from down west has recently been taken on as a shift captain and he brought his family here with him. It would seem a great many of the more experienced mine workers believe there are more prospects for them in this part of Cornwall.'

Goran had been looking forward to introducing Nessa to his mother and Mabel was aware of his disappointment. Although he had said little to her about the Pynes' middle daughter, a mother's intuition told her he had met someone he regarded highly.

Her suspicion was strengthened when Annie Pyne said, 'She is particularly hoping to see you because I believe she has a book to give to you, one that belonged to Morwenna. I overheard her offering to exchange a bracelet she has for it. I could probably find the book, but I think I'd better leave it to Nessa to give it to you.'

She gave Goran a knowing glance and her meaning was so apparent that Goran coloured up, embarrassed. Jennifer added to his discomfort when she said in all innocence, 'It was Nessa's favourite bracelet! She let me wear it once . . . but only for a little while.'

'I expect Nessa will bring the book down to you at the farm. I believe you've suggested she brings Jennifer down there to see some piglets you have there — that's if the farmer has no objection, of course.'

The remark was an opportunity for Mabel to

tell Annie Pyne, with considerable pride, that there could be no objection because *Goran* was now the farmer at Elworthy.

The mine captain's wife was impressed. She already realized that Nessa was strongly attracted to Goran and although she herself liked him, she had hoped it was merely a passing fancy on the part of her daughter, no more than a phase of growing up.

Unfortunately, Nessa was a strong-minded girl who took life a little too seriously and the ambitions Annie and her husband had for her were aimed higher than a young farm labourer husband, albeit a very likeable one. However, a *farmer* was a far more acceptable prospect!

12

Annie Pyne and Jennifer accompanied Goran and Mabel to the mean structure on the moor that was the Bolithos' home and, much to Goran's surprise, they found Albert Bolitho seated outside on a rock that had been rolled to the spot, a pair of crudely constructed crutches propped beside him.

With the aid of the crutches he struggled awkwardly to his feet when he saw the visitors approaching, ignoring their pleas for him to remain seated. Finally succeeding, he balanced precariously upon the crutches, a triumphant expression on his face as he faced the visitors.

When Annie Pyne introduced Mabel as Goran's mother, the injured man beamed, 'I'm very pleased to meet you, ma'am. Your son saved my life and I'd be honoured to shake your hand if I was just a little bit more sure of myself on these crutches that young Jenken made for me. It's the first time I've used them and I'm not too steady just yet, but I soon will be, I promise you.'

While he was talking, Harriet Bolitho had come from the moorland shelter, the youngest of their boys in her arms. The child looked pale and undernourished and while introductions were being made he had a coughing fit that left him gasping for breath.

Harriet, whom Goran thought looked only a little less strained than when he had last seen her, apologized for her son's condition, saying there had been a cold wind blowing across the moor for the past forty-eight hours and it was something that always seemed to affect the child's chest.

'I've brought some milk from the farm with me; it might help build him up a little. It's in a can here in the basket, together with a few other things I thought might be welcome.' Mabel lifted the milk can from the basket as she spoke.

Albert Bolitho frowned and Goran, remembering what had once been said about the miner being too proud to accept charity, sought to divert his attention by asking, 'Where's Jenken? I was hoping I might find him here today.'

'He's gone off to Caradon to see if he can find a day's work on one of the mines there. Sometimes a bal maiden goes sick and they might take him on until they can find another. Being a maid's pay it doesn't amount to much and the work seldom lasts longer than a day but it's better than nothing while I'm like this. Why were you hoping to find him? You're not thinking of starting haymaking earlier than expected?'

There was an eagerness in Albert's question that Goran recognized and, although the course of action he was about to propose had been little more than a vague idea, thought up on the way here, he suddenly made up his mind and said, 'It's not *quite* time yet, although it won't be long now, but there have been changes at Elworthy Farm. The man I've been working for isn't up to managing the farm any longer and has gone to live with his sister on the neighbouring farm.

She actually owns both farms and has asked me to take over the tenancy of Elworthy. I've agreed, but I'm going to need help. The problem is that for much of this first year I'm not going to be able to pay a man's wages. If you'd let Jenken come and work for me for a boy's wages he'd be fed at the farm and I'd try to add to his pay with eggs, the occasional chicken and bits and pieces like pork and mutton — potatoes too when I'm able to get some into the ground.'

Mabel and the food she had brought from the farm forgotten, Albert was genuinely excited by Goran's proposal. 'You mean you're offering Jenken a permanent job on a farm?'

'That's right, but as I said, I'll only be able to pay him a boy's wages to begin with, say three-and-six, or thereabouts, a week. Although, if things go the way I hope they will, I'll raise it before too long and if ever Agnes Roach wants work done at her farm I'll let him go there to earn a little extra — and there'll be more from both of us come haymaking.'

Suddenly doubtful, Albert Bolitho said, 'You're a bit young to be taking on the tenancy of a farm. Do you really think you'll be able to make a go of it?'

'I wouldn't be taking it on if I thought otherwise, and I'll do my damnedest to make it work.'

Looking at Goran seriously, Albert said, 'Yes, boy, I think you will and I'd like to see our Jenken learn to do something more than mining for a living. So would his mother. She'd help on farms down west when we were first married and

93

always said working on a farm was far better for a man than spending his life burrowing underground like a mole, which isn't what God intended for us. I've been mining for too long to change now, but it's time *something* went the way she wants, I've not been able to do very much to make her life any easier these last few months. Having our Jenken working on a farm would be a dream come true for her.'

'Then send him down to me as soon as he feels able to start and I'll take him on.'

While he was speaking, Albert had been looking to where his wife was feeding milk to their sick child who was taking it greedily from a handle-less cup and Goran realized from his expression that the miner genuinely loved his wife.

★ ★ ★

Mabel had already come to the same conclusion about Harriet Bolitho's feelings towards Albert. Aware of the impression Mabel must have been given by the conditions in which her family were living on the inhospitable moor, Harriet had insisted her husband was not to blame for their situation, declaring vehemently, 'He's a good worker . . . a good miner. Captain Pyne knows it and it's why he said he'll take Albert on when Wheal Hope begins working and it's why we came here in the first place. Albert's just had bad luck this last year, that's all. Three of the mines he worked for closed down, putting hundreds of miners out of work. Many of the other miners declared Cornish mining was too uncertain and went to foreign lands like Australia, America and such places. Albert would have liked to go, I know he would, but he wouldn't leave me and the boys here to fend for ourselves never knowing where he was or what he was doing.

'Besides, we haven't always lived like this,' she had added, defensively. 'When we were first married we had a little cottage that was as nice as anyone could wish for, but the mine was played out and we needed to go to where there was work for Albert. Things have just gone from bad to worse since then and this last year in particular has been a nightmare.'

As though aware of the depressive nature of her narrative, Harriet made a conscious effort to shake off the mood, saying, 'I'm sorry. You don't want to listen to me carrying on about something that's affecting others even worse than us. I've got a caring husband, a son to be proud of and a family who give me some very happy moments. Then there are people like you, Goran and the Pynes who couldn't be kinder.'

Despite her resolution, Harriet was close to tears when she added, 'It's more than a lot of women ever know.'

Mabel had already decided she liked Harriet Bolitho. She had fewer material possessions than anyone Mabel had ever met with and was so weary from caring for five boys and an invalid husband it was a wonder she was able to remain on her feet, but she was not a broken woman. She had a quiet strength within her that refused to admit defeat and there appeared to be no resentment towards those who possessed things she lacked.

On her way to the moor with Goran, Mabel had entertained a number of doubts about his ideas for the Bolitho family, but now, having met Harriet, she was in full agreement with him and before leaving she obtained a firm commitment from Harriet to come and visit her at Elworthy Farm in the next day or two, pointing out that Albert had now recovered sufficiently to be left alone for a couple of hours. Mabel would put Goran's proposal to her then.

★ ★ ★

'Have you thought any more about having the Bolithos move into our cottage once we're in the farmhouse?' Goran put the question to his mother as they were walking home from Wheal Hope after saying goodbye to Annie Pyne and Jennifer.

'Yes.'

When nothing more was forthcoming, Goran prompted, 'And?'

'I think Harriet Bolitho is a remarkable woman. Not only is she raising five boys in almost impossible circumstances, but coping with an injured husband who she refuses to blame for any of her problems. She obviously loves him very much.'

'You still haven't answered my question.'

'I'd be perfectly happy having the Bolithos living at Elworthy. There are bound to be a few problems having a family living there who know nothing of farming ways, but I believe Harriet is someone I can talk to, so we'd be able to sort things out.'

'Actually, Albert Bolitho was telling me that Harriet *has* worked on a farm and it's always been her dream that the boys would do the same instead of taking up mining.'

'There you are then!' Mabel spoke triumphantly, as though the idea of having the Bolithos come to live at Elworthy had been her idea in the first place. 'And judging by the look of her youngest, moving to a proper house can't come a moment too soon. He looks consumptive to me. Living in the way they are on the moor won't be helping him at all.'

'Well, Elworthy should be moving in with Agnes this weekend, so if Harriet comes to see you as she's promised, the family could move into the cottage almost immediately, which will be just as well for all of them. There's cloud building up out to the west and I think there's rain on the way . . . but this looks like Captain Pyne heading towards us from Roach Farm and the solicitor isn't with him. I wonder how they got on with Agnes.'

When they met the mine captain he explained the absence of the solicitor, saying, 'We took his horse with us to Roach Farm and he's returning to his office in Bodmin direct from there. We had an interesting meeting with Agnes Roach, *most* interesting. She is a very shrewd woman — as her family must have been before her. It seems it was her grandfather, or great-grandfather who obtained the mineral rights she holds. They are not only for the two farms but he somehow obtained the same rights, 'in perpetuity', for common land on the moor itself. I thought it was most unusual but Mrs Roach has the documents to prove her claim and Mr Foster confirmed they are indisputable. There is good news for you too. She tells me you have taken the tenancy of Elworthy Farm?'

When Goran nodded confirmation, adding, 'That's right, Agnes offered me terms that made taking the tenancy easy for me.'

'I can believe it, she would seem to be a most generous woman — and is obviously very fond of you. She also has great confidence in your ability to make a success of Elworthy Farm and the agreement we reached should ensure that you will.'

'An agreement? You mean about the rights that are due if your mining takes you beneath Elworthy?'

'That and more. She named you as recipient of fifty per cent of the dues for Elworthy land but said you are also to receive twenty-five per cent of any dues in respect of the common land for which she owns the rights. If the lode we've come across carries on in the direction I think it's heading, you'll end up quite a wealthy young man. It's likely to bring in more for you than farming, even in the best of years.'

Aware of his mother's delight at Pyne's words, Goran said, 'That really is very exciting, but I'll still be working the farm as though my livelihood depends on it.'

Captain Pyne nodded his agreement, 'I

wouldn't expect a sensible man to do anything else, but now I had better be heading back to the mine. I plan to carry out some blasting but I want to check everything first. We seem to be getting more water than I expected into the workings. I need to make certain we're not going to divert the course of an underground stream and so make things difficult for ourselves.'

'It would be easy to do,' Goran commented, 'There are a great many springs and streams around here.'

'So I believe.' With a knowing and amused smile, Captain Pyne added, 'I believe you and my daughters first met when they had found one of them.'

About to stutter an embarrassed apology, Goran was saved by Mabel. Addressing the mine captain, she asked, 'Before you go I wonder if I might speak to you about the Bolithos?'

'Of course, you've been to see them today, how is Albert coming along?'

'He's up on his feet with the aid of a pair of crutches, but it's the whole family I'd like to ask you about.'

Mabel proceeded to explain to the mine captain the plans she and Goran had for the destitute family's future and asked for his opinion of them.

'It would be a wonderful thing to do!' Captain Pyne replied, sincerely. 'Whatever Albert may say, or think, his days as an underground miner are over. I saw his leg when it was first injured and have since discussed it with the doctor. It will never be strong enough for him to negotiate ladders beneath grass so I'll need to find surface work for him . . . as an engine-man, perhaps. Until then Annie and I will see they never starve but unfortunately there are a great many miners without work right now and I can't afford to support all of them. If Goran is able to offer work to Jenken and a proper home to the family they'll get by and I don't think they'll let you down. Albert has always been a hard-working and honest miner and in Harriet he has a very good wife. Take them in and let me know if there is any way I might be of help to you.'

After telling Captain Pyne she had not yet discussed the proposal with Harriet Bolitho, Mabel was satisfied that their decision to house the Bolithos was a sound one, and she and Goran made their way back to the farmhouse, both proudly aware that the land over which they were walking would soon be theirs to farm.

13

Jenken Bolitho was so eager to begin work at Elworthy Farm that he arrived there the next morning ready to begin work while Goran was still dressing!

Goran had not intended taking him on until Elworthy had moved out of the farm, but the boy was so excited at the prospect of starting full-time work that Goran did not have the heart to disappoint him.

For his first morning Jenken accompanied Goran around the farmyard, learning the daily routine of releasing livestock that had been shut in overnight; feeding, watering and cleaning their pens and houses then checking on the well-being of a number of cows which were in various stages of pregnancy. After this it was time to bring in the milking cow and place it in a stall, ready to be milked by Mabel.

During the course of these chores Jenken was introduced to Elworthy who seemed bemused by the young boy's presence on the farm. However, so much was changing in the simple farmer's life that he accepted without question Jenken's right to be there.

Their early morning chores completed, and in accordance with the established farm routine, Jenken accompanied Goran and Elworthy into the cottage for a breakfast cooked for them by Mabel.

The fact that such a meal was a rare treat indeed for the boy was evident by the enthusiasm with which he devoured the extra large portion placed before him.

His enjoyment of the meal was not shared by Elworthy who merely picked at his food. It was so unlike the usual gusto he exhibited at meal times that Mabel commented upon his apparent lack of appetite.

'It's because I'm unhappy,' Elworthy replied, his lower lip thrust out in an expression of childlike misery, 'I won't be having breakfast here after tomorrow . . . and I like your cooking.'

'You'll like Agnes's cooking too, Elworthy: she bakes some of the best cakes you'll ever taste anywhere.'

'It won't be the same . . . and I won't have you working with me.'

Goran had worked and lived close to Elworthy for long enough to know the simple man often indulged in bouts of self-pity. On such occasions nothing anyone said could dispel the mood but, acutely aware that Elworthy would soon be leaving the comfortable familiarity of the farm that had been his home for so long, he said, sympathetically, 'I'll be coming to Roach often enough to keep you in touch with what's going on here, Elworthy, and you're welcome to come visiting as often as you like — although I know you'll soon be just as involved with everything that's happening at Roach Farm as you are here. When Agnes sees how well you look after animals she'll wonder how she ever managed before you came to live there. Besides, it will be really nice for a brother and sister to be working together.'

★ ★ ★

With breakfast over, Goran took Jenken to check on the farm's sheep, most of which were grazing on land well away from the farmhouse. He was also able to point out the boundaries of Elworthy Farm. Along the way, Jenken said, 'I feel sorry for Elworthy, having to leave a farm where he must have lived for so many years.'

'I do too, and if Sir John Spurre hadn't tried to swindle him out of the farm Elworthy might have been able to go on for another year or two, but he's been getting more vague and forgetful than ever lately and needs watching in case he does something particularly silly, so Agnes decided she wanted to keep a closer watch on him. If she hadn't I wouldn't have taken over the farm and you wouldn't be working here with me.'

'I'm *very* glad about that!' Jenken squirmed with delight as he added, 'Ma's very happy about it too and she hasn't had much to be happy about lately. Still, now I'm working for you I'll be able to make life a bit easier for her and for the whole family.'

'That's perfectly true . . . and it reminds me, she said she would come visiting Elworthy Farm soon, but *my* ma says you are to tell her she wants to see her urgently, tomorrow if possible.'

Alarmed about what Mabel could want to speak to his mother about that was a matter of

103

such urgency, Jenken asked, 'It . . . it's nothing about me working here, is it? I mean . . . your ma doesn't think I won't be able to keep up with the work on the farm?'

'No, it's nothing like that,' Goran said reassuringly, moved by the boy's genuine anxiety, 'I'm the one who decides whether or not you can do the work, and I'm satisfied there's no problem. No, she wants to see your ma about something I think will please you, but I won't say any more because it's something for your ma and mine to discuss . . . but talking of folk coming visiting, isn't this Morwenna Pyne walking down off the moor? What's she doing here?'

It *was* Morwenna and she was carrying something bulky beneath her arm. As she drew nearer Goran could see it was a large, leather-bound book.

On the occasions when they had met before today Goran had found Morwenna's attitude uncomfortably confrontational, but today she was surprisingly friendly, although she did not seem particularly pleased to find Jenken accompanying him. Ignoring the young boy, she addressed Goran.

'Hello, I was just coming down to the farm to see you.'

Taking the large book from beneath her arm she held it out to him, 'I've brought you this, it's a dictionary I was given a long time ago. I heard you wanted one and as I have no use for it I thought you might as well have it.'

It was a present Goran would have been delighted with had he not been told by Annie Pyne that giving him the dictionary had been

104

Nessa's idea and that she had been willing to exchange her favourite bracelet for it. As Morwenna held out the book to him, he noticed she was actually wearing an attractive silver-coloured bracelet decorated with pale-purple quartz-like stones and he felt uneasy.

Something was not quite right and he could think of no reason why it should be Morwenna and not Nessa bringing the book to him . . . unless something was wrong with Nessa.

He was about to ask after her when some indefinable instinct stopped him from asking a direct question. Instead, he said, 'It's kind of you, Morwenna . . . very kind. I shall make good use of it. I must say, I've never seen you without Jennifer and Nessa with you, I hope they're both well?'

'We may be sisters but we're not tied together. I like to do a lot of things without having them around. Anyway, Jennifer didn't sleep well last night and she's too irritable this morning to take anywhere, while Nessa's up at the mine office helping Pa go through the mine accounts. I was left on my own so I thought I'd come here to see you and bring the dictionary. Ma told us yesterday you'd become a yeoman farmer and as I'd nothing better to do I thought I'd come down to see you and let you show me over the farm.'

'I'd like to do that, Morwenna, but I don't have time today. I've got a lot of things to do this morning — and this afternoon I need to go and work at Roach Farm.'

Assuming an expression that was more in keeping with the person Goran believed her to be, Morwenna said peevishly, '*You're* supposed to be the farmer now. Jenken can do whatever needs to be done while you show me around the farm.'

'This is Jenken's first day working here. I need to tell him where everything is. Besides, I don't take over the farm until Elworthy leaves — and he's still here.' Goran had realized on the first occasion he had met the oldest Pyne sister that she liked getting her own way and she was not happy at being thwarted today.

'It seems I've walked all this way for nothing! I thought you'd at least show me around the farm. You told Jennifer you'd let her see some piglets you have in the farmyard.'

'I'd be very happy to show you *all* the piglets, but not today. Come back another time bringing Nessa and Jennifer with you and I'll show you all the animals. You've just chosen a bad day to call — but your journey certainly hasn't been wasted, I'm delighted to have the dictionary and will make very good use of it.'

'I suppose that will have to do, but you could at least give me a kiss for coming all this way with it.'

Goran hesitated. Morwenna was being particularly bold in asking him to kiss her, but Jenken was here with them so it would go no further.

Stepping forward he gave her a quick kiss on the cheek then stepped back quickly as she brought up her arms to draw him to her.

Dropping her arms to her side, she said scathingly, 'Well, that wasn't much of a kiss, but I suppose it will have to do . . . for now.'

14

That evening, in the Pynes' cottage at the Wheal Hope mine, the family were waiting for Piran Pyne to return home when Nessa, who had been upstairs in the bedroom she shared with her sisters, returned to the living room wearing a puzzled frown.

'Has anyone seen the dictionary I bought from Morwenna for Goran Trebartha? I can't find it upstairs.'

'Oh, I took it down to the farm and gave it to Goran while you were working at the mine office,' Morwenna said, casually.

'*You did what?*'

Although Nessa's disbelief was mixed with a very real anger Morwenna merely shrugged. 'I felt like taking a walk so I thought I might as well go that way and take the book to him. You were so eager to get it for him I thought it must be urgent.'

'It wasn't yours to do *anything* with any more, I'd given you my bracelet for it.'

Still behaving with almost insolent nonchalance, Morwenna said, 'I thought you'd bought it because Goran needed a dictionary, I didn't realize it was the actual *giving* of it that was so important. But if you want to get the dictionary back from Goran you can have your old bracelet again, I don't care.'

Speechless, Nessa stood staring at her sister

uncertainly for a long time before turning away and hurrying from the room without uttering another word.

Aghast at the actions of her eldest daughter, Annie said, 'That was *very* mean of you, Morwenna . . . and quite deliberate! You knew Nessa wanted that dictionary as a special gift for Goran, giving it to him mattered a lot to her. That is probably the most spiteful thing you have ever done and it will be a long time before I forgive you for it.'

'Why? What's so special about Nessa and a boy *she* cares for? All she really wants is to look clever and be a teacher. Anyway, no one thought twice about how much *I* cared for Alan Toms when you brought me here — and *he* wanted to marry me.'

'That isn't true, Morwenna, and it's no use you deluding yourself about Alan. We had to come here because your father's work demanded it, but before we left he spoke to Alan and offered him work on Wheal Hope, even though he didn't particularly like him, but Alan said he didn't want to come, despite knowing he would be more secure working here. Anyway, even if he had wanted to marry you it's no excuse for what you've done to Nessa, that is quite unforgivable — and I've no doubt your father will think so too.'

'I don't care what any of you think. If Goran likes me better than he does Nessa I'm not going to do anything to discourage him. *He* might want to marry me and being a farmer's wife would be better than being here where no one cares what *I* think about anything, or what it is *I* might want.'

With this, Morwenna rushed from the room, her footsteps loud on the new wooden staircase leading to the two upstairs rooms.

In the bedroom shared by the three sisters Nessa was lying fully clothed on top of her bed, staring up at rough, bark-clad timbers supporting the roof, her hands clasped behind her head.

She turned her head when Morwenna entered the room but seeing who it was immediately turned over on her side, facing away from her sister.

The movement prompted Morwenna to say, 'I can't do anything right in this house, I don't know why I even try!'

When her statement prompted no response, Morwenna added, 'I thought you *wanted* Goran to have the book, that's why I took it.'

For a moment Nessa wondered whether the explanation might be genuine, but then Morwenna added, 'At least the kiss that Goran gave me showed that *he* was grateful.'

Turning on the bed so that she was looking at her sister, Nessa said, with disbelief, 'Goran kissed you?'

'You mean he's never kissed *you*? I don't believe it! When he kissed me I thought it must be what he was used to doing with all the girls he knew. If it isn't . . . ? Well, perhaps he really meant it when he said he'd like me to come to the farm so he could show me around now *he's* the farmer and can find more time to do the things he really wants to do.'

Satisfied with the effect her words had upon her sister, Morwenna walked from the room, leaving a shaken and very unhappy Nessa behind her.

★   ★   ★

'Where are the girls?' Piran Pyne asked the question that evening as his wife put out plates for only three on the kitchen table.

'Nessa is upstairs in the girls' bedroom and says she doesn't want anything to eat, but I don't know where Morwenna is. I thought she was in the bedroom too, but Jennifer said she went out of the back door saying she was going for a walk.'

Frowning, Piran asked, 'Has anything happened to upset them?'

'Yes . . . ' Annie told her husband of the incident involving the dictionary.

After listening with increasing anger, Piran said, 'That really would have upset Nessa, she was talking happily to me today at Wheal Hope about taking the book to Goran at the farm tomorrow. It's most unthinking of Morwenna to have done that.'

'Sadly, I don't think there was any lack of thought in what she did. Morwenna is bitterly resentful about leaving Alan Toms behind when we moved here. She's convinced herself he would have asked her to marry him if we'd stayed down west.'

'We couldn't have stayed there, she knows that. The mine was played out and I was very lucky to have been asked to start up the Wheal

110

Hope, otherwise we could very well have been in a similar plight to the Bolithos. Besides, I offered Alan the opportunity to come here to be near her if that's what he really wanted. Had he accepted he would have been far more secure than he is there. I'll have serious words with Morwenna, she shouldn't have done what she did to anyone — certainly not to her own sister.'

'I've already made that point to her and I've no doubt the reason she's gone out is because she knows what you'll say to her about it.'

'I'll say what's needed anyway — although she may get away with it tonight, I have to go back to the mine after supper. We've hit hard rock in the shaft and are falling behind so I need to get the men working nights but I'll go upstairs and speak to Nessa before I go. I think Goran is a nice lad and a solid one, he and Nessa would be a good match. But I do have some good news to tell you. On my way home I met with young Jenken Bolitho returning from his work at the farm. He was happier than I've ever seen him. It seems he's going to enjoy working on a farm. He was carrying a basket of things he'd been given to take home. I think the family will be happy too — and even happier when they learn what Goran and his mother have in mind for them . . . '

★   ★   ★

Piran Pyne did not want to exacerbate the disagreement between his two daughters, so he used Jennifer's early bedtime as an excuse for going to the shared bedroom with her in his arms. Here he found Nessa lying on her own bed, still fully clothed.

Lying staring up at the ceiling she took no notice when he entered the room.

'Hello, aren't you feeling too well this evening?'

'I just don't feel hungry, that's all.'

'Well, I have some news that might help cheer you up. I met young Jenken Bolitho coming home from his work at the farm and he was bubbling over with delight about his work and although he doesn't know it yet, Goran has hinted that the family could be moving into the farm cottage. Mabel Trebartha wants to talk to Harriet Bolitho about it. When it's settled you might like to go up to the Bolithos' place and see if there's anything you can do to help with the children during the move. It's high time that family had some good luck come their way.'

'I'm pleased for the Bolithos, but I'm sure they'll be able to manage without my help.'

'I thought you might welcome an opportunity to go to Elworthy and congratulate Goran on taking over the farm? It's a great achievement for such a young man.'

'I think he'd rather see Morwenna than me and she no doubt passed on our family's congratulations when she went to the farm earlier today.'

'She might have done, but I'm convinced it would mean more to him coming from you — but where is Morwenna, Ma tells me she wasn't at supper either?'

'I've no idea . . . unless she's at Elworthy Farm.'

Realizing nothing he said to Nessa this evening would shake her out of her present despondent mood, Piran said, 'Oh well, I'm putting Jennifer to bed now, perhaps you'll read her one of your stories, she'd like that — and it might cheer you up a bit. I have to return to the mine for a couple of hours.'

15

When Morwenna left the Wheal Hope cottage she was nursing a sense of determined grievance, yet although fully aware she had been underhanded with her sister in respect of Goran, she had no regrets. The family had shown little sympathy to her when they insisted that she accompany them to this part of the country against her wishes, even though it meant parting her from the man she had intended marrying.

Morwenna's resentful ambition now was to marry and move away from her family. In Goran she felt she had found someone with whom she could not only achieve that aim but who could also offer her a more comfortable life than she would have within the mining community.

She shrugged off the knowledge that her sister was enamoured of the man she intended pursuing. Nessa had hardly had time to get to know him and would no doubt find someone else in due course.

The fact that Goran had shown no interest in her did not worry Morwenna unduly, there were ways of making a man with principles believe he *should* marry a girl. It had almost worked with her previous sweetheart and she believed she could do the same with Goran.

She did not feel the least pang of conscience about her intentions. She would keep Goran as happy as any man deserved to be and they would no doubt enjoy a comfortable life together. Besides, there were other considerations — serious ones — but Morwenna did not want to dwell on them and successfully pushed them to the back of her mind.

★ ★ ★

Morwenna's plans received a setback when she met up with Jenken who was on his way home from his work on Elworthy Farm. In reply to her question he informed her that Goran had left him to finish off the work at Elworthy while he went to Roach Farm to carry out some chores there.

Morwenna thought of going to Roach Farm to find Goran but changed her mind immediately. She had never met Agnes Roach but had heard enough to think twice about annoying her by interfering with Goran's work on her farm.

However, she had no intention of returning home just yet, the upset she had caused within her family was still fresh enough to erupt again and she would no doubt be blamed for its cause. It would take a while for their resentment against her to subside, so in the meantime she decided to explore a part of the moor she had not yet visited, the area beyond the upper limits of the two farms owned by Agnes Roach.

Reaching the section of Spurre land which extended on to the high moor from the large estate she followed the boundary wall until it was replaced by a recently plashed hawthorn hedge which was little more than waist-high.

Reaching the hedge, Morwenna was startled to see a young man, perhaps three or four years older than herself, walking on the estate side of the barrier. Unseen, he must have been keeping pace with her as she walked along the other side of the wall.

He appeared equally surprised, but was the first to speak.

'Hello, what are you doing up here, and where are you from? I don't remember seeing you around this way before.'

'That's because I haven't been up here before — and I hope you've got permission to be over there. There's a gamekeeper who's threatened to shoot anyone he finds trespassing on the Spurre estate.'

The young man smiled, 'You must be talking about my uncle Marcus. His bark is far worse than his bite, I don't think he's ever *actually* shot anyone.'

'That's where you're wrong! He shot a young dog just because it was friendly with me and my sisters — and he did it while we were watching. It upset my little sister so much she had nightmares about it, so don't tell me he's not a bad person!'

'He must have had a reason for doing what he did and you've seen a side of him I haven't, but you still haven't told me who you are and what you're doing up here on the moor.'

'It's none of your business, but my name is Morwenna and my pa is captain of the Wheal Hope.'

'Wheal Hope? Isn't that the name of the new

116

mine, a little way along the edge of the moor? It means we're almost neighbours.'

'Does it?' Morwenna shrugged, but her apparent indifference was carefully feigned. The Spurre estate gamekeeper's nephew was quite good-looking and, unlike Goran, did not seem entirely uninterested in her.

'Yes. My name is Tom, Tom Miller. I'm staying with my uncle Marcus because he's teaching me about gamekeeping. As soon as he thinks I know enough I expect to be given a cottage on the estate. There are one or two empty at the moment. The one I particularly like isn't far from here. It's hidden in that clump of trees over there . . . '

He pointed to where the tops of a number of deciduous trees could be seen rising above an apparent shallow hollow in the grounds of the estate, adding, 'It was lived in by an old retired gamekeeper who died a couple of months ago. It still has all his furniture there and would suit me very well. I'll show it to you if you'd like to see it.'

'I'm sure you would but as we've only just met and all I know about you is what *you've* just told me, you're not taking me anywhere!'

There was just sufficient indignation in Morwenna's reply to indicate to Tom Miller that she was not devoid of all morals, but the look that accompanied her words was bold enough to suggest that she did not value virtue as highly as was being implied.

'I'm sorry, I was being a bit forward, wasn't I? It's a long time since I had anything to do with girls. I worked in a saw-mill for my father until he died only a month ago, and my mother, Marcus Grimble's younger sister, died when I was only fifteen.'

'Oh! I'm sorry to hear that.' Morwenna's sympathy sounded genuine. 'Do you have any brothers or sisters?

'No, the only relative I have left now is my uncle Marcus. How about your family?'

'My parents are both alive and I have two sisters, both younger than me . . . '

For some minutes they talked about families until, displaying apparent reluctance, Morwenna said, 'I'd better be getting home now, before it gets dark, my ma will be wondering where I've got to.'

'That's a pity,' Tom Miller said, 'we were just beginning to get to know each other, but do you come out walking the moor very often?'

Her mind working rapidly, Morwenna said, 'I spend a lot of time walking because there's not very much to do about the mine, but I'm out much earlier as a rule, usually early in the afternoon. As I said, I haven't been up this way before so I don't know my way around at all, but it's nice and quiet and it's good to get away from all the noise about the mine.'

'I shall be on this part of the estate for most of tomorrow afternoon. If you're around I could show you the gamekeeper's cottage then. It's in a lovely spot, I'm sure you'd like it. There's a fishing lake close to it and usually a few geese and other water birds there. It's beautiful, really.'

Morwenna left Tom Miller knowing they were

both aware she would be returning the following afternoon. She knew, too, she would accept his offer to see the gamekeeper's remote cottage on the Spurre estate, fully aware of what the inevitable consequence was likely to be.

16

Piran Pyne left his eldest daughter in no doubt of his displeasure the next morning. However, his admonishment was less severe than it might have been because of his need to return to the Wheal Hope and supervise the work on the main shaft being sunk through hard rock ground.

Only a couple of hours later Harriet Bolitho returned from a meeting at Elworthy Farm with Mabel and called in at the Pyne home to happily confirm that she and her family would be moving to the farm cottage the following day.

Annie and Nessa immediately volunteered to go to the moorland hovel to help Harriet prepare for the move and they went from the house taking Jennifer with them, leaving Morwenna to clean and tidy-up in their absence As a result Morwenna had no need to think of an excuse to leave the house. Completing the chores to her own haphazard satisfaction, she made her way to the high moor above the Spurre estate, soon after noon, aware that upon her return any altercation would be about the manner in which she had cleaned the house and not about where she had spent the remainder of the day.

When she arrived at the hedge which had separated her from Tom on the last occasion they had met, the gamekeeper's nephew was nowhere to be seen. For half an hour she walked up and down the boundary becoming increasingly agitated until, much to her relief, she spotted him coming towards her along a path that cut through the middle of the strip of Spurre land.

Unaware of her anxiety, Tom waved gaily and, when he was closer, called cheerily, 'Hello, I was hoping I might meet up with you again. I've just been to have a look around the old cottage. It's in a far better condition than I realized, it will be a great place to live. Would you like to come and see it and tell me what you think? I would appreciate a woman's opinion on any possible drawbacks of living in such an isolated place.'

'Are you quite sure that's the only reason you want to take me to the cottage?'

'It is . . . unless you can think of something more exciting we might be able to do there?'

There was a thinly disguised implication in the bold question that required no answer and Morwenna said, 'I'll come and give you my opinion, but I doubt whether it will make any difference, you've probably already made up your own mind what you want to do.'

'That's just it, I *haven't*, so your opinion could make all the difference.'

'Well, first of all I need to get to your side of the hedge — and I'm not going to try to climb over it.'

'There's a gate not far ahead and we can talk to each other across the hedge on the way there.'

As they kept pace with each other on either side of the trimmed hedge their conversation was of generalities: the moor, its animals and birds, and places of interest in the area which Morwenna had not yet discovered but which Tom thought might prove of interest to her.

They were subjects with which neither of Morwenna's parents could have raised any objections. However, once she had passed through the gateway to the estate and they were walking together they both sensed an indefinable and unspoken change in their relationship, especially when the path occasionally narrowed and their arms brushed against each other.

It was nothing that either could have expressed in words but the conversation between them was now of a more personal nature.

'Are there many young men working at Wheal Hope?'

'None. My pa brought only the most experienced miners with him from down west. I don't think any of them are younger than he is.'

'That can't be much fun for you. What do you and your sisters do to keep yourselves amused?'

'Jennifer's quite happy playing with toys — and Nessa's always got her nose stuck in a book.'

'It sounds as though life must be very boring for *you*.'

'It is, that's why I spend so much time walking around the moor, but I expect *you* know lots of people — men and girls — and if ever you get bored you can always go off drinking with your friends.'

'I don't have any friends. At least, not hereabouts. We were living some miles away when my pa died so I don't really know anyone around here, not of my own age, anyway. That's why I was so pleased to meet up with you

— although I suppose you must have a sweetheart *somewhere*, you being so pretty.'

As he had hoped, Morwenna was flattered by his egregious compliment.

'Chance would be a fine thing! Anyway, I wouldn't want a miner for a sweetheart. I've spent all my life among miners and mines. I'd like to find someone who does something else, something *interesting*.'

'Yes, I suppose it must make a man boring if he's working down a mine all the time with nothing more than a candle or two to give him light. My work is very different. As a gamekeeper there's always so much to see and do, dealing with animals and birds and taking care of the estate . . . but here we are at the cottage. What do you think of it?'

The cottage he had brought her to had a steeply angled and heavily thatched roof which came down low enough for a man to reach up and touch it from ground level, its symmetry broken by two diamond-paned windows. They had approached the rear of the cottage, passing through a copse of trees which protected it on three sides, yet being far enough away for there to be a kitchen garden behind the cottage. It had not been tended for some time and was struggling to hold its own against the onslaught of seasonal weeds. Nevertheless, there was an air of complacent timelessness about the cottage which shrugged off the evidence of recent neglect.

'It's a *lovely* cottage!'

For once Morwenna was being completely

honest, expressing an opinion that was not motivated by self-interest.

'It is, and such a pity there's no one living in it. The inside is just as nice, come in and have a look around.'

The interior of the cottage was low-ceilinged and snug and surprisingly neat and tidy. When Morwenna commented on this, Tom explained, 'When the old gamekeeper died the housekeeper at Spurre Hall sent a couple of the maids here to give it a thorough clean, and as he had no known relatives to claim the furniture it was decided to leave it in place.'

'And this is the cottage you'll be moving into?'

'I don't know. I could if I wanted, but I'll need to think about it. Where I am now one of the maids comes in and keeps the house tidy and we're both fed from the kitchen of the Hall. If I came up here it would be too far for a cleaning woman to come in and I'd need to be cooking for myself.'

Shrugging with feigned nonchalance, he added, 'Perhaps I'll see if I can find a wife from somewhere.'

Disappointed when Morwenna made no reply he changed the subject abruptly. 'The last time I was here I found traces of a rat outside in the shed and put poison down to kill it. While I go and check whether I've caught it why don't you have a look around? There's a wonderful view upstairs from the big bedroom at the front.'

When he had gone Morwenna began her inspection, going from room to room, finding many features to admire including the stout oak beams in the downstairs rooms and a spacious inglenook fireplace complete with slate-slab seats in the kitchen. At the same time, she was disappointed Tom had not chosen to accompany her on her tour of his prospective home.

Climbing the narrow wooden staircase, she made her way to the front, east-facing bedroom that was surprisingly large for such a small cottage. Tom had not exaggerated about the view from here. The River Lynher curved through the valley that was part of the Spurre estate. The land rose on the far side, but the cottage was above the height of this rise and it had a panoramic view of a landscape which extended to the heights of Dartmoor, far off in the neighbouring county of Devon.

Suddenly she heard footsteps on the stairs and, a few moments later, Tom entered the room, coming to stand just behind her, looking over her shoulder to share the view from the window.

Despite being very aware of his closeness, her first words were far from romantic.

'Did you kill the rat?'

'I can't be absolutely sure but the poison has been taken, so no doubt it's lying dead somewhere.'

There was a brief silence between them before he leaned forward so that his cheek was touching hers and pointed to the far horizon. 'That's Dartmoor. It's far bigger than our moor here. Have you ever been there?

'No, I've never been out of Cornwall.' Very aware that his other arm had passed behind her and his hand was now resting on her shoulder, she added, 'You were right, it is beautiful.'

'Not as beautiful as you.' As he spoke the hand tightened on her shoulder and she was awkwardly pulled around to face him, her body against his.

This was the moment when she should have made a protest, Morwenna knew it, and so did Tom. When none came he kissed her, lightly at first but when she responded it became more demanding. Pulling her even closer he made a clumsy attempt to move her backwards towards the bed.

Now she *did* object. Pulling her head — but not her body — away from him, she said, 'You'd better save anything you have in mind for when you've found that wife you were talking about.'

'Perhaps I've found her . . . '

He tried to kiss her again, but she twisted her head to one side, away from him, saying, 'Don't be foolish, this is only the second time we've met.'

'What's time got to do with anything?'

He did not release his hold on her and with their bodies pressed hard against each other Morwenna was fully aware of the desire in him.

He spoke again. 'I believe that if you meet up with the right person you know it right away.'

'You might know straightway but it doesn't mean you get what you want there and then.'

'Why not, what's the sense in waiting? It's just wasting time if you both feel the same way.'

'You would say that because when you get what you want you can go away and forget all about it, leaving the woman to face the consequences.'

'I would never do that. If I felt strongly enough about a woman to want to do it to her I'd want to marry her anyway.'

'So you say. It would be a very different story if it came to *having* to marry because of what you'd done.'

He shook his head. 'No, it wouldn't. Like I said, I wouldn't do it to anyone unless I felt I'd like to be married to her. Mind you, I'd never get married to anyone I *hadn't* done it with. I'd want to know she loved me just as much as I loved her.'

Sensing that Tom was not quite as feverishly eager as he had been a few minutes before, Morwenna believed she might have overplayed her apparent virtuousness. Relaxing her body so it was still pressing against his, but less rigidly, she was able to excite him once more.

'How do I know you mean it?'

'I *do* mean it. What else do you want me to say?'

'Do you promise that if I let you and anything happens to me, you *will* marry me?'

'I promise! I knew when I first saw you that you're the sort of girl I want to marry. Even though I've only known you for a couple of days I'd like to marry you and bring you here to live.'

She said nothing while his body explored hers through the thin summer dress and his excitement increased. Then . . . 'All right, you can . . . but only because you've said you'll marry me if you get me into trouble . . . You *do* promise?'

127

'Of course I do, I wouldn't do it if I didn't want to marry you.'

Even as he was speaking he was propelling her backwards to the bed. Reaching it she fell backwards on to the hard, straw mattress.

After fumbling with his trousers he pulled her dress clumsily up about her waist.

'You're not wearing any drawers!'

'I've never worn any since I was a little girl. I don't like them.'

'That's all right, it makes everything much easier . . . '

He was lying on top of her now and she gave a gasp as he thrust inside her, then her body was responding to his and she abandoned herself to the love-making she had been missing so much since she had left Alan Toms behind in Cornwall's far west.

17

Goran had been surprised it was not Nessa who had brought the dictionary to him at Elworthy and disappointed that the middle Pyne daughter had not come to congratulate him on taking over the tenancy of the farm, but he was given little time to dwell upon her apparent unexpected lack of interest in him. It was time for haymaking on both farms although first it was necessary to take Elworthy Coumbe and what possessions he required to Roach Farm, to begin life there with his sister.

There was also the move to the farmhouse with his mother and, only twenty-four hours later, the Bolithos arrived to take up residence in the vacated Elworthy farm cottage.

Harriet Bolitho was ecstatic at the move from the hovel on Bodmin Moor. Assisted by three miners from the Wheal Hope she and her family arrived early in the afternoon, the injured Albert being conveyed in an iron-wheeled wheelbarrow with the sickly youngest Bolitho child in his arms.

Goran was not there to greet them on their arrival, but when he returned from working at the Roach Farm, he was greeted with a warm kiss from an emotional Harriet who declared, 'Goran, you are the best thing that's happened to the Bolithos for more years than I care to remember! What you have done for Albert,

Jenken and the whole family has given me . . . no, given *all* of us, new hope for the future. The cottage is *lovely* and Jenken is so happy to be working with you!'

Goran was forced to back away from her before she kissed him again and her happiness smothered him. 'I'm glad you're pleased with the cottage. I hope it leads to a change for the better in the fortunes of everyone.'

'How could it be otherwise? The very first thing Albert did was to limp to the back door and stand there telling me what he intends planting for us in the garden, and where it would go. All this while he was propped up on two crutches, barely able to stand! It's lifted his spirits as nothing else could have done.'

Embarrassed by such effusive gratitude, Goran said, 'I hope having you here will suit all of us. I'm certainly very happy to have Jenken working for me, I've never known anyone try so hard to please as he does. I've had to tell him to slow down otherwise he'll exhaust himself!'

'He's a good boy and I would be very happy if I knew his future was on the land and not burrowing beneath it.' Suddenly looking beyond him, she said, 'But where's Morwenna Pyne? I was hoping she might take care of the boys while I sort out the rooms, ready for their bedtimes.'

'Morwenna? What made you think she would be here?'

Now it was Harriet's turn to show surprise, 'I thought Annie said Morwenna was spending a lot of time here, at the farm. I must have got it wrong.'

At that moment there was a shout from one of the boys. He had just seen one of the farm cats in the back garden and Harriet hurried off to ensure he did not do anything to make the cat scratch him, leaving a puzzled Goran wondering why Annie Pyne should think that Morwenna was spending time at Elworthy.

★ ★ ★

Within a few days all thoughts of Morwenna and most other problems had been forgotten as haymaking began in earnest on the two farms. It was hard and concentrated work, involving far more than could be achieved by Goran, even with the assistance of Elworthy Coumbe and Jenken and he needed to recruit a number of helpers from the local workhouse.

Their daily wage, paid to the workhouse, was four pence for the men and two and a half pence for the women. The paupers enjoyed food cooked for them by Agnes Roach and Mabel and ale rationed out to them by Goran but, in spite of such incentives, they had neither the will nor stamina for the work involved and Goran ended each day thoroughly exhausted, his only thoughts being of sleep and the hope he could complete haymaking before the weather broke — a prospect that had been threatening and receding with a baffling frequency for a number of dry weeks.

Every countryman whose everyday life was dictated by the weather agreed that although the continuing absence of rain was important for haymaking, a drought such as was being experienced had serious long-term implications.

Older denizens of the countryside gloomily related stories of past periods of drought which had inevitably been followed by violent storms and torrential rain, as nature sought to right the imbalance it had brought about.

Eventually, much to Goran's relief, haymaking was completed, the hay cut, dried and built into ricks in which hay would be cured and compressed by its own weight and waterproofed from the onslaught of inclement weather by the skills of rick builders, a craft at which the simple Elworthy excelled. Lofts above the stables at both farms were piled high with hay, to be used when severe winter weather made access to outside ricks impossible.

With hay safely gathered in and the celebrations funded by Agnes over, Goran should have been able to relax a little, but it was now time to advance the plans he had for Elworthy Farm.

Jenken was by now sufficiently acquainted with the routine running of the farm to be left to carry out the work without supervision, so Goran felt able to go ahead with preparing two of his fields for crops, beginning with potatoes which would help clean the ground, but first the fields would need to be ploughed and prepared for growing crops. For this he would have to buy a second-hand plough with one, or perhaps two, good plough-horses to carry out the work, and learn how to use a plough. It was something he had never been required to do while Agnes dictated how the two farms should be worked.

In a few days' time a fair was being held in the town of Liskeard, some nine miles away and Goran thought he might be able to purchase a second-hand plough there and possibly find someone to teach him how to use it.

★   ★   ★

The night before the fair was due to begin, when Goran returned from an afternoon and evening spent working at Roach Farm, he called in at the Bolithos' cottage to find Jenken. The family was in a jubilant mood. All except Albert and the two youngest boys had been able to earn a few pence during haymaking and this, together with a variety of foodstuff donated by Mabel and Agnes, had enabled Harriet to cook more substantial meals than they had known for a very long time. They were even able to offer Goran a mug of ale.

Aware of the pleasure it gave to the head of the family to be able to offer something to a guest instead of being forced to accept their charity, he accepted, even though he would rather not have had a drink this late in the evening.

Sipping the drink, Goran said to Albert, 'I must go sparingly with this . . . and so must you, Jenken. I want you up at the crack of dawn tomorrow to get the farmyard chores done as quickly as possible.'

'That's all right,' Jenken replied. 'I don't like ale very much anyway, but are we doing something special tomorrow?'

'We certainly are! We're going to take the

horse and a light wagon to Liskeard. It's Fair Day and Agnes has loaned me money to buy a plough and harrow — if I'm able to find them at the right price. If they're too expensive I'll need to pay someone to do the work for me, but I'd rather not do that. I'll also need a plough horse . . . probably two, but I should be able to get them cheaper at a market a bit closer to home.'

'Do you have any experience of ploughing?' The unexpected question came from Harriet.

'No,' Goran confessed, 'but I expect I'll be able to pick it up as I go along.'

'It would be much easier if you were able to learn straightway from someone with experience of the work. I know from when I used to work on a farm that ploughing's a skilled job. A man who can plough is paid more than the other men on a farm. You'll have to be sure the horse you buy knows what it's doing. You can't set any old horse to a plough and expect him to get on with the job. You'll need to know when to rest him too, ploughing's hard work, even for the strongest horse, especially if you're working land that's never been ploughed before.'

'Perhaps I ought to take you along to the fair with us.' Goran suggested, only half-joking. 'You obviously know more about ploughing than I do!'

Harriet gave him a wry smile and shook her head. 'All I know comes from listening to farm talk when I was working down west, I'd be no good to you even if I was able to come to the fair. Anyway, I couldn't leave Albert to look after the boys by himself all day. But I'm serious about you finding someone to help you choose the things you're going to need. You can't afford to buy any old rubbish.'

Goran knew she was talking sense. He did not have the necessary knowledge himself, but hoped there might be farmers at the fair willing to express an opinion on the worth of farming implements being offered for sale.

18

'Have you ever been to Liskeard Fair before?'

The question came from Jenken as he and Goran were driving the horse and wagon to the fair the next morning. Despite the clouds overhead and an ominous dark mass gathering in the sky to the west, the young boy was thrilled at the prospect of attending something as exciting as a 'fair'.

'A couple of times, but never to buy anything, I was only looking around.'

'What's it like, what goes on there?'

'It's noisy, with a lot of buying and selling going on and men and women hoping to find work on farms, although this isn't the best time of year for that, most of the hiring takes place at the early spring fairs. There's a lot of fun things going on too: sideshows, dancing bears and monkeys, music, fire-eaters, sword swallowers — and there's usually a band and the hurdy-gurdies.'

'Do you need to pay to see these things?' Jenken asked anxiously, adding, 'I've got seven pence but I'd like to use it to buy something for Ma, she never gets anything.'

'You have to pay to see a lot of the things but there's always something going on you can look at for nothing.' Looking sideways at the excited boy on the wagon beside him, he added, 'Anyway, Agnes gave me a shilling to give you to spend at the fair because you've worked so hard for her during haymaking — and I'll give you a shilling too, for the same reason.'

It was not a vast amount, but it was more than Jenken had ever possessed before to spend on himself, all the money he earned on Elworthy Farm being given directly to his hard-pressed mother. He wriggled in pleasure as he thought of what he might be able to purchase with his new-found wealth.

★ ★ ★

The fair was everything Goran had promised and more. It was being held on open ground on the edge of the town although stalls sprawled over into the adjoining streets which were crowded with horses, carts and people, all seemingly moving in differing directions.

Goran was obliged to leave the pony and cart some way from the fair in a field, the owner of which was making more from this one day than a bumper crop would have fetched after a year's labour.

As he and Jenken moved among the crowd thronging the fair, Goran suddenly pulled Jenken to a startled halt. He had recognized a man he would rather not meet up with today. It was Marcus Grimble, the Spurre estate gamekeeper and he was accompanied by a younger man whom Goran had never seen before.

When Jenken saw the gamekeeper he began trembling. Laying a hand on the boy's shoulder, Goran said, 'It's all right, Jenken, he's never seen enough of you to recognize you, but try to steer clear of him and I'll do the same. There's nothing he can do to either of us with so many folk around, but he's nasty enough to be unpleasant if he met me. I wonder who the young man is with him, I've never seen him before.'

Controlling his fright, Jenken said, 'I have . . . at least, I *think* I have. I believe I saw him talking to Morwenna up by the Spurre estate, when I was out looking for that lamb we lost.'

'Morwenna with a friend of Grimble? No, you must have been mistaken.' Dismissing the suggested link between the two, Goran said, 'You go off and enjoy yourself now and forget all about Grimble. Meet me in a couple of hours over by the stall where they're selling pasties. I'll buy one for you before we head back home. If it starts raining we'll meet up there earlier.'

Not entirely reassured, Jenken set off on his own, a final warning from Goran about the danger of pickpockets ringing in his ears, although he was far too excited with everything going on around him to pay much attention to his words. Besides, although he *felt* rich there was hardly enough money in his pocket to attract the proficient and highly professional pick-pockets Goran had said frequented the country's fairs.

★   ★   ★

When the two parted company, Goran made his way through the crowds towards an area where he believed he would find farming implements for sale. Unlike Jenken, he *did* carry a great deal of money on him, money that Agnes had loaned him for buying a plough and harrow. He had it in a leather bag hanging from a long leather thong tied about his neck, the hidden bag a comforting weight beneath his shirt. He also had a few pounds of his own money tucked inside a pocket to spend on other things.

On one of the many stalls he passed a man who was offering cheap jewellery for sale and with a particular present in mind, Goran decided he would return to the stall after concluding the purchase of a plough.

Pausing only momentarily at some of the pens where pigs, sheep and cattle were being offered for sale, he eventually reached a clear space on the edge of the fair where various farming implements were laid out for inspection. Some were new, but a great many more were used, some obviously very well worn.

He found he was able to browse here at his leisure, his youth saving him from the attention of the implement vendors who dismissed him as being too young to be a potential buyer.

He had stopped to admire a new three-bladed iron plough when he was joined by an old, bearded man who had the weather-beaten appearance of someone who had spent a long lifetime working in the open air.

Standing beside Goran and looking at the plough, the man said, ' 'Tis a beautiful thing, no doubt about it, but it'd need at least four horses to pull it, and that's too many for good ploughing.'

'You know about ploughing?' Goran queried.

'I should do, it's how I've earned my living since I was only a little older than you are now, but it's not usual to find someone your age interested in ploughs and ploughing. It's too much like hard work for youngsters these days.'

Goran smiled to himself at the other man's comments. He had yet to meet a farmer who gave young men credit for working as hard as they claimed to have been obliged to labour when of a similar age.

'Well, I've just taken the tenancy of a farm that's never seen a plough and I hope to change that.'

Looking at Goran sceptically, the old man said, '*You*'ve taken on a farm? You're a bit young for such a responsibility. Your family must have plenty of money to give you a farm of your own.'

This time Goran laughed out loud, 'It would make life a whole lot easier if that were so . . . but I mustn't grumble, I've got the next best thing. I've worked for a generous widow since I was eleven and she's not only given me the tenancy of a farm she owns, but has made certain I have enough money to make a success of it.'

'Is that so? I wish I'd met someone like that when I was your age, but I've nothing to complain about. I was a ploughman for more than twenty years for as good an employer as you'd be likely to find anywhere, and he left me a sum of money when he died. It wasn't a huge amount but enough for me to buy a plough and two good horses and set out on my own when I fell out with his son and one of his favourite gamekeepers — who I've seen today for the first

140

time in years, right here in the fair.'

Remembering whom he and Jenken had seen when they first arrived at the fair, Goran said, 'You're not talking of Marcus Grimble, head gamekeeper on the Spurre estate?'

'That's him. Do you know him? Is he a friend of yours?'

All affability left the old man's voice when he voiced the questions and Goran said hastily, 'I know him and saw him when I arrived at the fair today, but he's no friend of mine, quite the opposite! The farm where I've worked is next to the Spurre estate and I've upset Grimble so often he's threatened what he'll do to me if he ever gets the chance.'

'It seems he hasn't changed, but what's the name of your farm, boy?'

'I've been working at both Roach and Elworthy Farms, but I've taken over Elworthy now — although I still put in time at Roach.'

His expression one of delight, the old man said, 'You've been working at Roach Farm? Is Agnes still there? I haven't heard a thing of her for years. But why have you taken over Elworthy Coumbe's Farm? Has something happened to him? No, don't bother to tell me here, come to the inn just across the road, you can buy me an ale and tell me all about what's been going on there.'

'But I want to look at the ploughs, that's the reason I'm here at the fair.'

'They're not going to go away, boy . . . and there's nothing here worth your money, but buying an ale or two for me might prove the best investment you're ever going to make . . .'

19

There were so many customers at the inn that Goran and the old man were forced to sit on a wooden bench outside, amidst a constantly changing crowd of noisy and hard-drinking fair-goers.

Goran ordered a tankard of ale for his companion and a lemonade for himself from an overworked and harassed serving-girl. The non-alcoholic drink was a treat, one rarely enjoyed on the farm and it meant he would have a clear head for their conversation.

When introductions were exchanged, Goran learned the old man's name was Horace Rundle and it transpired that as a young man he had courted Agnes Roach — or Coumbe, as she then was — but had been jilted in favour of the man who eventually became her husband.

'It was probably just as well,' Horace reminisced, 'Agnes was always a strong-willed girl, determined to get her own way about most things, although I don't remember her ever doing anyone a bad turn if she could do a good one.'

'She hasn't changed,' Goran said. 'She still likes to have her own way and is sometimes so positive she frightens the life out of folk who don't know her, but she's the kindest person I've ever met.'

'That's pretty much how I remember Agnes,

and she thought the world of that husband of hers. Mind you, I got married and had a happy life too, even though, like Agnes and her man, we never had any children of our own.'

The ale and lemonade had arrived and, with the pewter tankard to his lips, Horace seemed lost in his memories, until Goran prompted him with, 'When was the last time you saw Agnes?'

'Eh? . . . Oh, it was years and years ago. It must be more than twenty years since the present Sir John inherited the title and returned from the wars to take over at Spurre and I hadn't seen her for some years before that . . . but what's happened to her brother Elworthy, whose farm you've taken on, is he dead?'

'No, he's gone to live with Agnes at Roach . . . '

The conversation about Agnes, and Horace's reminiscences of his days working at the Spurre estate in the 'old days' lasted for another ale before Goran said, reluctantly 'It's been good meeting you, Horace, and I've really enjoyed talking to you, but there's a storm to the west that will be here within the hour. I came here to buy a plough and I must get on with it . . . '

'Don't be in such a hurry, boy, you just listen to what I have to say before you make up your mind about anything.'

Raising the tankard to his lips and looking over the rim thoughtfully for the length of a long draught, Horace eventually lowered the drinking vessel. Speaking seriously, he said, 'You came to Liskeard Fair to buy a plough because you want to grow crops at Elworthy, but there's more to arable farming than owning a plough. A whole lot more, especially if you want to show a profit at the end of the farming year. After being a ploughman for almost all my life I've not given it up because I want to, but because rheumatics won't allow me to work the way I need to and I can no longer put in a full day's work. Mind you, that doesn't mean I can't show anyone who wants to learn the way it *should* be done. I wouldn't do it for anyone mind. In fact there are very few I'd even try to teach the right way to go about it, but you have a head start on most all of 'em. You're starting out on a farming life at a much younger age and, most important of all to me, you've spent years working for Agnes Roach. I'm living out near Callington right now and although I can't do a full day's work I still have the plough and harrow I used to work with and own two of the finest plough horses you'll find anywhere. They'd almost plough a field without having anyone to drive 'em. If we can reach some agreement I'm willing to bring them to Elworthy with the plough and harrow, show you how to use 'em and set you on your way to arable farming.'

It was a remarkable offer and far more than Goran could possibly have anticipated, but Horace had earned a living as a ploughman and would expect to be paid for his services.

'That's very good of you, Horace. Having you teach me what to do would be just what I need, but I'd still have to buy horses, a plough and a harrow. How much would it cost me? Agnes has been more generous than I could ever have hoped, and I can't ask her for more. There *will* be money coming in if the Wheal Hope extends its workings beneath Elworthy — and the mine captain is fairly certain they will — but that's not likely to happen for a while yet. Until then money is going to be tight.'

'I don't think I've mentioned money, boy! Mind you, I'm so forgetful these days I can't remember what I've said more than half an hour after I've said it. How much land do you reckon on ploughing?'

Making a rapid mental calculation, Goran replied, 'I'm hoping to get about five acres ploughed and put in at least an acre of potatoes. If I could manage more, so much the better. There are rumours of a rich copper strike at Caradon. If they're true it will mean more mines and a lot more miners, so there should be a market for as much as I can grow.'

'I've heard the same talk, so your thinking is sound and potatoes are a good cleaning crop for ground that's never been ploughed before. Mind you, there's a lot of work to be done before you put them in but if you have turnips and mangel-wurzels growing along with 'em you'll be able to feed your animals through the winter too.'

Repeating his earlier question, Goran asked, 'If I was to hire you to do the ploughing and harrowing how much would it cost me?'

Horace shook his head. 'I told you, I'm not up to that much work, boy, but I'll put an offer to you. It's costing me good money to keep my two horses idle and there's a plough in my barn

145

that's better than any I've seen offered for sale today — even those newfangled ones that'll need so many horses to pull 'em that whoever buys one will never see his money back. I've also got a harrow I had a blacksmith make specially for me and it'll still be working the ground when both you and me are underneath it. I'll bring the lot over to you at Elworthy and spend a couple of days showing you the right way to plough and harrow then let you get on with doing it for yourself. When you've got the ground fit and ready, you plant not one acre of potatoes, but two, one for you and one for me, and I'll see you get the right potatoes for planting and show you how they should be cut to get the best from 'em.'

'Are you saying you'll let me have the horses, plough and harrow for nothing? You don't want actual money for them?'

'I'm not saying that. Potatoes for planting are going to cost you money, although I'll get them at a price a sight cheaper than you'd be charged for the amount you're going to need. Then, you'll be feeding the horses through the winter months and I'd expect you to keep 'em as fit and healthy as they've always been with me. As for actual money changing hands . . . Well, we'll talk about that when we see what sort of a crop of potatoes you grow for me and when you've got money coming in from this mine that's started up. I'd expect you to settle up something with me then, but I won't be robbing you, boy. I'll take into account the money I get from the potatoes and the money you'll have spent on them.'

It needed very little time for Goran to realize that Horace was offering him a great deal more than he had expected to return home with when he left Elworthy Farm that morning. Extending his hand to the old man, he said, 'We have a deal, Horace. You show me what it is I need to do and it won't be my fault if we don't produce the best crop of potatoes to be found anywhere in Cornwall.'

'I hope you're right boy, but . . . ' — pointing up to the heavens Horace added — 'never forget there's someone up there who has far more to do with the success of farming than you or me and it's not going to be long before He's sending us a reminder.'

20

Walking back through the fair with Horace, Goran saw the stall where he had seen jewellery on display. In the excitement of all he and the old man had been talking about he had forgotten it, but now he stopped to look at what was being offered for sale.

His eye was caught immediately by a bracelet which reminded him of the one he had seen Morwenna wearing and which Nessa had given to her in exchange for the dictionary Morwenna had brought to the farm for him. Picking it up he examined it carefully before deciding it was cheap and ill-made and replacing it on the stall.

'Doesn't it suit you, young sir? It would look very nice on the wrist of your young lady, I'm quite sure.'

Goran shook his head, 'It's not what I'm looking for.'

'And what *are* you looking for, something cheaper, or something of *real* value?'

'I'm looking for a bracelet that's a little better than anything you have here.'

'Ah! Then the young lady must be someone who's very special and nothing's too good for the true love in your life . . . No, don't go away. I have a few items here that I don't show to everyone. I keep them hidden away and only show them to discerning customers like yourself.'

The stall was covered by a heavy and rather

threadbare green chenille cloth, which reached to the ground on all sides. Lifting the edge closest to him, the stallholder lifted out a small, stiff leather case.

He opened the lid to reveal a number of compartments, each filled with differing varieties of jewellery, necklaces, rings, bracelets and more.

'Now, if it's a special bracelet you're looking for, here's the best in the box — and you'll not find a more precious one anywhere, it's solid gold.'

'I don't want a gold bracelet. I'm looking for a silver one with jewels in it. Purple jewels.'

'Purple? You don't mean blue . . . sapphires?'

'No, *purple*!'

'Ah! Then you must mean amethysts, and they're *very* expensive.'

'Oh well, that means I won't be able to buy her an amethyst bracelet then.'

'Don't be quite so hasty, young sir. I just happen to have an amethyst bracelet — but only one. Mind you, I wouldn't still have it had I showed it to every young man who wanted something special. It would have been bought by the very first one to see it, but I was waiting for someone to come along I felt would appreciate it, and I think you might be that very young man. Just look at this, ain't it the most beautiful bracelet you've ever seen? Not only that, I know the young lady you want it for will never have seen another like it because I doubt very much whether there *is* one.'

It *was* a very beautiful silver bracelet, set with a number of finely cut amethysts, but Goran realized immediately it would probably cost far more than he could afford, however much he wished to find something with which to impress Nessa.

'How much is it?'

'Ah, well may you ask! If I was to wait until I got back to London I could name my own price for it. There's gentlemen around Covent Garden as would happily pay fifteen — or even twenty guineas for it.'

'Then you'd better keep it until you get back there because I can't afford that sort of money.'

'And I wouldn't dream of asking such a price from *you*, young sir. No, for someone like yourself who wants to buy it for a young lady he thinks a whole lot of, I'd let it go for, say . . . *ten* pounds?'

'Even that's too much. I'm just a tenant farmer who hasn't even reaped his first crop yet.'

'I understand what you're saying, young sir, and I realize times is hard, here in the countryside, so I'll tell you what I'll do — and I wouldn't do it for anyone else — you can take it away with you for five guineas! Now that's being more than generous, as I'm sure you'll agree.'

'I'm sorry, I don't even have *that* much in my pocket.'

Frowning, the stallholder asked, 'Well, how much were you thinking to spend on this very special girl of yours?'

Rapidly calculating how much of his own money he had and what he thought he might be able to afford, Goran said, 'I think I could just about afford to give you two pounds for it.'

150

'*Two pounds*? That's less than I paid for it. I might just as well *give* it away to the first pretty girl who walks past my stall! Can you read?'

Goran nodded.

'Well, just look here then, see what it says on the inside? 'Silver' it says, that's real silver on that bracelet, silver and jewels — and for *two pounds*?' He shook his head in exaggerated disbelief.

Goran was disappointed. He felt Nessa would have really appreciated such a gift, but he could not afford the five pounds the stallholder was asking. He turned to walk away, but the man reached out and took hold of his arm.

'I'll tell you what I'll do. I can see you've set your heart on having this bracelet, and it shows you to be a young man of uncommon discernment, so it's yours for three pounds, young sir. How does that sound to you?'

'It sounds good, but two pounds is all I can afford — more, in fact.'

'Make it two pounds ten shillings and the bracelet is yours.'

'I'll go to two guineas, but I daren't part with a penny more.'

Holding out his arms in a gesture of mock despair, the stall-holder said, 'You're wasted as a farmer, young sir, give it up and I'll employ you right here, on my stall. I've never known anyone strike such a hard bargain. All right, it's yours for two guineas — and may I never meet with another young man like you!'

Horace had been observing the keen bargaining with considerable interest, but he said

151

nothing until the deal was completed and Goran had the bracelet, then, addressing the stallholder, he said, 'Seeing as how you're in a benevolent mood, how much is that bracelet you have on your stall — the plain silver one?'

Switching his interest immediately to Horace, the stallholder said, 'For you, sir, ten shillings . . . no, as you're with this business-minded young man I won't even attempt to make a profit. It's yours for eight!'

Chortling, Horace said, 'I may be with my young friend but I'm older and seen many more fairs than the both of you, so you'll need to do a whole lot better than that!'

Throwing up his hands in a mock gesture of resignation, the stallholder said. 'Oh no, not another one! All right then, for you I'll make it five shillings. After all, what right have I to come all this way and expect to make any profit?'

'Now if you'd said two and sixpence I'd have bought it from you as a present for my grand-niece's birthday, but I couldn't spare a penny more than that on her . . . good as she's been to me.'

'Two-shillings-and-sixpence? That's not hard bargaining, it's downright robbery! That's solid silver, that bracelet is . . . but I've no doubt she's a pretty young thing and as she's been so good to an old man who's very careful with his money, it's yours for *four* shillings.'

Horace put his hand into his pocket and pulled out a number of coins. Counting them slowly and carefully, he put them back into his pocket and, shaking his head, said, 'I could go no

152

higher than three shillings, so as we're not going to reach agreement I'll bid you good day and be on my way before the rain comes and you need to pack up your stall.'

Casting a quick glance up at the heavy clouds gathering above the fair, as Horace turned away, the stallholder said quickly, 'All right, it's yours for three shillings — and I must remember to give Liskeard Fair a miss next year or I'll end up in Newgate debtors' prison.'

Chuckling as they walked away, Horace said to Goran, 'I think I'm going to enjoy working with you, Goran. You and I make a good pair — too good for the likes of that London stallholder, for all that he thinks he's so clever!'

Goran said nothing, but he gripped the boxed bracelet that was safely ensconced in his pocket, thrilled with the gift he had bought for Nessa, impatient to see her delight when he gave it to her.

21

The storm that had been threatening for much of that day broke soon after Goran and Jenken left Liskeard. Within minutes rain was falling with a ferocity that indicated it intended making up for the many weeks of drought Cornwall had experienced.

Goran had brought along a couple of old oilskin capes that had been hanging in a farm outhouse but these, with the hats both he and Jenken wore, afforded only partial protection against such a fierce storm and they were soon soaked through.

They had not travelled far when they came upon Marcus Grimble, battling his way on foot through the storm. He stood to one side as they came up to him and from his expression it was evident he was hoping to be offered a ride in the cart where he could gain some relief from the wind and rain that was battering him.

His hopes vanished when he recognized who was driving the cart and he turned away to trudge after them as they passed by. Despite his intense dislike for the gamekeeper, Goran felt a twinge of conscience about leaving the man to walk home in such atrocious weather but, remembering how Jenken had reacted when they saw him at the fair, he knew he could not have taken pity on Grimble.

The rain eased off slightly before they reached Elworthy Farm, although they were aware that the storm was still raging on the high moor, accompanied by thunder and lightning that provoked an occasional frightened whinny from the rain-sodden pony.

Despite their soaked condition, now talk was possible, Jenken was full of all he had seen at Liskeard and it seemed he must have seen everything the fair had to offer, his experiences including fire-eaters, dancing bears and a bearded lady. Yet he had not forgotten his family. He had come away with a clay pipe for his father, an embroidered handkerchief for his mother and sweets for his younger brothers.

While the boy was happily chattering Goran was very aware of the bracelet he carried in his pocket and he felt obliged to surreptitiously check it occasionally to satisfy himself it was still there. He also tried to tell Jenken about his own success with ploughman Horace but eventually gave up, aware his information would need to wait until his young companion was in a more retentive state of mind.

When both he and Jenken were drying off the pony in its stall, Goran said, 'I wonder how long it will take Marcus Grimble to reach home? I detest the man, but I couldn't help feeling guilty about not offering him a ride in the cart.'

'It's a good job you didn't,' Jenken replied fiercely. 'If you had it would have been *me* still walking home. I wouldn't have stayed on the cart with *him*! I'll always hate Grimble for what he's done to Pa and if he's caught his death of cold because of the storm it's no more than he deserves.'

Fully aware the young boy had good cause to hate the game-keeper, Goran said, 'You're right; offering to be nice to Grimble wouldn't have changed the man he is, but I wonder what happened to the young man who was with him, the one you think you saw talking to Morwenna. He probably decided to remain at the fair, it's an event that's more likely to appeal to someone his age. In fact I'm surprised Grimble was there at all.'

'Grimble going to Liskeard had nothing at all to do with the fair. He'd gone there to see his nephew off on the Plymouth bound coach because he was going to America.'

'How do you know that?'

'There was an inn on the far side of the fair and it had a coach and horses standing outside. I went across to have a look at the coach because I'd never seen one before. That's when I saw Grimble with the young man, who was riding outside on the coach. As it pulled away he called out, 'Goodbye, Uncle, I'll write to you from America,' and Grimble waved to him.'

'I'm surprised that even close relations would want to stay with a man like Grimble, but perhaps he's different with them.'

Goran wondered how Morwenna could have met up with a man related to Grimble, but Jenken was chattering about the fair once more and how his family would be delighted with what he had bought for them and the question quickly passed from his mind.

★ ★ ★

Goran knew there was little that could be done outside of the farmyard during the continuing wet weather and Elworthy would have carried out all the work that was needed at Roach Farm. Nevertheless he went there the following day to tell Agnes of his meeting at Liskeard Fair with Horace Rundle.

She was delighted to learn that the ploughman was going to help Goran on Elworthy Farm. 'He's a good, honest man,' she declared. 'I came close to marrying him when I was a young girl, and could have done a lot worse, but he spoke of nothing but ploughing all the time and I'd have soon tired of that. Come to think of it, it could explain why I've never wanted you to start ploughing anything here! But then I met my future husband and knew right away that I didn't want to marry Horace anyway. But if you're going to learn about ploughing from anyone then Horace is the man to teach you. He was the top ploughman in the county in his day.'

'He's also made me a very good offer,' Goran said, and went on to tell her what Horace had suggested.

'You take him up on his offer,' Agnes said, firmly. 'You'll never get a better one, and the hay has been so good this year there's more than either of us will need, even with two working horses to feed, but if you do find yourself running short there'll be plenty here for you to call on.'

Waving aside his thanks, she asked, 'How is the family of that young mining lad you took on making out?'

'They are all very happy at Elworthy and I'm particularly pleased with Jenken. He's keen and hardworking, and seems to enjoy farm work.'

Goran went on to tell Agnes about Jenken's day at the Liskeard Fair and of the presents he had bought for his family from the money they had given to him to spend there.

'Did he buy anything for himself?'

'No, although I believe he spent a few pence looking at some of the attractions they had there.'

Agnes made a sound in her throat which might have indicated either approbation or disapproval before saying, 'Would you have room at Elworthy for that young calf that was born to my Devon-cross cow last week? It's only just been weaned but it should be a good milk cow when it's grown.'

'I'll have no shortage of grazing with all the rain we're having, but if it's only just weaned it's going to need a bit of extra care for a while.'

Aware that Agnes also had ample grazing land, Goran added, 'Wouldn't Elworthy be happy to take care of it?'

'He would, but as you say, it's going to need a bit of tending for a while. I thought it would be good experience for the boy and that he'd take extra interest in it if it actually belonged to him.'

'You're thinking of giving the calf to Jenken? He'd be over the moon to have a calf of his own to rear, but it's very generous of you, Agnes.'

Embarrassed by his words, Agnes said, 'There's no generosity involved. Having a calf to rear would cost me both money and Elworthy's

158

time — and the price calves are fetching in the market today doesn't make it worth the trouble involved in taking it there. Let this young mining lad learn what's involved in bringing up farm animals before he gets all starry-eyed about farm work.'

Goran knew better than to smile openly at Agnes's attempt to pretend the gift of a calf to Jenken was an economic decision and not a philanthropic gesture.

He left Roach Farm in a happy frame of mind, not least because talking about the Liskeard Fair had reminded him of the present he had bought there for Nessa. As soon as the weather improved he would go to the Pyne cottage and give it to her. He had become increasingly enamoured of her in the brief time they had known each other and hoped the bracelet might prove sufficient to bridge the gulf that seemed to have opened between them in recent weeks.

22

'Why don't you and Morwenna like each other any more?' The unhappy question came from Jennifer when Nessa closed the book she had been reading to the young girl in their bedroom. It was the youngest Pyne girl's bedtime and, as the rain had seemingly exhausted itself for the day, Morwenna had just come into the room to change her shoes before taking a late evening walk on the moor, a pleasure she had been unable to enjoy for a couple of days due to the severe weather.

Morwenna had entered the room, changed her shoes and left without saying a word to anyone, carefully avoiding looking at Nessa and giving only the merest semblance of a smile when she glanced at Jennifer.

'It's nothing for you to worry about, Jen. Families don't agree with each other all the time.'

'Is it because of Goran? When I asked Morwenna whether that was the reason she wasn't talking to you she said there was no need for you to quarrel about him any more because you can have him back any time you want.'

'Morwenna said that?'

'Yes, but she said she didn't think it would make any difference because you were really only angry because of some silly old book. But you wouldn't quarrel with her about a book, would you, 'cos we like books.'

'Yes, we do.'

It was a half-hearted reply because Nessa was wondering what was in Morwenna's mind. She felt her sister must be planning something. She had been obsessed with the thought of marriage for almost as long as Nessa could remember and she felt the obsession had grown to the exclusion of almost everything else in recent weeks. If Morwenna believed there was even the faintest chance of Goran marrying her she would have pursued it with a vigour that was otherwise lacking in her everyday life.

If Morwenna had declared she was no longer interested in Goran it must mean that either Goran had made it very clear there could never be anything between them — or Morwenna had found someone else.

She dismissed the second eventuality immediately. It was most unlikely Morwenna could have got to know anyone well enough to consider him as a prospective husband without the family knowing about it — and the alternative excited her.

★   ★   ★

When Morwenna told her mother she was going out for a walk because she had been stuck in the house for so long if she didn't get out she felt she might suffocate, Annie Pyne commented only that she should take care where she walked because there were some notorious bogs on the moor that might prove treacherous after all

161

the rain that had fallen in recent days.

Weary of constant arguments with her eldest daughter about the time she spent away from the mine cottage, Annie Pyne had arrived at a compromise with her that seemed to be working. Morwenna would spend the mornings helping in the house, her duties including caring for Jennifer, the ironing and mending of the family's clothes, tending the kitchen garden and helping with the general housework.

If this work was carried out to Annie's satisfaction Morwenna would be free to do as she pleased for the remainder of the day.

Morwenna would take needlework with her and when her father asked her where she was going when she left the house she replied that she intended finding a quiet spot on the moor in order to carry out her needlework without interruption. However, when she left it behind one day and Annie examined it, she discovered the piece of tapestry was certainly not of a standard she would have expected from something on which so many hours had been spent.

Annie said nothing to her daughter about the standard of her work knowing that to put her thoughts into words would have led inevitably to another of the bitter quarrels that had so disrupted the family in the past. She hoped that by showing a trust towards her daughter she sadly did not feel, Morwenna might eventually settle down once more as the loved eldest daughter of the family.

When Morwenna returned to the mine cottage that evening, she spent some time repairing a tear to the hem of her dress that she said had been snagged on a low-lying gorse branch during her walk and, as she did not seem in a mood for conversation, Annie left her to it, busying herself by ensuring that the meal she had prepared for her husband did not spoil because he was delayed at the Wheal Hope.

★ ★ ★

Upstairs in the darkness of the girls' bedroom, Nessa lay in bed, hands clasped together on the pillow behind her head, wide-awake and still thinking of what Jennifer had said to her.

When Morwenna eventually came to bed, Nessa waited while she undressed in the darkness and got into bed before speaking to her.

'Morwenna?'

All sounds of movement ceased as Morwenna, surprised at having her sister speak to her, decided whether or not to reply.

Finally making up her mind, she said curtly, 'What?'

'Jennifer told me today you're no longer interested in Goran. Is that true?'

'I don't see it's any business of yours, whether it's true or not.'

Nessa realized that any conversation between her and her sister was not likely to be amicable, but she wanted an answer to her question and was trying to think how she could learn what she wanted to know without starting a bitter argument when Morwenna unexpectedly spoke again.

'Yes, it's true, I've got no interest in Goran at all any more, he's boring. So you can have him back again, if that's what you want.'

Angered by the condescending nature of her sister's reply and, despite her intention of trying to avoid an out-and-out argument, Nessa snapped, 'I have no intention of bothering myself with one of your cast-off lovers. I just wanted to know if what Jennifer said was true, that's all.'

'Well, now you know and I don't care whether you take him back or not, any more than anyone in this family cares what it is *I* want, or what it is that *I* might care about.'

There was silence in the room for a full minute before Nessa, regretting that she had reacted so angrily to Morwenna's declaration that she could take back Goran now she no longer wanted him, tried to placate her sister.

'That isn't true, Morwenna, we *all* care about you and the things you want. Ma in particular worries that you're not happy here and Jennifer was almost in tears tonight because she's so unhappy you and I aren't talking to each other.'

Nessa waited for her sister to reply but all that came was a mock snore that succeeded in bringing all further conversation to an end.

Lying in her own bed and thinking about the gulf that was widening between her and Morwenna, and what had been said about Goran, it was a long time before Nessa's troubled thoughts allowed sleep to come to her.

23

After two days of heavy, albeit intermittent rain, the storms moved on from Cornwall and Morwenna was able to make her way across the moor to the Spurre estate to keep her tryst with Tom once more — but the gamekeeper's nephew did not put in an appearance.

She waited by the hedgerow boundary for two hours before telling herself that the heavy rain had undoubtedly caused disruption at Spurre Hall and there would be work for Tom to attend to, perhaps closer to the big house. Disconsolately, she returned to the cottage at Wheal Hope.

When it was a similar story on the second day she began to feel uneasy. Perhaps something had happened to him! After all, his work meant he spent a great deal of time among the trees and woods of the estate. There had been many severe storms — and lightning was known to strike trees! But how could she find out?

When there was still no sign of him on the third day after the storms had passed on, she decided to check whether he was at the cottage among the trees, where he used to take her. Tom had told her she was never to go onto the estate unless he was with her, but she was so concerned she felt she had no alternative.

The relationship she had with Tom had been a carefully calculated one after their first casual

165

meeting, but she had grown to like him a lot. She decided she would be a good wife for him and had no doubts about his potential as a husband — and father.

If there was no sign of him at the cottage Morwenna knew she would need to think of something else, but she had felt utterly frustrated outside the estate hedge, waiting in vain for him to put in an appearance.

On the way to the gamekeeper's cottage the thought came to her that perhaps he was actually moving in to the cottage. If this was so he was no doubt being helped by his uncle and it would be very difficult for him to leave him and come away to meet her.

The thought buoyed her spirits until the cottage came into view and she slowed her approach, no longer certain of what to do next. The cottage looked deserted with no sign of anyone in residence.

There had been a musty unlived odour inside the cottage and, although it had never dampened the ardour of either of them, Tom had commented on it and, had he taken up residence, she would have expected him to open every window to allow the fresh air from outside to clear the mustiness.

Arriving at the front door of the cottage she paused. Should she go inside and see whether Tom, or any of his belongings, was there? What if somebody else had moved in . . . ?

This possibility had not occurred to her before but the cottage was on the estate and Sir John Spurre might have had other plans for it.

'What do you think you're doing here?'

The voice startled her and, turning to see where it came from, she was dismayed to see Marcus Grimble standing at the corner of the cottage. He had come from the rear of the building and was standing looking at her, nursing the gun he was in the habit of carrying whenever he walked the estate.

'I asked you what you're doing,' he repeated. 'This is private property and you could be prosecuted for being here.'

'I . . . I came here looking for Tom — Tom Miller. I usually meet him by the hedge to the moor but I haven't seen him for a while and wondered whether he was all right. He brought me here to show me the cottage, but it was only the once,' she lied, hoping Grimble would believe her.

'He shouldn't have, but Tom won't be showing anything to you any more, he's gone.'

'Gone? Gone where? When will he be back?'

'If he *ever* comes back it won't be for many a year, he's gone to America.'

Morwenna knew little about America, but she was aware it was somewhere across the sea and a very long way from Cornwall. 'But . . . he told me he was going to be a gamekeeper and would be moving into this cottage!'

Morwenna's distress was patently genuine and, looking at her speculatively, Grimble said, 'Now why should Tom have told you a story like that, unless . . . ?'

Leaving the sentence unfinished, he said, 'I think we'd better go inside the cottage, young woman, and you can tell me what it is you and my nephew have been getting up to.'

'I'm not going inside there with *you*!'

Grimble's revelation that Tom had left the country had come as a great shock, but it had not stripped her of her common sense.

'I'll be getting home before my pa wonders where I am and comes looking for me.'

'I shouldn't think your pa's *too* particular about where you get to or you wouldn't have been able to get to know young Tom well enough to have him show you places like this. Who are you, anyway, and where do you come from? You're not from these parts or I'd know you, although your face seems familiar.'

'Who I am is none of your business — but my pa is captain of the Wheal Hope.'

'Oh, so you're a mining girl? I've heard all about what they get up to around Caradon way . . . but you're still trespassing on Spurre land, so I think you'd better come inside the cottage and we'll decide what we're going to do about it.'

At that moment they both heard a muffled explosion. It came from the direction of the Wheal Hope and there was nothing unusual in the sound. Black powder was used to blast through the granite in the deepening shaft and also pursuing tin lodes which already showed great promise at two levels.

The sound had hardly died away when the ground beneath Morwenna seemed to tremble and it was accompanied by an ominous rumbling. The sound disconcerted both those at the cottage — but only Morwenna was

168

immediately aware of its significance.

When she was a very young girl her father had been a shift captain on a coastal mine. A tunnel extending seaward had come too close to the sea-bed and during a storm sea water had broken through, flooding the mine with a terrible force that carried everything before it, rocks, machinery — and men. The Wheal Hope was a long way from the sea, and not close to the place where she and Grimble were standing, but she had no doubt that something similar had occurred at the Wheal Hope.

All other considerations immediately forgotten, Morwenna turned to run back the way she had come.

'Stop! Come back or I'll shoot you.'

Running as she had never run before, she did not slow even when she heard the sound of his shot. But Grimble had fired into the air and neither slowing her pace nor looking back at him Morwenna kept on running.

24

When the disaster at the Wheal Hope occurred, Goran had just returned to Elworthy Farm on the pony after checking on the well-being of his sheep which had been grazing on the moor during the recent storms.

He had dismounted in the farmyard and was holding the reins of the pony and talking to Albert Bolitho when they were interrupted by the same sounds and sensation experienced by Morwenna and Marcus Grimble.

The feeling of the ground trembling beneath their feet frightened the farmyard animals and the pony almost pulled free from Goran but, as had Morwenna, Albert realized immediately what had happened.

'The Wheal Hope must have broken through into water,' he cried. 'If Cap'n Pyne wasn't prepared for it he'll be in serious trouble.'

Succeeding in bringing the frightened pony under control, Goran said, 'I'll ride up there and find out what's happening.'

'Take me with you.'

When Goran looked at the crippled miner, his expression showed clearly his disbelief that Albert could possibly be anything but a hindrance if there was an emergency at the mine, and Albert said fiercely, 'I may not be able to help physically but the only man on the mine who knows more of mining than me is Captain

Pyne and I don't think he's ever experienced a serious break through into water. I have!'

A granite mounting-block, accessed by three steps stood close to where the two men were standing and Goran said, 'I'll help you up there. If you can get yourself into the saddle I'll mount up behind you.'

The pony objected to carrying a double burden but, holding the reins with his arms about the miner, Goran heeled the animal into motion, calling out a brief explanation to Harriet Bolitho who was emerging from the farm cottage as they passed by.

*   *   *

The mine was in a state of turmoil but around the head of the shaft miners were busily attaching a pulley and rope to a rapidly erected wooden tripod. The previous apparatus used to bring dug earth to the surface had collapsed and it was intended that a man should be lowered down the shaft to assess just what had happened.

'Is anyone trapped down there?'

Albert called the question to a harassed miner whom he knew would be employed as a shift captain when the mine began full production. He appeared to be organizing all that was going on now.

'Cap'n Pyne's down below with a four-man team. They've been following a copper lode that was found while the shaft was being dug. John James has come up from the thirty fathom level where he was checking on another lode and says

171

he thinks the cap'n and the others might have been sheltering in one of the tunnels on the other side of where they were blasting. It should have only been a small blast but it broke through what was either some old workings or a reservoir. Jack tried to go back down to find out where the others were but the water had carried the ladders away and he couldn't get down to them.'

'This lode that was being followed — was it down towards the bottom of the shaft? Would the water have hit them right away?'

'They'll probably be safe for a while, but water's coming into the shaft above them and judging by the sound of it there's a whole lot of it. If it keeps up at its present rate no one can possibly get through and it will flood the whole of the Wheal Hope's workings — including the place where they're sheltering. To be honest I can't see any way we can help them.'

The miner made a gesture of hopelessness that horrified Goran, but Albert was speaking again.

'We know there must be plenty of water down there because of all the springs in the area — and recent storms won't have made things any better, but if you've broken through into old workings there would have been an adit coming out somewhere by the river.'

'An adit? Isn't that some sort of a mine tunnel?' Goran put the question to Albert.

'That's right, most of the old-time mines had them — many of the newer ones too whenever possible. They're tunnels dug to take off water from a wet mine without the expense of having a

172

pumping-engine and having to buy fuel to keep it working.'

'There's an adit coming out in a copse of trees down at the bottom of Agnes Roach's farm. It must have been dug by the miners who worked on the big mine that was once on Spurre land. The mine was worked a very long time ago, possibly as long as hundred years or so, but some of the older folk still talk about it. You can see by the ground in front of this adit that it once carried a whole lot of water, but Elworthy Coumbe said his father told him the roof had caved in when they were cutting down a great oak, a bit farther up the slope. He's probably right, you can see the hollow in the ground where it fell in. I once went along the adit and came to where a lot of earth and stone was blocking it. There was a bit of water coming through too, although it was little more than a trickle.'

Suddenly excited, Albert asked, 'How big is this hollow in the ground where you think the roof of the adit collapsed?'

'Not all that big, perhaps half the size of your cottage and if I stood in it I'd probably still be able to look over the edge.'

Albert and the Wheal Hope miner exchanged glances, but their two reactions were very different.

'It's too much of a long shot,' the miner said, shaking his head dubiously. 'Even if it is the old adit and we could clear the roof fall it would take time.'

'If we packed explosives into the fall we could

blow a hole big enough to loosen up the blockage. If there's as much water in there as we think there is it would do the rest for us.'

'It would still take more time than we have.'

'Not if *I* did it. There's not another man in the whole of Cornwall with my knowledge of explosives, you've heard Cap'n Pyne say so — and I'm telling you it *can* be done.'

'You do it? You're forgetting your leg . . . '

'Let *me* worry about my leg. While you're finding reasons why it *can't* be done the water's rising up the shaft. If I have a try at clearing the blockage in the adit we'll feel we're doing *something* — and it might save the lives of Cap'n Pyne and four men.'

Albert's fervour finally convinced the other man. 'What will you need, and where is it to go?'

'I'll need a whole barrel of black powder and as much safety fuse as you have ready, candles, Lucifer matches, pipes and packing for the powder. I'll also need the best drill team you have — get Jim Darley and his two boys — and tell them to bring the longest borers they have.'

Turning to Goran, Albert, now very much the man in charge of the situation, asked, 'Where is this adit?'

'Come down through Elworthy land to the river and follow it upstream to the small copse on Roach land. The adit is in there.'

'Right.' Turning to the miner, he said, 'Get things moving with all the speed you can. Goran and me will go back to the farm to collect as many lanterns as we can find and go in and inspect this adit. We'll meet you there . . . but hurry, there's no time to waste.'

Riding away from Wheal Hope in the same manner as he and Albert had arrived, Goran caught a glimpse of Nessa . . . and his heart went out to her. With Jennifer in her arms she looked pale and on the verge of tears standing with her mother, a hot-looking and dishevelled Morwenna and two other women on the edge of the crowd about the shaft.

She was not looking in his direction and he could not tell whether or not she was aware of his presence at the Wheal Hope, but now was not the time to even think of speaking to her. She and the members of her family would be greatly distressed at the knowledge that Piran Pyne was trapped deep down in the mine and in imminent danger.

25

The roof of the adit was not quite high enough to enable a tall man to stand upright and was so muddy underfoot that Goran was concerned for Albert who needed to lean heavily on a makeshift walking stick for support as the two men made their way along the adit, guided by the light of one of the lanterns taken from the milking shed at Elworthy Farm.

As they were leaving, Harriet Bolitho had needed to bite back the objections she wanted to raise against her husband's projected attempt to unblock the adit of the ancient flooded mine. She knew miners were always ready to risk their own lives when incidents such as this occurred, accidents being a constant hazard in underground mining.

She was aware, too, that knowing he would be doing something useful — something *vital* — would give her husband back much of the self-esteem he had lost during the long period of being unable to provide for his family and the injury which had left him feeling hopelessly useless as a husband and provider for them.

Meanwhile, Mabel had hurried to Roach Farm to tell Agnes what was happening on her land.

Before entering the adit, Albert asked to see the depression in the land that was believed to have been caused by the collapse of part of the

176

adit roof. Looking at it thoughtfully, he had Goran pace out its length then, still thoughtful, he limped after Goran to inspect the drainage tunnel itself.

'It's muddy in here,' Goran commented, as they neared the place where the roof had collapsed. 'Won't it make setting explosives difficult?'

'Not necessarily. If it's very wet I'll seal the gunpowder inside a pipe but if the water is seeping beneath the fall and not coming through the roof or walls it won't be too bad — and might even work to our advantage. It could mean there are faults in the fall. If I can place the explosive in the right place and cause rocks in the fall to shift, the force of the water piled up behind it should be enough to force its way through.'

'But once you've packed in the explosive and lit the fuse will you have enough time to get clear of the tunnel? I'm thinking of your bad leg.'

'I don't intend even trying,' Albert said, cheerfully. 'That's going to be *your* problem. While the Darleys are drilling the hole I'm going to need, I'll be preparing the charge. When they're done I'll ram it home, put the fuse in place and get out of the adit, leaving you to light the fuse and get yourself out!'

His unexpected involvement in the plans Albert had made left Goran speechless for some moments. When he did find his voice, it was to ask, 'How long will I have to get out between lighting the fuse and the explosion?'

'It depends how much fuse I think it's going to need, but don't worry, we'll be using the new safety fuse and that burns at about half-a-minute for each foot of fuse. I'll make certain you have enough time to get clear — and I don't think you'll want to waste any time!'

When they reached the roof-fall Albert inspected it carefully before expressing optimism that he would be able to create an explosion that would do all that was necessary to clear the adit, adding, 'It's better than I thought it was going to be. I'm pretty certain there's a powerful lot of water on the other side. All I need do is loosen up the fall a little and the water will do the rest, but there'll probably be a fair-sized hole up above, where the hollow is, so you're going to need to fence it off to stop any of your animals from falling down it.'

'That will be no problem, the copse is fenced off anyway and the only time there'll be animals in here is when Agnes turns her pigs out in the copse in the autumn. I'll tell her to get Elworthy to fence it off — but let's hope the explosion does what we need it to do.'

'It will,' Albert said confidently. 'I only hope we're going to be in time . . . '

He did not amplify his statement and there was no need for Goran to make a reply. They both knew what the outcome was likely to be for the trapped Wheal Hope miners if Albert's plan was not successful.

★   ★   ★

It seemed an age before miners from Wheal Hope arrived with all the things Albert had

178

asked for. They also brought the depressing news that the miner sent on the end of a rope down the shaft at the mine had been unable to reach the tunnel where it was thought Captain Pyne and the four miners were trapped.

The unsuccessful rescuer had reported that water was cascading from a breach in the mine wall 'Like them Niagree Falls they talk about in America', and he believed the water might already have reached the place where the five unfortunate miners were thought to be.

The father and two sons from Wheal Hope wasted no time getting down to the task of boring a hole in the place where Albert decreed it should be and Goran was astonished at the speed at which the three men worked and the skill they displayed in their work in the comparatively cramped space of the adit.

They worked with the father lying on his back, first of all holding a short drill which he twisted after each sledge-hammer blow delivered alternately by his two powerfully shouldered sons with a fast rhythm and accuracy that Goran found awesome. Very soon the short drill was replaced by a larger one with hardly a break in the hammer blows and, finally, an even larger and longer drill to complete the hole.

When the hammer blows ceased and the long drill was removed, Jim Darley spoke to Albert. 'I think you might be lucky, Albert. Just before we finished the drill went through an empty space I believe to be between a couple of rocks. I couldn't judge how big it is but if you pack enough powder in it you'll likely cause an explosion that should shift more than it otherwise might.'

As the three skilled miners made their way back to the adit entrance and Albert was busily tamping gunpowder into the hole they had made, Goran asked, 'How could he tell about the space between the rocks at the end of the hole they'd made? Do you think he's right?'

'If Jim Darley says it's there, then it is. There's no man in Cornwall knows more about his job ... Now, pass me more of those packs of powder. Fortunately it's bone dry inside the hole so we'll not have to waste time drying it out before we set the charge.'

For the next few minutes Goran kept passing Albert all the items he needed to expertly pack the hole full of black powder explosive and set the fuse.

When all was done and Albert ready to leave the adit, he gave final instructions to his companion. 'Now, listen carefully, Goran. I want you to count slowly to three hundred, to give me time to clear the adit before you light the fuse. Make absolutely certain it's burning, then waste no time getting out yourself. I've given you six feet of fuse which gives you three minutes to get out. It should be plenty enough time — as long as you don't dawdle. I'd give you longer, but every minute counts if we're to save Cap'n Pyne and the others. When you're clear of the adit go up the slope well to the side and above the hollow where the roof fall is. You'll no doubt see me up there somewhere. Good luck now!'

With this, Albert was gone, and Goran began

counting slowly, aware that his heart was beating faster than the count. As the count reached 250 he began to worry that the crippled miner might not have reached the adit entrance. What if he had slipped and fallen and been unable to get up, would he, Goran, be able to help him out in time . . . ?

Goran needed to be firm with himself, but when the count reached 300 he paused . . . but only for a moment. As Albert had said, every second counted if the trapped miners were to be saved. Following Albert's instructions he struck a Lucifer against the metal striker — and the thin stem broke and the head of the Lucifer fell to the ground, fizzling and throwing out sparks. Quickly, he struck another, applying its ensuing flame to a candle . . . then the candle flame, in turn, to the safety fuse. At first nothing seemed to be happening, then the gunpowder-filled rope hissed and the ensuing red glow began travelling slowly along the fuse. Satisfied it was burning the way it should, Goran grabbed the lighted lantern that Albert had left for him and began to run.

He was making good progress and could just make out the dim light from the wooded entrance to the adit when he slipped — and lost the lantern, the flame from the candle inside it going out.

In a moment of panic he began groping around in the mud for the lantern before remembering the smouldering fuse behind him and the reason *why* he had been running. He realized that even if he found the lantern he would have no time to replace the candle and relight it.

Scrambling to his feet he began running blindly towards the glimmer of light which grew as he drew closer and eventually he stumbled out into the shaded light of the copse — but not before he had grazed himself a number of times against the rough stone on either side of the adit and slipped over twice more.

'Here, Goran, up here — quick!'

Hurriedly climbing up the steep bank of the copse, to where Albert was standing leaning heavily upon his stick among a group of the Wheal Hope miners, Goran arrived gasping for breath, his heart pounding.

He had no sooner reached them when it felt as though the ground erupted beneath his feet and there was a sound like the rumble of a frighteningly close thunderclap. Looking back to where the hollow had been, he saw earth, rock and water being flung into the air.

It subsided as quickly as it had appeared, although water still spewed from the spot and the thunderous noise continued. Suddenly, Goran and the watching miners saw a torrent of water gush from the adit entrance with such force that rocks as heavy as a man were flung out with it as easily as if they were corks.

The sheer power of the suddenly released water was fearsome and for a moment the miners were stunned into silence. Then a cheer went up that challenged the noise of the torrent and they crowded about Albert, telling him he had lost none of his skill and that despite his injury he was still 'The best explosives man in the whole of the West Country.'

Goran came in for a share of the praise, both for knowing where the adit was situated and for his part in firing the gunpowder that had succeeded in reopening the adit and drastically reducing the amount of water flooding into the Wheal Hope mine.

The congratulations over, the miners wanted to hurry back to Wheal Hope to check on the results of their efforts. Goran said he would come with them until Albert suggested it might be better if he returned to Elworthy Farm and cleaned himself up first.

It was only then he realized he was covered virtually from head to foot with mud from the adit floor. He also became aware for the first time of the many grazes and bruises he had received along the way from the rough adit walls.

26

Mabel Trebartha was dismayed by the state of her son and, after he had stripped off his muddy clothes and used two buckets of water from the butt at the rear of the farmhouse to clean off the mud before changing into fresh clothes, she dressed his cuts and grazes with a home-made salve concocted from yarrow and other herbs found on the moor.

It had taken Goran a long time to reach home with Albert who was almost exhausted by his exertions, but the crippled miner insisted on accompanying Goran to the Wheal Hope.

Using the farm pony once more, the two men reached the mine to find an air of excitement among the gathered miners there. Water was still pouring into the workings from the old mine but it was apparent from the reduced sound emanating from the shaft that it was easing off and while preparations were being made to send a man down to find out what was happening, ladders were brought to the shaft, ready to replace those that had been washed away. When these were secured it should be possible to reach the level where it was hoped Captain Pyne and the four miners with him might still be alive in the tunnel.

There were other tunnels leading from the shaft, both here and at lower levels too but it was not thought any of the missing miners were in these. Had they been, they would have undoubtedly perished. The hopes of everyone at the head of the shaft was that Captain Pyne had kept to his intention of checking on the rich lode that ran in an upward incline from the main shaft.

If the men had managed to reach the far end of the tunnel — and if there was sufficient air to keep them alive for the time they had spent there — they might have survived.

The imponderables divided opinion among those above ground at the mine surface, but at no time was there disagreement about the need to press ahead at all possible speed in the hope their efforts would meet with success.

Goran and Albert were greeted at the mine as heroes for the part they had played in clearing the adit, with Annie Pyne, a wide-eyed and confused Jennifer in her arms, foremost among those showering them with praise.

Embarrassed, Goran changed the subject by saying, 'I saw Nessa here before Albert and me left, has she gone back to the cottage?'

'Yes, Morwenna was out on the moor when she heard the sound that brought us all here to the mine. Realizing what it was, she ran back in such a blind panic that she made herself ill. Nessa has taken her home and I told her to stay with Morwenna until we have more news of what is happening here.'

*　*　*

Morwenna, pale and trembling, was helped home to the Wheal Hope cottage by Nessa, but instead of allowing herself to be taken to the bedroom she shared with her sisters, she insisted upon first going alone to the small wooden privy situated at the far end of the cottage's as yet unproductive garden and she came close to hysteria when Nessa expressed reluctance to leave her alone.

Giving in to her sister's wishes, Nessa went inside the cottage and prepared her sister's bed and night-clothes. However, when time passed and Morwenna had not put in an appearance she became concerned.

Returning to the privy she could hear no sound from inside and, tapping on the rough-board wooden door, called, 'Morwenna, are you still in there?'

Receiving no reply, she called again — and this time she thought she heard what sounded like a low moan from inside.

There was no bolt on the inside of the door and, alarmed, Nessa pushed it open, fearing what she might find inside.

Her fears were fully realized. Seated on the crude lavatory, Morwenna was slumped sideways against the rough planking of the wall, breathing heavily and, to Nessa's alarm it seemed there was blood everywhere.

'Morwenna . . . What is it? What's happened to you?'

'Nothing!' Morwenna was in obvious pain, but speaking between clenched teeth, she said, 'Just help me to get cleaned up, then take me into the house.'

It was so unlike Morwenna's usual dramatic

manner when there was even the slightest thing not right with her, that Nessa realized something was seriously wrong. Suddenly a number of things fell into place and she realized what had occurred.

It explained Morwenna's moodiness, the deliberate distancing of herself from the rest of the family — and the occasions when Nessa had heard her sister being sick when she and Jennifer, desperate to relieve themselves, were waiting for her outside the privy first thing in the mornings.

'You're pregnant!' It came out as an accusation.

'Not any more, thank God!'

'How long have you known?'

'That doesn't matter now. I'm not pregnant any more.'

'Does Goran know?' It was a question Nessa felt compelled to ask, although she did not really want to know the answer.

'Nobody knows — except you now. But stop talking about it. Get me a bucket of water to clean myself up, then help me into the house and hide these clothes until I can get rid of them.'

'Ma should know about this . . . '

'Don't you think she has enough to worry about right now? If Pa is all right — and I've been praying he *will* be — there'll be a lot of things to be put right at the mine, even if they are able to save it.'

Morwenna had rarely been known to think of anyone but herself and Nessa did not doubt she was using the catastrophe at the mine to divert attention from the trouble she was in, but she knew her sister was right. The calamity at the Wheal Hope was of far greater importance than the temporary distress of Morwenna's present condition.

'Start stripping your clothes off and I'll bring water and a towel out here for you. When you're cleaned up I'll help you to bed indoors then clean up out here and get rid of your clothes. But this isn't the end of it. You and I have a lot to talk about.'

27

Two hours after Goran and Albert arrived on the mine, Captain Pyne and the four missing miners were located, safe and well. As was hoped, they had been inspecting the upward sloping lode when water from the old mine broke into Wheal Hope. Although the lode tunnel had been flooded for the whole of its length the water was no more than waist high at its furthest extent and there had been a sufficient pocket of air remaining at the end of the tunnel to keep the men alive — but it would not have lasted for very much longer.

The miner sent down the shaft on the end of a rope risked his own life to find them, needing to go underwater along much of the lode tunnel in order to reach them, not knowing whether he could surface and find air enough to breathe at the far end.

Once there he organized their rescue, accompanying each man along the flooded tunnel and having them hoisted as far as the ladders that had not been affected by the sudden torrent of water, then waiting for the rope to come back down to him and repeating the operation.

Captain Pyne was the last of the men to arrive at the surface and he was greeted with emotional relief by Annie. His youngest daughter, unable to comprehend the great danger he had been in, protested at being hugged by her father who wore soaked clothing, her indignation helping to break the tension which had been felt by all those gathered around the flooded shaft.

Even as he was being embraced by his wife, Piran Pyne was thinking of how soon he could have the Wheal Hope returned to normal working, but soon afterwards the shift captain who had been in charge of the rescue operations told him how it had been possible to slow the flow of water into the shaft and he realized the adit dug to drain the ancient mine could be utilized to take away the water from the Wheal Hope and keep it drained without the need for a pumping engine until his own mine's workings had extended beyond the depth at which the adit began.

When the mine captain was told of the part played in his rescue by Goran and Albert he looked for them in order to express his gratitude, only to learn that once it was confirmed the missing men had been located and were being brought to the surface, Goran had returned to the work that awaited him at Elworthy, taking Albert with him.

Piran Pyne wasted no time setting in motion an operation that would have the Wheal Hope working again as soon as possible and before making his way to the Pyne cottage to change out of his wet clothes and have something to eat, he left instructions for the old workings to be explored with a view to breaking through lower down the existing Wheal Hope shaft and using the reopened adit to drain all the water from both mines.

On the way home Annie told him of Morwenna's collapse, the result, so she believed, of the state she had got herself into due to the accident involving her father.

Moved by the reported concern of his eldest daughter, Piran went up to the girls' room as soon as he arrived home to assure Morwenna he was none the worse for his ordeal, but came downstairs again to say she was fast asleep and looking very pale.

Soon after eating, unable to settle and despite his wife's protests, the mine captain returned to Wheal Hope to check that his instructions were being carried out.

⋆   ⋆   ⋆

Late that evening, his chores completed for the day, Goran tramped up the slope to the Wheal Hope once more, this time with Jenken, for confirmation that the mine captain was safe and well. He was given a personal assurance from Piran Pyne who was effusive in his thanks for Goran's part in the rescue operation.

Aware of the pride Jenken had in his father, Goran said, 'It's Albert you should really be thanking. For a man who almost lost a leg only a few weeks ago he was truly magnificent.'

'So I've been told, and I intend showing my gratitude to him in a practical way. The engine-house is nearing completion and the engine on its way from Hayle with the engineer. When they arrive I'm hoping Albert will be able to come up here to watch it all being put together and have the engineer give him instruction on how to work it. He'll be my chief engine-man, with a couple of helpers to carry out any heavy work and do the climbing about for him.'

Jenken had great difficulty hiding his delight and Goran said, 'Albert will be happy with that — but you're going to lose a very experienced explosives man.'

'True,' Captain Pyne agreed, 'but he'll be on hand to give advice when it's needed — although I hope it won't be for anything similar to what's happened here today. It's quite obvious the old mine must have been extensively worked beneath Agnes Roach's land. I'm surprised she said nothing about it.'

'I doubt very much if she or her family before her ever knew. The main workings would have been on Spurre land and I doubt whether the family was any less reluctant to have anyone know anything about its business then than Sir John is today.'

'Well, we'll know more when the water's gone and I can get into the old mine and map it out. We were lucky the accident today wasn't far more serious. We can't rely on that luck being with us if it should happen again. As it is, the only people who seem to have really suffered are yourself with your cuts and bruises . . . and Morwenna.'

'Yes, Mrs Pyne told me Morwenna had been taken ill because she ran home in such a hurry, is she going to be all right?'

'I hope so. She was asleep when I got home

but she certainly looked pale and wan. I suppose she was with you when she became aware of the accident?'

Surprised by Captain Pyne's assumption, Goran replied, 'I haven't seen her for weeks. What made you think she would have been with me?'

'I thought she was seeing you . . . I must have mistaken something she said.'

Shaking his head, Goran said, 'I haven't seen her since the day she came to the farm and brought the dictionary Nessa had bought from her for me . . . ' A sudden thought struck him. 'Is that why Nessa hasn't been to the farm to see me, because she believed there was something between Morwenna and me?'

Thinking fast, Piran Pyne said, 'I believe there might have been a little misunderstanding about it, but I don't know how serious it was.'

'I'm sorry about that. I was surprised when it was Morwenna who brought the book to me, and not Nessa. I understood she'd exchanged a bracelet for the dictionary to give it to me.'

Hesitating for a moment, wondering whether he should tell his secret to Piran Pyne, Goran decided he would. 'I bought Nessa a replacement bracelet when I went to Liskeard Fair and was hoping to give it to Nessa as a thank you, but what with taking over the farm and haymaking I've been kept so busy I haven't been able to get around to it. To be honest, I've been disappointed that she hasn't been to see me at the farm.'

Captain Pyne explained that now Nessa knew

he was safe she would be spending the next day or two at Caradon with her recently arrived friend whose birthday was being celebrated, but he promised to suggest that she visited Elworthy Farm on her return.

He realized that Goran cared more about not seeing Nessa than he did about Morwenna being taken ill, and it raised the question of why Morwenna had said she was seeing Goran when it was quite apparent she had not. He sincerely hoped it was not one of his eldest daughter's malicious little games. But if Morwenna had not spent her time at Elworthy, where had she been when she was away from home so much?

It was something he needed to think about seriously, but not now. The immediate concern was the future of the Wheal Hope.

28

On a wet afternoon, two days after the Wheal Hope was flooded, Goran was in the milking-parlour repairing a wooden manger when Jenken hurried in and said, excitedly, 'There are a lot of men coming along the track towards the farm, Goran . . . they look like miners.'

'Are they from Wheal Hope? I wonder what they're doing down here.'

'I don't recognize any of them and they don't look particularly friendly. They're coming from the direction of the village and not from the moor.'

Abandoning the manger, Goran stepped outside the milking-parlour and saw a group of some fifty or sixty men heading along the track towards Elworthy. Dressed in the manner adopted by miners, many of them carried sticks and although they were approaching quietly there was an air of aggression about them that made Goran immediately uneasy. But he could think of no reason why they should want to cause him any trouble.

The gate to the farmyard was open. Entering, the men fanned out in front of him, one of their number stepping forward to confront Goran, saying, 'We're here to see how much corn you've got.'

Puzzled, Goran said, 'I doubt if I have half-a-sack left in the store, I'll need to buy some in later this week.'

'We're not interested in what you've got for feeding your animals, we're here to buy what you've got to sell, but we intend paying no more than thirty shillings a bushel, none of the fancy prices you're selling it for in the market.'

Goran shrugged. 'You'll find no corn here apart from what I've already told you about. I'm hoping to begin arable farming soon, but Elworthy and Roach Farms have never been anything but pasture land for as long as I've known them.'

'Then you won't mind if we have a look for ourselves to see whether you're telling the truth, will you?'

It was phrased as a question but Goran realized the miners were going to search his farm whatever he replied and it angered him.

'Yes I *do* mind, same as I mind you coming here and stopping me from getting on with my work. I've told you there's no corn here and I'd be grateful if you went about your business and left me to carry on with mine.'

'Well now, it's my experience that when there's money to be made it's greed and not the truth that comes first with farmers so, like I said, we'll have a look around for ourselves.'

'That won't be necessary, Jacob Barlow.'

The voice was Albert's and it came from a corner of the milking-parlour, where he had arrived, unseen, and stood leaning heavily upon his stick.

The leader of the party of miners was as surprised as Goran at his appearance, but it was apparent he knew the injured miner and he

196

demanded, 'Albert Bolitho! What are you doing here?'

'I'm recovering from an injury that ended my mining days and would have put an end to me too had it not been for Goran here — and, if it hadn't been for him, Cap'n Pyne and four of his miners would have been dead when water from an old workings broke through into Wheal Hope. So if you're here to cause trouble, you'll find yourself coming up against Cap'n Pyne, me, and every man at Wheal Hope.'

'We're not here to make trouble for anyone, Albert, but as you know well enough, times are hard down west and farmers are making them harder by pushing the price of wheat sky high. We're going around buying up all the wheat we can — but at a fair price. Fair to us, and fair to the farmers. We've just bought some from a reluctant farmer who tried to put us off by saying there was a farm along this way which had harvested a brave wheat crop this year. We thought it must be this one.'

'Well it isn't. Goran's only just taken over Elworthy Farm after working this and the next farm since he was a boy and neither has ever grown crops — am I right, Goran?'

'Yes, and although I hope to have some arable land for next season the first crop has to be potatoes, so I'll not have wheat for a couple of years yet. I think that farmer might have been talking about Colonel Sir John Spurre. The wheat I saw growing on his Home Farm fields, beyond the skew bridge on the other side of the estate was some of the finest I can ever

197

remember, but you'll need to be careful how you check on what they have stored at the farm. Sir John is both a magistrate and commanding officer of the local militia. He also has a gamekeeper named Marcus Grimble who's fond of boasting about the number of poachers he's peppered with small shot and who would as soon shoot a miner as a magpie if he found them on Spurre land.'

'Is that so?' The miners' leader spoke above the angry murmuring of the men with him. 'Perhaps we'll be lucky enough to meet up with this gamekeeper. I don't think we'll need to search your buildings after all, young man, but remember us when you start growing corn. We're happy enough to pay a fair price for it. After all, you need to make a living, same as we, but there are enough folk getting rich at our expense. We'll not have farmers added to the list.'

Nodding to Albert, the miners' leader turned and walked back the way he and his companions had come to the farm. Some of the miners following in his wake raised a hand in a farewell salute to Albert as they departed, but one of their number did not go with them. Only a year or two older than Goran he spoke to Albert whom he quite obviously knew well.

'Hello, Albert, it's a surprise meeting up with you.'

'I could say the same about you, Alan Toms,' Albert said, with little warmth in his voice. 'Although I'm not surprised to find you in the company of Jacob Barlow, you were never one to choose your friends wisely, as I remember, even though you were a good enough miner. Barlow's more interested in making a name for himself than helping miners, for all his talk of miners' rights.'

'I'm not with him because I want to be, Albert, but things got far worse down west after you left. Miners are leaving from Falmouth by the shipload, going to places they've only heard of, and them as stay are desperate for work. Those who follow Jacob Barlow can at least be certain of getting one meal a day.'

Albert snorted scornfully. 'I doubt if it's Barlow who pays for it. With a mob behind him he scares someone else into providing the wherewithal. One day he'll come up against a man powerful enough to refuse him, and Barlow and all those with him will end up in chains on their way to Botany Bay.'

'I know that, Albert, and if I can find work I'll have no more to do with him. Do you think Cap'n Pyne might have anything for me?'

Goran was about to go back to the work he was carrying out in the milking-parlour when Albert's next words brought him to a halt.

'After the way you treated his daughter I doubt it very much — especially with what's been happening at the mine . . . ' Albert told the other man of the flooding from the ancient mine, adding, 'All the Wheal Hope men will be working hard to get the engine-house completed so they can bring out some ore and get a pump working. But you can go and see Cap'n Pyne if you want to. He might take you on just to cheer up Morwenna. His being trapped underground upset her so much she's been in bed ever since.'

'What's wrong with her?' Alan Toms sounded genuinely concerned and he confirmed this by adding, 'To be honest, I've been hoping to meet up with her again. When we were seeing each other, down west, she talked about marriage so often it scared me. I didn't *want* to be married, but since she left with her family I've missed her so much I've come to realize it might not be such a bad idea after all.'

'Well, that's your business, son, and no one else can sort that out for you, but if you're going to keep up with Jacob Barlow you'd better hurry, he'll be out of sight soon.'

Looking to where the departing miners had almost passed from view, Alan Toms said, 'I won't have any problem finding Jacob if I need to. How do I get to the Wheal Hope?'

Goran directed the young miner by the shortest route, through Elworthy farmland. When he had gone on his way and Albert had returned to the cottage, Goran suggested Jenken should help him complete the work in the milking-parlour.

Once inside, he asked, 'Was that Morwenna's sweetheart when you and the Pynes were living down west?'

'He was the latest one, and the one she seemed really serious about. So serious that everyone thought she'd get him in the end and make him marry her.'

Grinning at Goran, Jenken said, 'She might get him, even now, but it might spoil her chances if he learns about Grimble's nephew. The more I think about it the more certain I am that it *was* him I saw with her up by the Spurre estate and I heard Ma talking to Pa about her, the other night. She said that Morwenna has been telling her ma she's been spending a lot of time down here, but we all know that isn't true, so I bet she was seeing Grimble's nephew instead. Alan Toms said it was her talk of marriage that frightened him off, but there were lots of rumours about the type of girl she was — and had been. If he thought she was up to her old tricks again he might think twice about what being married to her would be like!'

29

'Well, look what we have here! I never expected to see you again, Alan Toms. What are you doing at the Wheal Hope?'

Piran Pyne was standing with the engineer who had arrived with the giant cast-iron beam from the foundry which would be hoisted in due course to its place in the engine-house, being positioned half inside and half outside the tall building. Once connected to engine and pitwork it would become the beating heart of the mine complex.

'I've come to ask if you have any work going on the Wheal Hope, Cap'n?'

When the engineer had tactfully made his excuses and moved off to join the men from the foundry, Piran Pyne asked, 'What's brought about the change of heart, Alan? You weren't interested when I offered to bring you here with my other miners.'

'It wasn't that I didn't want to work for you, Cap'n, but, as you know, my ma is a widow, I was reluctant to leave her on her own and thought I had a steady job.'

'So, what changed?'

Alan shrugged unhappily. 'The mine folded, like so many others down there and instead of bringing money into the house I was adding to her problems.'

'Did you come here especially to find me?'

Alan hesitated for a few moments, wondering whether he should lie. Deciding against it, he said, 'No, I came this way with Jacob Barlow. We called in at the farm down by the river, looking for corn and I met Albert Bolitho there. He said you were here and I thought I might find work with you.'

'Didn't Albert tell you the mine has been flooded so badly we've had to stop working?'

'Yes. I realize you won't have work for a miner right away, but I was hoping you might need help ridding the mine of water and getting it working again.'

Changing the subject, Piran Pyne asked, 'What were you doing with Barlow? The man's a dangerous troublemaker.'

'I can't argue with that, Cap'n, but he makes certain the men who go along with him get to eat and that meant my ma wasn't trying to make what little she has stretch to feed the two of us. As I saw it I could either throw in my lot with Barlow, or leave the country like so many others, leaving her to fend for herself and I didn't want to do that.'

Piran Pyne was fully aware that similar problems were being faced by very many miners in West Cornwall and Barlow with one or two others were taking advantage of the situation to stir up trouble for their own ends. Barlow was a Cornish miner who had been working in the Durham coal mines until returning a year or so ago with the declared intention of promoting 'Unionism'. The current problems had brought him the support of a few hotheads, but he had not won the support for which he had been hoping.

While Piran Pyne was thinking about the would-be miners' leader, Alan asked hesitantly, 'How's Morwenna?'

Returning his attention to the young man standing in front of him, the mine captain said, 'She was upset that you weren't with us when we came here, but she's moved on, so it really isn't any business of yours any more.'

The question had been a tentative attempt by Alan to improve his chances of being given work. Realizing it had failed, he said, lamely but honestly, 'I know that, Cap'n. I also know I made a mistake by not coming with you for Morwenna's sake. I've found myself thinking of her more and more since you all left to come here. I'm sorry . . . I just wondered how she is.'

Piran Pyne thought rapidly of the possible ramifications of having Alan Toms back on the scene. He had never particularly liked him but Morwenna *had* been far less difficult to have around when she was seeing Alan . . .

He felt he needed to have a discussion with Annie about Alan's reappearance, but that would have to wait, there was a great deal going on at the Wheal Hope right now.

Drawing a coin from a pocket, Piran Pyne proffered it to the young miner. 'Here's a florin, it should get you a meal and a bed at the inn you'll find in the village. Come back to the Wheal Hope in the morning and I'll let you know whether I can offer you work — but stay clear of Jacob Barlow.'

Piran Pyne's warning to Alan was well founded. After leaving Elworthy Farm the grain-seeking miners paid a call on the Spurre Home Farm but news of their approach had been given by a stable-hand who had passed them on the road while exercising one of Sir John's riding horses.

Anticipating trouble, the landowner had promptly sent a messenger to Launceston to call out the local militia. Then, mounted on one of his hunters and flanked by a party on foot which included a number of estate workers and two armed gamekeepers, one of whom was Marcus Grimble, Sir John made his way to the entrance of Home Farm. He was aware of Barlow's actions in forcing farmers to sell corn at greatly reduced prices and realized that with the known agitator in the area his Home Farm might become a target.

The corn-seeking miners had as yet caused no serious trouble in the county, most farmers having already sold their stocks of grain, but those who still held some, anxious to avoid trouble, had reluctantly sold to the miners what little they held, at the price dictated by Barlow.

Sir John's farm still had a considerable amount of wheat in its granary, crops grown on the slopes of the moor being harvested later than lowland ones, but Sir John had already made arrangements to have the grain shipped out from a North Cornwall port to markets offering a price far in excess of that being dictated by Barlow.

When the miners put in an appearance their numbers took Sir John by surprise. They were more numerous than he had been expecting, but he and his employees were inside the estate with a closed gate between them and the miners — and the two game-keepers were armed.

Arriving at the gate the miners halted uncertainly and Sir John, seated on his horse called out, 'This is private land. I will prosecute anyone who tries to enter, so state your business and go on your way.'

'We represent men, women and children who are starving while farmers and landowners grow fat by selling corn at a price no working man can afford. We believe you have corn at your farm and we are willing to buy it at a fair price for those in desperate need.'

Barlow spoke loudly and confidently. He and his miners outnumbered the estate employees by at least six to one.

'There is no corn on my farm and even if there was I would sell it to whomsoever I wish and not be dictated to by some unlawful rabble!'

There was an angry murmuring among the miners at Sir John's words and Barlow replied, 'We are reasonable men, Sir John. If you allow a couple of us to check the farm buildings and satisfy ourselves there is no grain there we'll apologize and go on our way peaceably. On the other hand, if you're mistaken and there *is* corn there, we would expect you to sell it to us at a fair price in order to feed our starving families.'

'I'll be damned if I do anything of the sort! You'll go on your way now before I read the Riot

Act and have every one of you arrested by the militia — who have already been summoned. What's more, if anyone tries to enter the estate he'll be shot by my gamekeepers. Now, on your way before I lose patience with you and have them shot anyway.'

The fury of the miners was evident now and suddenly one man shouted, 'What are we waiting for? He's lying because he knows there's wheat in his farm granary. Who's coming in with me . . . ?'

With this the miner who had shouted defiance lifted the latch of the gate and pushed it open.

There was an immediate surge forward by the miners and a cheer went up. It faltered when Gamekeeper Grimble raised the gun he carried to his shoulder and peered down the length of its long-barrel. Then, with a shouted assertion from Barlow that Grimble would not dare open fire on them, they moved forward again . . . albeit more cautiously.

The gamekeeper's finger tightened noticeably on the trigger . . . and then he *did* fire, but at the last moment he raised the barrel very slightly so that the only damage was to the leaves of a tree that overhung one of the pillars of the gate.

The report caused the miners to come to a halt, but only briefly. Then, with a concerted howl of outrage they fell upon the luckless gamekeeper and he was knocked to the ground and kicked savagely by a dozen feet encased in the heavy boots favoured by miners.

The incident released all the frustration and sheer desperation that had been simmering in

207

the miners during a long foray through the lanes of Cornwall and their fruitless search of empty granaries. Furious, they fell upon the remainder of the Spurre employees.

The second gamekeeper, ignoring Sir John's furious command for him to 'Shoot!' fled the scene without firing a shot — and the Spurre men fled with him, deaf to the furious orders of Sir John to stand their ground.

Aware he had lost the day, the landowner backed his frightened horse away from the uproar, mouthing what he would later claim in court to be the Riot Act, before turning the horse and galloping away to the safety of Spurre Hall.

30

The area was soon agog with news of all that had occurred between Barlow's miners and the estate employees. After the encounter at the entrance gate, the miners set out for the Home Farm but had no sooner reached it than a shout went up that armed militia were approaching in carts and carriages, led by their officers mounted on horses.

The miners fled empty-handed, without even a glimpse of the wheat filling the granary. Scattering as they went they would be hunted down relentlessly, mainly by the mounted militia officers — of whom there seemed to be more than there were rank and file — in the manner of true fox-hunting country gentlemen.

No one outside the estate, and very few of its employees were unduly upset at the punishment meted out to the unpopular Marcus Grimble — and the humiliation of Sir John was hailed by many as being long overdue. Nevertheless, the actions of Barlow's miners had caused alarm among farmers in the area for whom a rise in the price of the various cereals they harvested had eased their financial burdens considerably.

The man-hunt continued the following morning and was going on when Jenken went down to the Elworthy Farm gate to scrub out the wooden churn kept there to hold the milk for collection by the villagers. He returned hurriedly and, in a state of great excitement, sought out Goran.

'I've just seen some of the militiamen. They've arrested Alan Toms for being one of those who fought with Sir John's men.'

'But he couldn't have been there; we saw him going to the Wheal Hope when he left here and that's in the opposite direction!'

'I know, and Alan called out to me to tell Captain Pyne that he's been arrested, so he must have been up there to speak to him.'

'Did he say anything else?'

'No, he had his hands tied behind him and one of the militiamen hit him with his gun and knocked him over before he'd even finished talking to me, then he told me to be on my way or I'd be arrested too.'

'It sounds as though they're arresting anyone they don't know. Where do you think they were taking Alan Toms?'

'They were following the river upstream, so I should imagine it would be to Spurre Hall.'

'Run to Wheal Hope and tell Captain Pyne what you've just told me. While you're doing that I'll take the pony and go across the moor beyond the estate. I won't be able to do anything to help, but I'll be able to see whether the militia take anyone away to Launceston.'

★   ★   ★

Piran Pyne listened to a breathless Jenken in silence before asking, 'How long ago did this happen?'

'Not much more than twenty minutes . . . I've

210

run all the way here.'

'And you think they were taking Alan to Spurre Hall?'

'That's the way they were heading.'

'Then I'll go straight there now and take two of my soundest men with me to witness what's said. I'm not over-fond of the boy, but there's no way he could have been mixed up in anything that went on and I'll not see him arrested for no other reason than that he's a miner. Find Goran and tell him to let me know immediately if they take Alan away. If they do we'll need to get to Launceston before they haul him before a magistrate.'

Piran took a short cut to Spurre Hall, going across the moor and not entering the estate via either of the two lodge gates which were being guarded by zealous militiamen, eager to perform a duty that seldom came their way.

Because of their route to the hall the arrival of the three miners came as a surprise to Sir John who, with a militia captain, was supervising a manacled Alan Toms being placed in an open cart for transportation under escort to the decaying cells of Launceston Castle.

The militia captain moved to block the miners' advance as they approached but Sir John stopped him and, addressing the mine captain, asked pompously, 'Have you come to offer your apologies for the disgraceful conduct of your miners, Pyne?'

'I have nothing to apologize for, Sir John. The conduct of the men who came here yesterday was regrettable, albeit understandable, but none

211

of my miners were involved — and that includes Alan Toms, the man you have in chains. He was at Wheal Hope talking to me at the very time you were having your problems here. It's a fact that my two companions will verify.'

'I have no doubt they will, miners are notorious for supporting each other — whatever the truth of the matter might be.'

'I am not a liar, Sir John. Alan Toms was with me at the time of the incident for which he's been arrested, *unlawfully* arrested. After talking to me he went straight to the inn in North Hill village where he took board and lodging, paying for it with a florin I gave him. Had there been a place for him to stay at the mine he would have spent the night there. As it is I will have the landlord of the inn, his servants and every one of my miners called to give evidence that Toms could not have been involved in the troubles here on Spurre land. Furthermore, should my word be questioned in court I'll call witnesses to testify to my integrity, among them the adventurers for whom I've managed mines. They include the present Sheriff of Cornwall, a past sheriff and a number of peers of the realm. Your militiamen have made a mistake and it's in everyone's interest for that mistake to be acknowledged and Toms released, here and now.'

'I doubt if any mistake has been made. When the militia appeared on the scene the rioters scurried off across the countryside like scared rats and the militiamen went after them, catching up with a great many.'

Alan Toms had been listening to the exchange

212

between the two men and now he called out, 'I wasn't scurrying anywhere, Cap'n. I was arrested this morning when I was on my way to Wheal Hope from the North Hill Inn where I'd spent the night.'

Sir John Spurre was the commanding officer of the North Cornwall militia and, as such, ultimately responsible for their actions. When Alan Toms had been brought in as one of the 'rioting miners', Sir John had not questioned the arrest which had been made by a platoon of militiamen led by the enthusiastic but not very intelligent son of another wealthy landowner.

Had not Piran Pyne raised objections, Toms would have been found guilty of rioting and transported as a matter course. With the exception of the convicted man it would have been of little concern to anyone and soon forgotten.

Captain Pyne's intervention had put a different complexion on the situation. Not only would the weight of evidence he could produce undoubtedly secure the acquittal of Toms, it would also throw doubt on the credibility of the whole militia operation.

This had become apparent to Sir John, but he could see no way of overcoming the problem without being humiliated for the second time in two days. However, it was the prisoner himself who had provided him with a solution — and he grasped it eagerly.

'Arrested only this morning? Is that correct, Lieutenant Spry?'

Taken by surprise at having his actions questioned, the young militia officer tried unsuccessfully to think of a reply that might justify the arrest he had made. 'Yes, sir, but he — '

'No 'buts', Lieutenant. I was given to understand the man had been arrested during the immediate pursuit of the rioters, not picked up only this morning. Release the prisoner immediately.'

Turning to Piran Pyne, he said, 'Thank you for bringing this to my attention, Pyne. Lieutenant Spry is a young and inexperienced militia officer and has perhaps been over-zealous in carrying out his duty.'

With this, the titled landowner turned and walked stiffly away, leaving the aggrieved officer to order that Alan Toms be released.

★ ★ ★

Rubbing his chafed wrists after being freed from the manacles, Alan Toms caught up with the mine captain who had not waited to witness his release, but was walking back the way he had come accompanied by the two Wheal Hope miners.

'I'll be forever in your debt for coming to my rescue, Cap'n. That militia officer told me to make the most of what I saw of the countryside on my way to Launceston Prison because it was likely to be the last I'd ever see of Cornwall as I'd be spending the rest of my life in Van Diemen's Land. I don't doubt he was right and I'd almost given up all hope of ever being released.'

'I'm not convinced I've done the right thing,'

214

came the unexpected reply.

Startled, Alan Toms said, 'What d'you mean, Cap'n? I'd done nothing wrong, you know that.'

'What I know is that if it wasn't for the support of fools like you, Barlow wouldn't be able to go around Cornwall causing trouble. Mines and miners have more than enough to cope with without having men like him stirring up the countryside against them.'

Piran Pyne made this observation without slackening his pace and not glancing at the young miner who was hurrying to keep up with him.

The small party walked on in silence for some minutes more before Alan Toms spoke anxiously and contritely, 'I'm sorry I've behaved so stupidly, Cap'n. I'll think long and hard before doing anything like it in future, but back there you told the owner of the estate I was one of your men. Does that mean you'll give me work on Wheal Hope?'

'I suppose if I'm not going to show myself up as a liar I'm going to have to!'

Looking at the young miner now, he added, 'Heaven help you if you let me down, Alan Toms. You do and you'll wish you had gone to Van Dieman's Land.'

31

When Jenken returned to the cottage occupied by the Bolithos for the family's midday meal, Jenken told Albert and Harriet about seeing Alan Toms being taken away by the militia and of running to Wheal Hope to inform Captain Pyne.

'I doubt if Piran Pyne would have wanted to do anything about it,' Harriet commented. 'Not after the way young Toms upset Morwenna.'

'He did though,' Jenken said, 'He went straight off to Spurre Hall taking two of the Wheal Hope miners with him.'

'I wouldn't expect Cap'n Pyne to do anything less,' Albert declared. 'He didn't care too much for the lad but young Alan is a miner — and a good one, for all his faults — and he was up at the mine talking to the cap'n when all the trouble was going on over at the estate. He wouldn't see the lad get into trouble for something he had no part in. Do you know where Alan is now, Jenken?'

'No. Goran said he went off with Cap'n Pyne and the others but I don't know whether he'll be working at Wheal Hope, or not.'

'I promised to take some sewing and mending I've done for Annie Pyne up to their cottage this evening,' Harriet said. 'I'll find out then. I'd like you to come with me and help me carry the things there when you finish work this evening, Jenken.' With this, she dished out the midday meal for her large family and no more was said on the subject.

That evening, leaving the younger children in Albert's care, Harriet and Jenken set out for the Wheal Hope cottage. Jenken protested that the amount of clothing they were carrying hardly merited the two of them being involved, but Harriet's reply was that it had all been cleaned and ironed and she had no intention of taking the risk of dropping anything along the way, or having it arrive at its destination in a creased condition.

Once at the mine cottage, Harriet asked after Morwenna and was told the oldest Pyne girl had been out of bed that day, sitting downstairs for a few hours, but had retired to her bedroom earlier that evening and appeared to be asleep when Jennifer had been put to bed.

Satisfied she and the mine-captain's wife could now settle down to have a good long gossip whilst enjoying the tea Annie had brewed, Harriet sent Jenken out of the house until she was ready to return to Elworthy.

Annie suggested that he make his way to a small copse not far away from the cottage where he would probably find Nessa. The middle Pyne daughter had surprised a badger with two cubs some days before and discovered their sett in the copse. Since then she had visited the copse frequently, hoping to see them again.

Jenken would have preferred to remain with his mother and the mine-captain's wife to learn what they had to say about Alan Toms, but he decided he would settle for an opportunity to see a badger with its family.

He found Nessa in the copse watching the sett from a little distance. She was not immediately pleased to see him but, relenting, she put a finger to her lips and, beckoning for him to follow her, led him away from the sett.

When she thought they were far enough away she explained, 'The mother badger is very wary. When she's ready to bring her babies from the sett she puts her head out of the hole and listens and sniffs about her for ages before letting the cubs out. It's still a bit early for them, but if you're patient and quiet enough we can go back there in a minute and might be lucky enough to see them . . . but what are you doing at Wheal Hope?'

A sudden thought came to her and she asked, 'Did Goran come up here with you?'

'No. Ma had some sewing to bring and I helped her carry it, but I think she and your ma want to have a good old gossip, so they sent me down here to watch for the badgers with you.'

'Well there's plenty to gossip about with all that's been happening at Wheal Hope.'

'I don't think it's going to be about the mine. They'll probably be far more interested in what went on at the Spurre estate between Sir John's men and Jacob Barlow — and talking about what happened to Alan Toms.'

Startled, Nessa queried, 'Alan Toms . . . Morwenna's old sweetheart? What's he got to do with the Spurre estate?'

Realizing she had heard nothing of Alan Toms's presence in the area, Jenken told her of his arrival and how he had been arrested and released by the intervention of her father.

'Pa has said nothing about Alan Toms being here, at least, not to me — and certainly not to Morwenna or I would have known. She wouldn't have been able to keep *that* to herself. Mind you, we haven't seen Pa today, he's been at the mine since dawn and Ma took something for his dinner up there. He probably said something to Ma then about Alan being here, but she wouldn't have mentioned it until they had discussed it properly and decided what they were going to do about it.'

Thinking hurriedly about Morwenna's behaviour in recent weeks, Nessa asked, 'Does Goran know that Alan was once Morwenna's sweetheart?'

'Yes, Pa told him.'

'What does he think about Alan coming here? I mean, Goran was seeing Morwenna for a long time, wasn't he?'

His confusion evident, Jenken said, 'What makes you think that? I'm pretty certain that the last time he saw Morwenna — probably the *only* time — was when she brought that book to the farm ... and he wasn't expecting her then. In fact he was embarrassed by her being there, especially when she made him kiss her as a 'thank you' for giving the book to him.'

'Morwenna made *him* kiss *her*?'

Grinning at the memory of the occasion, Jenken said, 'Well, it was *supposed* to be a kiss but he hardly touched her cheek and then jumped back as though he was frightened he

219

might catch something from her. I don't think Morwenna was very happy about it!'

With so many thoughts tripping over themselves in her mind, Nessa tried to put them in some logical order and, thinking aloud, said, 'But if she wasn't seeing Goran . . . ? Perhaps Alan has been around here for a lot longer than we realize. She was probably seeing him when we all thought she was with Goran. That's why . . . '

She almost mentioned Morwenna's miscarriage but stopped herself in time. It was a secret that should never go outside the family, but Jenken was shaking his head.

'I believe Alan only came to this part of Cornwall recently, with Jacob Barlow, and I saw Morwenna up on the moor with gamekeeper Grimble's nephew, but he's gone off to America now so she won't be seeing *him* again.'

Listening to Jenken, everything suddenly fell into place for Nessa. First Morwenna's claims that she was going to Elworthy Farm every day to meet Goran, then her unexpected taunt that Nessa could have Goran back. She would have been desperate to find a father for the child she was carrying before it became evident to everyone she was pregnant. That would mean she probably realized she was pregnant before coming to the Wheal Hope. What seemed certain was that it could not have been Goran who was responsible!

With this knowledge it felt as though a huge weight had been lifted from her mind. She believed that both Goran and Grimble's nephew had been targeted as prospective husbands because of Morwenna's desperate need to be married. The man undoubtedly responsible for her condition had to be Alan Toms and it would explain why she had been so upset when he had refused to come to the Wheal Hope with the other miners.

Putting all the facts together, Nessa suddenly felt desperately sorry for Morwenna and the problems she had been forced to grapple with alone, not daring to tell anyone else about them.

Then Nessa remembered the manner in which Morwenna had come between herself and Goran, and had made no real attempt to put matters right, even when she must have believed she had succeeded in persuading Grimble's nephew to marry her.

Turning to Jenken, Nessa said, 'You stay here and wait to see the badgers. I don't think I will be able to settle down enough to watch them tonight. I'd probably be so fidgety it would frighten them off. I'm going back to the cottage — and I hope Morwenna is awake: we have things to talk about!'

32

When Nessa returned to the mine cottage she hurried upstairs to the bedroom she shared with her sisters. Morwenna was asleep — but so too was Jennifer. Nessa knew that what she and Morwenna had to say to each other would be so heated it would certainly wake the younger girl. Frustrating though it was, she realized the showdown with her sister would need to wait until morning if Morwenna's miscarriage was not to be disclosed to the family.

Returning downstairs, she found Harriet Bolitho ready to return home and offered to go and fetch Jenken, but Harriet said she was quite happy to go home alone and leave him watching the badger sett, adding, 'He works hard during the day and has very little time to do things he enjoys. He loves all animals and birds and if he sees a badger it will be an unforgettable experience for him.'

When Harriet had left the cottage, Annie said to Nessa, 'I presume Jenken has told you Alan Toms is here, on the mine?'

'He told me Alan is around again, but he wasn't sure whether or not Pa had taken him on, or whether he's staying in the area.'

'He's been given work at Wheal Hope, but only to help clear water from the mine and not as a miner. Pa wants to know Morwenna's feelings about him before taking him on. In the meantime he's moved in with a few of the miners who have taken over a cottage halfway between here and the Caradon mines. But I heard you go upstairs when you came in, were you going to tell Morwenna about Alan being here?'

'I had a number of things to say to her and that was one of them, but she's asleep and I didn't want to disturb Jennifer, so it will need to wait until morning.'

Nodding approval, Annie said, 'I think we both have a few things we want to discuss with Morwenna, but I'd rather you left saying anything until your pa has spoken to her about Alan. He was hoping to do it tonight but she went to bed early and he's late home so that too will need to keep until morning.'

'Is what she says likely to make a difference to anything? I thought Pa didn't like Alan very much.'

'I don't think Pa is particularly fond of him, but he did say that Alan has gone up in his opinion for the way he's behaved over this business with Jacob Barlow. He said Alan wasn't taken in by Barlow's claim to represent the rights of the miner and left him as soon as he could. It would appear Alan has shown more common sense than Pa gave him credit for. But whether or not he's taken on as a Wheal Hope miner depends on what Morwenna has to say about him.'

Nessa thought that had Alan put in an appearance some days earlier Morwenna would have had him in church before the young miner knew what was happening to him . . . but now?

223

'Harriett told me Morwenna's story of spending much of her time at Elworthy isn't true and that she hasn't been near the farm,' Annie said.

'Jenken told me the same thing — and that's something I intend having words with her about,' Nessa said firmly.

'Well, save it until Pa has spoken to her, I'm sure we'll all be able to sort everything out.'

★ ★ ★

When Piran Pyne took his eldest daughter to one side after breakfast the following morning and asked her to walk to the mine with him, she was concerned about what he might have to say that could not be discussed in the presence of the other members of the family. Deciding it must be something to do with her state of health, she felt able to face such questioning with far more confidence than had it been a few days earlier.

Their conversation began very much as she had anticipated and she was able to tell her father with honesty that she was feeling much better and confident she was on the mend.

Then he said, unexpectedly, 'Have you got over feeling upset about leaving Alan Toms?'

It was an unexpected question, but carefully composing herself, Morwenna replied, 'I still think about him sometimes.'

'If the opportunity arose do you think you would take up with him again?'

'I'm never going to know, am I?' she retorted. 'We're not likely to go back down west again.'

'That doesn't answer my question. Would you, or wouldn't you?'

As Morwenna pondered the possible reason her father might have asked the question, he said, 'Perhaps there's someone else who's taken his place since you came here?'

The question caused her a moment of panic, thinking her father might have somehow learned about her affair with Tom Miller — from Nessa, perhaps?

She breathed easily once more when he added, ' . . . Goran Trebartha, for instance?'

Shaking her head, Morwenna replied, 'There's nothing between me and Goran.' Suddenly remembering she had used seeing Goran as a cover for the time she had spent with Tom Miller, she added hurriedly, 'Although I did think at one time there could have been, but why are you asking me about Alan now, after all this time?'

'Because he's here and wants me to take him on at the Wheal Hope.'

The reply left Morwenna stunned. For a few moments she struggled for words before asking, hesitantly, 'Have you . . . taken him on?'

'Not as a miner. I've said I'd use him to help drain the mine and get it working again before I made a decision. But I wouldn't employ him until I'd spoken to you. If you've found someone else it would be an embarrassment for you to have him around . . . and your feelings are important to me and your ma.'

'Has Alan mentioned me at all?'

'Yes, he asked after you and said he realized

he'd made a mistake in not coming with us when we moved here.'

'He would say something like that if he's desperate for work, wouldn't he?'

'He would,' Piran Pyne agreed, 'and there's always the possibility he could upset you again, but he told Albert Bolitho that the reason he hadn't come with us in the first place was because you were so keen on being married it frightened him. It was only after we'd left and he'd had time to think that he realized he'd made a great mistake in letting you come here without him.'

'He actually said that?'

'That's the gist of it, I think.'

'And you believe him?'

'I do — and the way he's conducted himself over the last couple of days has caused me to reconsider the opinion I had of him when we were down west.'

Telling Morwenna of the events involving Alan over the past few days, he added, 'But, as I've said, I'll not take him on if it's going to upset you.'

The answer to his original question had never been in doubt in Morwenna's mind and she suddenly felt happier than at any time for many weeks but, trying not to sound too eager, she said, 'I don't think he would have come to the Wheal Hope asking for work unless he meant what he's said and, if he *really* means it, I'm willing to give him another chance — although I shall make him prove to me that he is serious this time.'

226

33

Morwenna returned to the mine cottage in a state of euphoria — but she soon discovered that not everyone in the family shared her elation. The first person she met was Nessa, carrying water from the butt which caught rainwater channelled from the roof and taking it to the copper in the wash-house built on to one end of the cottage. When filled, a fire would be lit beneath the copper to boil water for the family's washing.

'Hello, do you want some help with that?'

The two sisters had hardly been talking for so long that Morwenna's cheerful and unexpected offer almost caused Nessa to drop the bucket she was carrying.

'I gather Pa has told you that Alan has been to see him about coming to work at Wheal Hope.'

'You know about it? Who told you — and when?'

Lowering the heavy bucket to the ground, Nessa said, 'I was coming to speak to you about it last night, but you were asleep.'

'For news like that I would have been happy to be woken up. Has Pa told you Alan's realized he made a mistake by not coming here to be with me in the first place? He'll marry me now, for certain.'

'Don't be too cocksure about it. He'll want to know what you've been doing since you came here — with Goran, for instance.'

'Oh, I'm not worried about that, I'll tell him all he needs to know.'

'I think you'd better tell *me* all I need to know about it, first.'

Belatedly realizing her sister was seething with scarcely concealed anger, Morwenna shrugged dismissively. 'What does it matter now? What's done is done.'

'That isn't good enough. You've told everyone so many lies about you and Goran that I don't know what to believe — so I want you to tell me. Was there ever anything going on between the two of you?'

'Why don't you ask him? Although he'll no doubt tell you only what he thinks you want to hear, men are like that, aren't they?'

As Morwenna turned to go inside the cottage, Nessa said, 'I don't intend asking Goran and since you won't give me an answer I'll get Alan to ask you. While he's about it he can ask you about gamekeeper Grimble's nephew too — and your miscarriage. I did believe that Alan had probably fathered the baby but I suppose when he knows the facts he might feel it was Goran's, or even Grimble's nephew's. Who knows?'

With this, Nessa lifted the bucket of water and began walking towards the wash-house once more.

Running after her, Morwenna demanded, 'Who told you about Tom Miller? What do you know about us?'

Responding in a similar manner to that adopted by her sister, Nessa replied, 'I'll tell Alan what I know and you can ask him.'

'You wouldn't, Nessa,' Morwenna pleaded, 'Not after all I've been through. You wouldn't spoil my chance of marrying Alan now — it would break my heart, truly it would!'

'Everything you've been through has been entirely your own fault, even though you behave as though you're the most hard done by person in the whole world and everyone is against you. They're not, but *I'm* going to be against you for the way you've behaved toward me and what you've deliberately done to upset *my* life.'

Entering the wash-house, Nessa raised the heavy wooden bucket with difficulty and the noise of the water pouring into the copper made further conversation impossible until the bucket was empty.

'*Please*, Nessa, I beg you. Please don't say anything to Alan. I want to marry him more than I've ever wanted anything. I always have. There was never anything between me and Goran, I swear it. It was *you* he was sweet on, not me.'

'But I thought he gave you a passionate kiss when you gave him the dictionary . . . that's what you told me.'

Desperately unhappy and close to tears, Morwenna pleaded, 'It wasn't true, I swear it wasn't. I didn't know what I was doing, or saying. I just wanted him — or anyone — to marry me. You know why. He *did* kiss me, but only because I demanded it as payment for taking the book to him and it certainly wasn't passionate. It was hardly a kiss at all. He just pecked my cheek, then stepped back so quickly I never had a chance to do anything in return. That's the truth, Nessa, honestly!'

'That's what I've been told, but I wanted to hear it from you. You're absolutely horrible, you know that? You must be the worst sister anyone has ever had. I really don't believe Alan deserves someone like you, he's not a bad person.'

'*Please*, Nessa! I beg you!' Tears were streaming down Morwenna's cheeks now.

Pushing past her in order to fetch a final bucket of water, Nessa said, 'You needn't worry, I wasn't going to tell anyone, anyway. All your nasty secrets are safe enough with me, but I don't think I'll ever be able to trust *you* again.'

Feeling almost sick with relief, Morwenna followed her sister to the water butt. 'I'll never do anything like that again, Nessa, I promise. I won't ever need to. If Alan marries me, and I'm certain he will, I'll try never to do a nasty thing to anyone ever again — especially not to you.'

Nessa knew her sister meant every word — at this moment — but she made no reply. Now she knew the truth about Morwenna's supposed affair with Goran she had other things to think about. There were plans to be made. Pleasant plans . . .

34

After a lengthy discussion that went on until far into the night in the privacy of their bedroom, Piran and Annie Pyne agreed they would not seek answers from Morwenna about what she had been doing during the time she claimed to have been at Elworthy Farm with Goran and the following morning when Piran went to the mine he sent Alan to the cottage to talk matters over with Morwenna.

Knowing the couple had a great deal to discuss, Annie agreed to allow them to walk together on the immediate moorland in order to settle their future relationship — if there was to be one.

The young couple were away from the cottage for two hours and when they returned Alan went to the mine and Morwenna joined her mother in the cottage. It was immediately apparent to Annie that there was a complacency about Morwenna that bordered on smugness.

She explained that Alan had apologized abjectly for not coming to Wheal Hope with her after the long and close relationship they had enjoyed together in West Cornwall. He had pleaded to be given another chance, declaring he had been thoroughly miserable during their time apart and had come to appreciate just how much she meant to him.

He further promised that if she forgave him he

would ask her father for permission for them to be married as soon as was possible and would do everything within his power to make her happy.

Although Alan was offering her everything she had ever wanted, Morwenna allowed him to think she needed time to consider whether or not to take up with him again — but she did not keep up this pretence for *too* long.

When she appeared to relent and agree she *would* marry him, Morwenna stipulated that a physical relationship would not be resumed until they had been made man and wife in a church — and *that* depended entirely upon her father accepting Alan as his future son-in-law.

When Annie queried why Alan had not returned to the cottage with her, Morwenna explained that he had work to do at the mine and intended finding her father and asking for his permission to marry her.

There were no doubts in the minds of either mother or daughter that Alan's offer would be accepted, but as time passed with no sign of either Piran or her would-be fiancé, Morwenna became increasingly agitated, remembering that in the past her father had never approved of Alan.

She would have gone to the mine to learn what had gone on between the two men but Annie pointed out this would be seen as unseemly eagerness on Morwenna's part.

Morwenna accepted her mother's advice. She had been able to dictate terms for her relationship with Alan that morning and, wishing to continue to hold the advantage, was forced to curb her impatience and wait until her father returned to the cottage at midday. He brought Alan with him, explaining that he had invited the young miner to come and eat with them.

The head of the family's announcement that Alan had asked for Morwenna's hand in marriage and had been accepted was greeted with delight by Morwenna, but when Piran said the acceptance was conditional she became suddenly apprehensive. But Piran explained.

'I've told Alan that in view of the fact he and Morwenna haven't seen each other for some time I feel they need to get to know each other again. I also want to satisfy myself that his foolish escapade with Jacob Barlow was no more than that — a foolish escapade. He now needs to prove to me that he's ready to settle down to what he does best — mining. I've agreed that Alan can marry Morwenna, but the wedding will not take place until spring next year. When that time comes and he's proved himself to my satisfaction I'll be pleased to welcome him into the family.'

Morwenna appeared dismayed, but Alan spoke directly to her. 'Don't worry, Morwenna, I'll prove myself to both you and your pa. I'll work twice as hard as any other miner so that we'll have a bit of money put by to get started in a home together. You'll be proud of me by then, you just wait and see.'

Warming to the fervent young man, Annie said, 'I am sure we'll all be proud of you, and it means Morwenna will have time to get some of the things together that you're both going to need in a home of your own.'

Morwenna had been hoping for an early wedding, but Alan had committed himself to marrying her and she was confident he would not go back on his word now. Besides, what he and her mother had said made a lot of sense. Setting up a home meant a lot of work, planning — and money. She would ensure Alan did more than his share to achieve at least two of the requisites. She had her own ideas of the sort of home she wanted. She smiled happily once more.

The only person in the room who did not share wholeheartedly in wishing the young couple well for their future together was Nessa. While she would do nothing to upset her sister's plans she had not entirely forgiven her duplicity in coming between Goran and herself.

Piran was aware of his middle daughter's lack of enthusiasm for Morwenna's betrothal and, after the meal, when the pots and plates had been cleared away and Morwenna and Alan were seated outside on a bench talking together, he suggested that Nessa walk with him to the mine, making the excuse he would like her to bring one of the mine's account books back to the cottage with her to check his figures.

As they walked side-by-side, he said, 'Are you happy that Morwenna and Alan are to be married?'

'It's what Morwenna's always wanted.' Nessa replied, ambiguously.

'It's going to feel strange having a daughter marry and leave the home, but I suppose it's something your ma and me will need to get used to. You'll no doubt be next.'

'I don't think you'll need to worry about me getting married for a while, if at all, but you know Uncle Cedric has asked if I'd like to travel to London to live with him and Aunt Joan? He's opened his own school and would like me to teach the girls there. He thinks I would be a good teacher with his tuition.'

'Yes, your ma told me. If that's what you would really like to do we wouldn't stand in your way — but I think Goran would be very disappointed if you were to leave.'

'I doubt it, we haven't seen each other for a long time.'

'Would that be because Morwenna gave everyone the impression she was seeing him?'

'Yes.'

Nessa could have said a great deal more on the subject but she chose to remain silent.

'Goran wasn't aware of any of that, you know. I think he's very hurt that you have never gone to Elworthy to congratulate him on taking over the farm.'

When Nessa made no reply, Piran added, 'Do you know that when he learned you had given your bracelet to Morwenna in exchange for a dictionary for him he bought you a bracelet to replace it?'

Startled, Nessa said, 'Are you sure, he's never brought it up here for me?'

'He told me himself but asked me to keep it a secret. He bought it when he and Jenken went to a fair in Liskeard to buy something that was needed for the farm. I think he's probably been waiting for the right moment to give it to you, but with all that's been going on and the hours he's been putting in on the farm I doubt whether he's had a moment to spare. I don't think that helping to rescue me and the other miners helped. I spoke to Albert a day or two ago and he says he's never known anyone work as hard as Goran; he's determined to make his farm a success.'

'I didn't know, Pa. I'll get down to the farm and give him my belated congratulations as soon as I can now that Morwenna's settled with Alan and there's no question of her being involved with Goran.'

35

Horace Rundle arrived at Elworthy Farm a few days after the excitement caused by Jacob Barlow and his disorderly miners had died down, those taken into custody having been remanded to appear at the next assizes.

The ploughman arrived with his two horses which were pulling a heavy wagon containing a plough, harrow and a number of other farming implements. It heralded a very busy time for Goran and Jenken when the general work around the farm would not cease, animals needed to be fed, their houses cleaned and general welfare attended to, but Horace would only be at Elworthy for a few days, lodging in the farm-house.

During his stay Goran would need to learn at least the rudiments of preparing land to take crops — initially root vegetables. Horace had suggested potatoes, turnips and swedes in order to clean the ground before sowing wheat, the crop Goran had been urging Agnes to grow for almost as long as he had been working for her.

Ploughing was hard work for both man and horses, but it was Jenken who was particularly eager to try his hand at controlling the plough. He swiftly learned he did not yet possess sufficient strength needed for the task and for the time being would have to be content to watch and listen to what was being explained.

However, he was allowed to lead the horses which were so experienced in their task that once the first furrow had been cut they needed little or no guiding.

On the second day of ploughing instruction, Horace received an unexpected visitor in the form of his great-niece, Victoria. A dark-haired girl who had just celebrated her sixteenth birthday, she walked to the farm from her home to find Horace and thank him for the silver bracelet he had bought for her at the fair, leaving it with her mother to be presented to her on her birthday.

She was taken to the field by Harriet Bolitho who brought along her two youngest boys to see their big brother working. After hugging and thanking her great-uncle, Victoria left Horace introducing Harriet and the two young boys to the large but patient and gentle horses and made her way to where Goran was cleaning off the ploughshare.

Waiting until he looked up she said, 'Hello, I'm Victoria, Horace's great-niece. You must be Goran, he's talked a lot about you.'

'He's spoken to me about you, too. I believe you've just had a birthday?' Victoria was a very pretty girl and Goran felt unusually tongue-tied in her presence.

'That's right and Uncle Horace remembered it. That's why I came here today, to thank him for buying me this lovely bracelet and leaving it with my mother for me.' She held out her wrist to show him the bracelet, adding, 'It's a very expensive present and must have cost him a lot of money.'

Goran was about to say that he was present when the bracelet was bought, but changed his mind hurriedly. He did not know whether Horace had exaggerated the value of the bracelet, or whether the girl had put her own value upon it. Instead, he said, 'It's very nice, he must think a lot of you.'

Pleased to have impressed him, Victoria removed the present from her wrist and handed it to Goran, saying, 'You look here inside, it says it's real silver — and that's worth a lot of money.'

'It is indeed.'

Taking the bangle from her, Goran made much of examining it properly before slipping it back on her wrist as she extended her arm to him.

When it was in place she gripped his hand and, smiling up at him coquettishly, said, 'Thank you.'

It was blatant flirting and Goran was amused — but it did not amuse everyone who witnessed it.

No one had noticed the arrival of Nessa Pyne on the scene. Hidden behind a tall, summer-luxuriant hedgerow until she arrived at the field gate, she had arrived in time to see Goran slip a bracelet on to the wrist of a very pretty young girl who appeared to be gazing up at him adoringly.

Suddenly, the volume of poetry she was carrying as a gift for Goran felt unbearably heavy. Turning away, she hurried back the way she had come, heading for the high moor but avoiding Elworthy Farm, from where Albert

239

Bolitho had given her directions to the field where Goran was ploughing.

Arriving on open moorland, out of sight of the farm, she found she was trembling and knew she could not go home immediately. She first needed to gain control of herself and put her scrambled thoughts into some semblance of order.

★   ★   ★

When Piran returned home from the mine that evening he was greeted by his wife who said, 'It seems it's not just one daughter we are about to lose, Piran, but *two*!'

Taken by surprise, Piran said 'Two? Why, has Nessa come to her senses and made it up with Goran . . . he hasn't proposed to her? She's still too young to be thinking of marriage, but I'm very pleased . . . '

He stopped when Annie rested a hand on his arm, bringing his happy chatter to a halt.

'I'm afraid it's nothing like that. In fact, it would appear that any chance of a romance between the two of them is over. Nessa has decided to take up Cedric's offer and go to London to teach in his school. It's something she's always said she wanted, you know that.'

'It *was* what she wanted, but that was before she met Goran.'

'I know, but things haven't been going well between the two of them lately. I think she went to the farm today with the intention of making it up with him, but she must have had second thoughts about what it was she really wanted.

When she came home she sat straight down and wrote a letter to Cedric accepting his offer.'

'Where is she now, I'll speak to her about it?'

Annie shook her head ruefully, 'It would make no difference, Piran. You know what Nessa is like when she's made up her mind about something. Besides, as soon as she'd written the letter she went out to send it off in the mail. Before she left she said she'd like you to make arrangements for her to travel to Falmouth where she'll stay with my sister until a respectable family can be found going by sea to London with whom she can travel. She says she wants to do it right away, before Cedric finds someone else to teach in his school.'

'What do you think about it, Annie?' Piran asked, unhappily.

'I think I feel much the same as you do. I was hoping she might marry Goran one day, but if that's not going to happen, we must let her go to London. After all, she has always said it's what she wants and she's worked hard at her schooling in order to achieve it. I don't think we can stop her now.'

Piran thought about it for a long time before nodding his head. 'No, you're quite right, Annie and, as you say, it's what she's always told us she wanted to do. The trouble is we're both going to miss her so much — and so too will Jennifer, but I suppose what will be, will be.'

36

It was eighteen months since Nessa had left Cornwall to take up a teaching post in her uncle's London school and, although England's capital city was an exciting place to be, it had taken her a long time to adapt to city life.

During the first few months she had assisted an elderly and stern woman teacher in instructing the few girls who attended the school and who were taught separately from the boys. Although never having married herself, the teacher firmly believed that the most important thing for her pupils to learn was how to become a good wife and mother and master social skills in order to attract a suitable man to elevate them to this highly desirable state.

For Nessa, to whom learning had much wider implications, such strictures were frustrating, especially when she came across the occasional girl whose views on education matched her own and who possessed a thirst for knowledge that extended beyond a home, a husband and a family.

It had been thought that the elderly teacher was ailing and that Nessa would take over from her soon after arriving in London but she seemed determined to continue teaching until senility deprived her of the ability to communicate with her young pupils. Because of her past loyalty, Cedric Couch was reluctant to retire her.

Aware of Nessa's increasing frustration, in January of 1839, her uncle called her to his study in the large house that was both school and home. Inviting her to take a seat across the desk from him he leaned back in his chair and said, 'I understand from Miss Brooks that you are not entirely happy with the breadth of the teaching given to our young ladies?'

Miss Brooks had been teaching at Cedric Couch's school since it first opened and enjoyed the full confidence of its headmaster. Because of this, Nessa made a cautious reply. 'There's nothing wrong with Miss Brooks's teaching methods for the majority of the girls, but she has little time for the occasional girl who is far more intelligent than the average pupil and who feels a need to learn more than how to become a good housewife.'

'I am inclined to agree with you, Nessa, and it may surprise you to know that when my school first opened Miss Brooks sat where you are seated now and made a similar complaint to me.'

The statement took Nessa by surprise, but her uncle was still talking. ' . . . I sympathized with her then, as I do with you now. Unfortunately it is the parents who pay their daughters' fees — sometimes with considerable reluctance. They feel education is advantageous only to their sons and we are forced to teach what is wanted by *them.*'

Nessa's inclination was to challenge her uncle's explanation, but she knew he was right.

She had offered special tuition for one particularly bright girl who showed great promise in mathematics, only to have her mother threaten to remove her daughter from the school if Nessa continued to put ideas unbecoming of a young lady into her daughter's head.

'I was unaware Miss Brooks shared my feelings,' Nessa confessed, 'but it doesn't change anything. I enjoy teaching, but so much of what I want to teach is impossible when all the parents want is for their daughters to marry men who expect little more from their wives than to behave as well-bred servants. So much of my work and the girls' intelligence is being wasted!'

'I have known for some time how you feel and am aware it's because you are a gifted and dedicated teacher. You *care* about what you are doing. For such a teacher there can be nothing more soul-destroying than feeling that his, or her, work is not being appreciated — but I can assure you it is not going unnoticed and it is not you who are at fault.'

Wondering why her uncle had called her to his study to express support for her, while at the same time declaring there was nothing that could be done to change their method of teaching, Nessa asked, 'Are you trying to tell me in a kind way that you feel I'm not suitable to teach in *your* school, Uncle?'

'Of course not, you are eminently suitable to teach anywhere. No, I asked you here because I have some *extra* duties in mind that I feel you might find rather more stimulating. I personally believe it to be most worthwhile but it poses a challenge that not all teachers are either willing or capable of accepting. I believe you are.'

Intrigued, Nessa waited for her uncle to explain further.

Leaning forward in his chair, he asked, 'You have heard of what have become known as 'ragged schools'?'

Nessa nodded. Ragged schools were free schools set up by philanthropic or religious bodies in the most deprived areas of British cities to provide education of widely differing standards to children who themselves had equally diverse views on what, if anything, they expected from life.

'Good. I have a friend, Father Michael Jaye, a fellow Cornishman, who is vicar of one of the most deprived parishes in the whole of London. He has asked me if I will give my support to a school he has opened there. He recently moved premises to an empty furniture workshop in order to expand the school. When he opened his first school, critics said he would never have any pupils, yet children have been falling over themselves to enrol and he has needed to expand, but is in desperate need of more teachers. Mind you, the fact that he provides soup and bread once a day for all his pupils and wherever possible cleans them up and provides them with second-hand clothing may have *something* to do with the school's popularity, but he is highly gratified at what he feels is a most unexpected success. In general it's rather simple teaching — reading, writing and basic arithmetic, but he has said to me that if someone showed exceptional talent he would do all within his power to help them go further. It is an enormous challenge, Father Michael says so himself, but without something to lift them out of their squalor he fears the only way out is either prison or the gallows . . . a path taken by a great many who reside in the Old Nichol. However, given a basic education he is hoping he might be able to find sponsors to send them to countries like America or Canada in order to make a fresh start.'

Aware of Nessa's uncertainty about teaching basic skills in such an environment, Cedric Couch said, 'Think about it overnight, Nessa. I promised Father Michael I would go to the Old Nichol tomorrow and see the school for myself. Come with me and we will see if there is anything we might do to help him.'

★   ★   ★

Leaving the wide streets flanked by tall well-kept houses far behind, the next day Nessa and her uncle, riding in a hackney-carriage, entered a part of London she had not seen before and could never have envisaged in her worst nightmare. There were no smart carriages drawn by well-groomed horses on the narrow streets here. Instead, most wheeled vehicles seemed to be handcarts of all descriptions and condition, being pushed or pulled by men, women or children whose dress was as varied as the carts.

The houses were small and dingy, seeming to lean in upon each other and in various states of disrepair. The people who occupied the streets and houses were different too. In the area of London around Kensington, where her uncle had his home and school, there *were* ill-dressed men, women and children, but they were few and far between. Here there were people who were actually clothed in what could only be described as 'rags'.

They were entering an area known as the 'Old Nichol' where there were no street cleaners, and roads and pavements — where the latter existed — were strewn with all manner of filth and litter.

The children they saw were in the main gaunt and thin, and Nessa thought that most of them had 'haunted' expressions. As the carriage passed by they paused to give it hostile stares, as though it had no right to be there.

Reaching a junction, the hackney-carriage came to a halt in a tight turn and the driver said, 'This is as far as I go, guv'nor. For Old Nichol Street you'll need to go up Boundary Road and you'll find it on your right — but if you've anything of value in your pockets I'd advise you to tuck it inside your shirt, and hide the lady's purse, or it'll be gone by the time you get there.'

Irritated, Cedric Couch said, 'Can't you take us up the street a while further? Boundary Street looks wide enough for your carriage.'

Shaking his head, the carriage driver said, 'Sorry, guv, but if I went up there they'd have the wheels off my carriage and my poor horse would be in a hundred cooking pots before I could get out of the Old Nichol.'

Still grumbling, Cedric Couch paid off the

247

driver and turned to find half-a-dozen urchins crowding Nessa with hands held out and clamouring for pennies.

Nessa was unused to such behaviour and Cedric Couch hurried to her rescue. When there was space around her, he asked, 'How do we get to Father Michael's school, in Old Nichol Street?'

The boys looked at each other before one of them, a boy of about fourteen years of age asked, 'What do you want with Father Michael?'

Aware of her uncle's indignation at being questioned by this urchin and believing it would not be sensible to alienate anyone in the Old Nichol if she was to work here — not that she was at all certain she would *want* to — Nessa said quickly, 'I might be teaching at Father Michael's school, but we need to find it first.'

The reply provoked immediate interest among the urchins and the boy who had questioned her uncle's reason for going to the school said, 'I'll take you there, but it's going to cost you.'

'Then we'll find our own way,' Cedric Couch snapped.

Ignoring her uncle's affronted response, Nessa asked, 'How much do you want?'

'I don't want your money, but there's been talk of Father Michael bringing in another teacher and starting up an extra class. If he does I want my sister Sally to be in it.'

'Only your sister? Don't *you* want to learn how to read and write?'

'Sally's the one who wants learning, I don't. Besides, I'm too busy getting money to feed the both of us, I ain't got no time to waste on things that don't matter to no one.'

'Yet you're happy for Sally to be taught?'

Momentarily discomfited, the urchin said, 'Our ma always wanted for Sally to get out of the Old Nichol and go into service with some rich family somewhere else. She wouldn't be able to do that unless she learns some of the things they'd expect her to know.'

'Where's your mother now?'

'She's been dead for nigh on three years, but . . . '

'And your father?'

The boy's discomfort increasing, he said, 'I dunno. Ma would never talk of him — or anyone related to him. There's some as said he was dead, others that he was sent to the hulks, but what's all that matter? If you won't take Sally into Father Michael's school I haven't got time to waste answering your questions.'

The young urchin and his companions were dirtier and more ragged than any child she had seen since coming to London and his dialect more extreme than any she had heard. He pronounced 'th' as though it was an 'f' and the letter 'h' seemed not to exist. He also ran words together in a manner that was sometimes confusing, yet she found his obvious affection for his sister touching.

'How old is Sally?'

He shrugged, 'I dunno. She's about a year younger than me so I suppose she must be twelve, thirteen . . . or even fourteen. Whatever it is she's not too old to go to school.'

'All right, I don't know for certain yet whether I *will* be teaching at Father Michael's school, but if I *do* start work there I'll take Sally into my class. Where do you live, so I can let you know?'

His delight disappeared at her question, but only for a few moments. 'We live here and there, but don't you worry, there's not much goes on in the Old Nichol that I don't know about. I'll know soon enough if you come to work for Father Michael and Sally be there on your first day. Come on, I'll take you to the school . . . '

*   *   *

The Old Nichol ragged school's founder was a much younger man than she had been expecting. Probably not yet thirty, Father Michael Jaye was a dedicated priest who, although having a wealthy background, had given up a lucrative living in a rich Kensington parish in order to dedicate his life to caring for the needy in this, the worst of London's slums.

His popularity in the previous parish stood him in good stead here in the Old Nichol, there always being someone he could turn to when he was desperate for funds in order to advance his work.

When Nessa told him of her meeting with the street urchin who was brother to the as yet unknown Sally, he said, 'That will be young Arthur Harrup, one of the Old Nichol's most hardened young criminals. He thinks the world of that sister of his and as far as I am concerned that is a saving grace for him — possibly his only

250

one! He has tried before to have his sister taught in the school, but he so upset the teacher who was taking the younger children at the time that she refused to have Sally in her class. That teacher left us some months ago. Unfortunately, there have always been more pupils than we can cope with and it is only now I have larger premises that it is possible to bring in more children like Sally. I only wish it was possible to have Arthur enrolled as well, he has a quick mind. I feel that with proper guidance he could make something of himself.'

The compassionate parish priest raised his hands in a gesture of frustration, 'But there, I can see potential in so many of the children. Sadly, all too few will ever be able to escape from the Old Nichol. I would very much welcome your presence here as a teacher, Miss Pyne and would be very happy to see Sally Harrup among your pupils.'

37

A week after her first visit to the Old Nichol, Nessa returned there to take her first class in Father Michael's ragged school. It was to be a mixed class of boys and girls who would, nevertheless, be strictly segregated when in the classroom.

It was with some trepidation that Nessa alighted from the hackney-carriage which, as on her first visit to the Old Nichol took her only as far as the edge of the notorious slum.

She learned immediately that there was no cause for concern. Waiting for her were Arthur Harrup and a gang of his fellow urchins to escort her to the new premises of the ragged school, taking a short-cut through a maze of evil-smelling, litter-strewn alleyways.

In answer to her question concerning the whereabouts of his sister, Arthur replied that she would be at the school for her lessons.

'How about you, why not come along too and see how you like it?'

She realized that she had probably made a mistake in putting the suggestion to him in the presence of the other urchins, it being immediately apparent that they awaited Arthur's reply with great interest. He was aware of it too.

'School's all right for them as having nothing better to do. I've got Sally to look out for and things that need doing right here, in the Old Nichol.'

It was a reply that seemed to meet with the approval of Arthur's followers and Nessa asked him no more questions on the way to the ragged school with her urchin escort.

Father Michael greeted Nessa enthusiastically and took her along to introduce her to the class she was to teach. He would have remained with her but she wanted to assume authority in the classroom from the very beginning and insisted upon being left alone with the forty pupils she was to teach.

Her first command was to have all the windows opened, despite the protest of those seated closest to them that it was a cold morning. It was doubtful whether water had touched the skin of her pupils either that day or on many previous days and the air inside the room was fetid.

In response to the protests, Nessa replied, 'It's far too stuffy to work in here with the windows closed, but it is quite chilly at the moment. Isn't that stove alight?'

There was a free-standing iron stove in the room and Nessa had thought she detected a glimmer of life in it when she entered the room. Checking it now she saw it contained a thin layer of faintly glowing embers, but if the coal was not replenished soon it would die and there was no fuel to be seen nearby.

'Does anyone know where the coal is kept?'

She put the question to the class in general and there was a quick affirmative reply from a boy of about ten whose grimy hands looked as though they might have had a long acquaintance with the fuel in question.

'Good, then go and find a bucket or something to carry it in and bring some coal back for the stove — and be quick, or it will be out.'

The boy turned to hurry away only to have his path blocked by an older boy. 'No, I'll go, miss.'

Nessa was about to say that *she* would delegate any tasks that needed doing during school hours when the older boy explained, 'If Micky went, by the time he got back here with a bucketful of coal he'd have twice as much hidden away to collect and sell after school. It's what he does best, nicking coal and selling it to them as can pay for it.'

The younger boy scowled at the speaker but made no attempt to deny the accusation and Nessa realized there was going to be a lot more to teaching these children than she had experienced at her uncle's Kensington school.

This was brought home to Nessa once again some minutes later when with the windows of the schoolroom open and a hopeful glow emanating from the open flap at the base of the coal-fuelled stove, she began making a register of those attending her class.

When she had recorded the last name she looked out over the class and frowned. 'Sally Harrup was supposed to be here, has anyone seen her?'

A few of the girls looked at each and one of them tittered. Silencing the culprit with a stern look, Nessa said, 'What do you know about her, why isn't she here?'

When the girl averted her glance and gave no reply, Nessa said firmly, 'When you are in my class and I ask a question I expect a reply. If you want to remain at school you had better remember that. Now, where is Sally Harrup?'

Realizing that Nessa was serious, the girl said, 'She's got nothing to wear, miss.'

'What do you mean, she has nothing to wear? No one expects her to dress up to come to school.'

'No, I mean she has *nothing* to wear. Her brother, Arthur, got her a dress to wear today — a *really* good dress — although it was a lot too big for her. Anyway, on her way here she met one of the women who hangs around the pub along the road and who'd been drinking all night. She liked the dress and offered Sally a whole shilling for it — so Sally sold it to her, there and then, and was left with nothing to come to school in.'

The explanation brought a number of amused and knowing smiles from the others in the class and Nessa decided she would take the matter no further. However it did not end there and then.

Her first lesson at the Old Nichol ragged school was no more than an hour old when Arthur Harrup entered the schoolroom unannounced and without so much as a knock on the door. The young, scowling girl with him looked as though the frock she was wearing had come from a ragman's barrow, which in all probability it had. Pushing her unceremoniously into the classroom, Arthur said, 'I've brought Sally here for you to give her some learning!'

With this blunt statement he turned to go but, recovering from her initial surprise, Nessa said, 'Just a minute! If Sally wants to attend my classes she'll need to arrive on time, the same as

255

all the others. I can't teach school if pupils are going to come and go as they please.'

'She'd have been here in time if someone hadn't knocked her down and nicked the frock I got for her specially.'

One of the girls in the classroom sniggered but the sound ceased abruptly when Arthur glared around the room at the assembled urchins.

Saying nothing of what she had been told earlier, Nessa said, 'Then she can find herself a seat — but I'll expect her to be the best timekeeper in my class from now on.'

'She will be.' With this Arthur turned and left the class and, when Nessa had silenced the hubbub that erupted immediately after his departure, she made various pupils repeat what she had been telling the class prior to Arthur's interruption and when this was done she continued with the remainder of her lesson.

When lessons came to an end after a two hour session Nessa dismissed the class and they promptly stampeded off in order to claim the bowl of soup and hunk of bread that was the sole reason for the attendance of many of the Old Nichol urchins at the ragged school.

Sally Harrup was among them, but before she could escape, Nessa put out an arm to bring her to a halt and keep her behind. When all the others had left, Nessa looked at the girl who stood reluctantly before her. She saw an under-weight, blue-eyed girl with long, lank brown hair who possessed fine features, but was so dirty and ill-clothed that all her finer points went largely unnoticed.

She stood fidgeting uneasily and looking down at her bare feet which were as dirty as the rest of her visible body. In spite of this, Nessa thought there was something indefinably appealing about the young waif. Speaking to her more gently than she had intended, she said, 'Arthur said you had been attacked and had your dress stolen?'

'That's right.' Sally's East London dialect was the equal of that of her brother.

'That isn't true, is it?'

Sally's glance flicked up to Nessa's face before she looked down once more without making a reply.

'You sold it for a shilling, I believe.'

'Who told you that? It's not true.'

'I think it is and I don't like pupils who lie to me, Sally, any more than I will tolerate pupils arriving late for my lessons and disrupting the whole class. It was despicable of you to sell a dress that Arthur must have worked hard to buy for you.'

Sally looked up again and said scornfully, 'You wouldn't catch Arthur *buying* a dress, he don't pay for nothing.'

After a moment to gather her thoughts, Nessa decided she was more disappointed than shocked. Arthur was a product of the time and place in which he lived, his concern for his sister had temporarily blinded her to the fact, that was all.

'All right, Sally, off you go and have your soup now. I'll see you in the morning — but don't be late.'

38

That evening, over a dinner which, with its venue, was far removed from the soup and bread dispensed from the kitchen at the Old Nichol ragged school, Nessa told her uncle about Sally, her brother and the events of the day.

His reply was philosophical. 'Sadly, thieving and dishonesty is a way of life for so many of the children you will be teaching there; they know nothing else.'

'It is such a shame,' Nessa said. 'Many of them are really quite bright. In spite of his apparent dishonesty, young Arthur Harrup is obviously very fond of his sister and accepts a great deal of responsibility for her. She, too, is exceptionally quick-witted and deserving of far more from life than she has now.'

'Then you have been given a great opportunity, Nessa. Teach Sally and the others about the world outside the Old Nichol and guide them towards a happier and more fulfilled way of life — but don't be too despondent if you fail with the vast majority. It will be well worthwhile if you succeed with only one or two. Think of yourself as a farmer, sowing the seeds of knowledge, having prepared the ground as best you can, but the results, as in farming, depend on circumstances over which you have no control and which are beyond our understanding.'

Nessa left the dining-room that evening having

assimilated the wisdom of her uncle's words, but her thoughts were not entirely of the Old Nichol and the children she was teaching there.

Cedric Couch's homily had not been entirely wasted, but his parable of a farmer sowing the seed of knowledge had made her think of Goran. She thought of him quite often but for some inexplicable reason today she had a yearning to see him that had returned with an intensity she had not known since her early days in London when he had been in her thoughts for many of her quieter moments.

She decided it had much to do with the last letter she had received from her mother. In it Annie Pyne mentioned that Goran's experiment of growing wheat had been so successful he intended sowing double or even treble the amount of acreage for the coming season, something which delighted the Wheal Hope miners and their families who were able to earn a few welcome extra shillings by providing the labour needed at harvest time.

Annie rarely mentioned anything about Goran's personal life in her letters and Nessa never asked questions about it in hers, but that did not mean she never wondered whether he would marry the girl to whom she believed he had given the bracelet her father said he had bought for her.

That night, when she eventually went to sleep it was Goran who was foremost in her thoughts and not the problems of the Old Nichol ragged school.

In spite of the many problems posed by her pupils, Nessa gained a great deal of satisfaction from her teaching at Father Michael's school as it became increasingly organized. The parish priest agreed to a great many of the suggestions put forward by Nessa and personally worked hard to ensure they were carried through.

As a result of this and a surge of interest from those living in the slum it had been decided that boys and girls should be taught separately. This decision was taken because as older boys were enrolled in the school many of them resented taking orders from a woman, so Father Michael took their classes.

It had also become apparent that some of the older boys were taking a reciprocated interest in the girls when two pupils were discovered copulating in the coal cupboard and urgent action needed to be taken.

Now the girls received schooling in the morning and boys in the afternoon with meal times staggered to fit in with the new routine. Then Father Michael came to an arrangement with the local workhouse to take worn-out children's clothing that would otherwise have been disposed of to a rag-and-bone man.

He had also hoped to persuade the children to make use of the workhouse facilities to bathe themselves, but workhouses were anathema to the residents of the Old Nichol — and all the other slums of London — so the resourceful priest had two wash-houses built at the rear of the school, where soap, water and towels were readily available.

The result was that there was less of an odour in the classrooms and that summer proved a very satisfying one for all those involved in the ragged school. There was a steady rise in the number of pupils, and to everyone's delight the police reported a drop in crime in the area.

It did not mean there was no longer *any* crime. For many of the Old Nichol families, stealing was as much a part of their lives as breathing and drinking — and more familiar than eating.

Then, as autumn grudgingly gave way to winter and the weather began its seasonal change, Nessa's life suffered an upheaval that could not have been anticipated.

It began when Sally failed to arrive for her lessons one morning. This in itself was unusual. Although never the best of timekeepers, she had never missed a day's schooling in all the time she had been a pupil.

When she failed to attend school the next day too, Nessa became very concerned. She asked the other pupils whether any of them had seen Sally, but learned nothing. However, she felt it was evasiveness on the part of the girls rather than a lack of knowledge that was the reason for their silence.

Sally had never shown any great friendliness towards any particular girl in the class but Nessa had occasionally seen her talking to a girl named Marie and when the class was dismissed that morning, she called the girl back.

261

'Just a minute, Marie, I want to talk to you.'

'Can't it wait, miss, I'm *starving*! If I'm late I won't get no dinner.'

'I'll see you don't miss it, but I want to know why Sally isn't at school — and it's no use telling me you don't know because I won't believe you.'

'You've already asked the class, I don't know any more than anyone else about her.' Marie spoke without looking at Nessa and it was clear she was lying.

'You're not telling me the truth, Marie. If Sally is in some sort of trouble I want to help her. Now, I suggest you tell so you can get on your way and have your soup.'

Marie was obviously reluctant to say anything, but when Nessa continued to wait without dismissing the girl she eventually said, 'It's not Sally who's in trouble but Arthur, her brother.'

Alarmed, Nessa demanded, 'What for? What's he done?'

'He was collared last Saturday after he'd broken into a shop and nicked some clothes.'

'Where is he now?'

'He came up before a beak yesterday and they sent him for trial, so I expect he's in Newgate . . . that's where my dad is.'

The fact that Marie's father was in Newgate Prison was expressed with a hint of pride that, having spent some time working in the Old Nichol, no longer surprised Nessa.

'Where does Sally stay? Where can I find her?'

'I don't know, nobody knows . . . except Arthur.'

When Nessa broke the news to Father

262

Michael about Arthur and expressed her concern for Sally, the Old Nichol priest was deeply saddened. He had always felt Arthur could have made something of himself had he only put his mind to it.

'Regrettably, Arthur has always been his own worst enemy, but you have worked hard improving the life of young Sally Harrup's life, we can't let her down now. I'll go along to the magistrates now and find out exactly what's happening and where Arthur is. While I'm away arrange for someone else to take over any duties you have and put on your coat, ready for when I come back.'

'Where will we be going?'

'Newgate Prison if that's where they've taken Arthur — but may the Lord help him if it is.'

*   *   *

When Father Michael returned from the magistrates court he confirmed that Arthur was in Newgate Prison and suggested he and Nessa should walk there. It would take them about half an hour, but he explained he had not left the Old Nichol for more than two months and felt an acute need for a change of air and scenery.

In the ragged school Nessa rarely had an opportunity for a lengthy conversation with the priest and she made the most of the opportunity on their walk to the infamous London prison.

'What made you come to work in the Old Nichol? Uncle Cedric says you could have had your pick of almost any parish in the country.'

'I came here for that very reason. I had always felt I have more than my share of the good things in life; a happy childhood and comfortable home and, as I grew up, the respect that came with being the son of a vicar well liked by his parishioners. It was never in doubt that I would go into the Church — especially as one of my uncles is a bishop — and another dean of a West Country cathedral. I would probably have taken a comfortable parish somewhere had I not attended a lecture given by a priest returning from a spell as a missionary in Africa. I spoke to him after the talk and mentioned I was soon to be ordained. I said that missionary work greatly appealed to me and asked where he believed there was most need for such work. Much to my surprise, instead of mentioning some rather romantic and exciting foreign land, he said the greatest need was right here, in London. Two days later he persuaded me to accompany him on a walk around Bethnal Green and Shoreditch to witness the poverty and lack of godliness to be found here. Later, soon after my ordination, I returned here and discovered the Old Nichol. Witnessing the utter degradation of those who live here — especially the children — I made a vow to dedicate my life to the betterment of their lives in every way possible, both spiritually and materially and . . . well, here I am!'

'That was very noble of you, Father.'

'Noble is not a word that comes easily to mind when talking about the Old Nichol, Nessa . . . and talking of mere words, when we are not in school I would prefer you to call me Michael

264

and not Father. But, to return to my work here, I feel deeply that it was never God's intention that men, women and children should suffer such misery as exists in the Old Nichol. I like to think I am carrying out His will by working to improve their lives.'

For perhaps the first time since coming to teach in the ragged school, Nessa realized her companion was a devout Christian priest whose missionary zeal was the equal of any of those better known men and women who forsook the comforting shelter of the Mother Church in order to bring Christian principles to those in far away lands.

She hoped Father Michael would not burn himself out in seeking to achieve more than was possible in one man's lifetime.

39

Newgate Prison was a formidable and grimly imposing building, its high walls towering high above the surrounding streets, giving comfort to those who lived in fear of having a colony of criminals living in their midst, but adding to the despair of those whose lives wasted away within its crowded and festering interior.

Nessa shuddered as she and the priest waited for someone to respond to the echoing sound of the huge iron knocker attached to the main road door, separated from the huge, solid gates through which vehicles carrying prospective inmates entered the prison.

The gaoler who opened the door recognized Father Michael as having visited the prison on a number of previous occasions and greeted him by name, but when they stated their business the warder shook his head dubiously.

'If he's only on remand there's no visiting allowed. I think you already know that, Father.'

'I do, but there are exceptional circumstances in this case. Arthur Harrup has been taking care of his young sister ever since their mother — the sole surviving parent — died. Since Arthur's arrest she has not been seen and has failed to attend my ragged school, where Miss Pyne is a teacher. We are both extremely worried about her. No one in the school is able to tell us where the girl might be found and we both feel she could be in some danger. Arthur is our only hope.'

'Sally Harrup is a bright girl who shows great promise,' Nessa added. 'I have every hope that, given a chance, she may be found respectable work outside the Old Nichol — but we need to find her quickly. She relied heavily upon the support of her brother.'

'Well, he's not going to be able to help her no more,' was the gaoler's pessimistic reply. 'It's transportation for him, for sure — if he survives the hulks. He'll be sent to one of 'em to wait for a ship to take him to the colonies and there's something like a two-year wait for a passage, the courts sentencing them faster than they can be carried away.'

'Then we need to find Sally very quickly,' Father Michael said, firmly. 'It's bad enough that she no longer has Arthur to take care of her, once he's sentenced she'll go to pieces completely unless she has Miss Pyne to support her.'

Looking from one to the other of them, the man said, 'Well, it's not *really* allowed, Father, but seeing as how it's you and it's a matter of life and death, I think we can bend the rules a bit. I can't leave the office for long enough to take you there, but you wait here and I'll go and find someone to take you to where he's being held.'

★   ★   ★

Nessa would look back on her walk through the prison as one of her life's most horrifying

267

experiences. The stench inside the building was highly offensive, as might have been expected in a building which housed an excess of unwashed bodies, both male and female, and which possessed a notoriously poor sanitation system but, adding to this was an indefinable odour of fear and despair.

Her presence as the small party passed by iron-barred cages crammed with men provoked ribald and obscene shouts and suggestions to which she tried hard to show no reaction. The cages containing women were only marginally less noisy.

Eventually they reached a cage no different to the many others in which there were about thirty fettered men, most attired as befitted vagrants.

'Arthur Harrup?'

The gaoler needed to repeat his shout a number of times before there was movement among the large cell's inmates and Arthur pushed his way towards the visitors, calling out, 'What d'you want?'

Reaching the bars and seeing Nessa and Father Michael, his surly indifference turned to concern, 'What are you doing here, has something happened to Sally?'

'She hasn't been seen since you were arrested, Arthur, that's why we've come to speak to you. Where have you both been sleeping?'

The young prisoner looked at Nessa uncertainly as she was speaking, then, habitual secretiveness coming to the fore, he replied, 'If Sally don't want to be found then that's her business.'

Making an awkward shuffling turn, hampered by the leg-irons he was wearing, he intended returning to the rear of the iron-barred cell but Nessa said desperately, 'If that's what she wants we'll respect her wishes, but I'm concerned for her, Arthur. You have a lot of friends in the Old Nichol — but you have enemies too. They'll know you've been arrested and no doubt some of them will know where to find Sally. Is that what you want?'

She put the question to him, at the same time trying to keep the desperation she felt from her voice.

'Sally can look after herself.'

Arthur's words lacked conviction and, pressing home her advantage, Nessa said, 'She could look after herself while you were around but you're not there for her now — and probably won't ever be again. I'd like to help her make a good life for herself and I think that's what you want for her too, otherwise you wouldn't have been so insistent that I take her on when I began teaching at Father Michael's school. I won't be able to do anything to help her if the wrong people get hold of her first, Arthur, and you don't need me to spell out what life will be like for her then.'

Turning back to her, Arthur said, 'You really will take care of Sally? Why . . . she's nothing to you?'

'I'll do it because she's a bright young girl, Arthur, bright enough to leave the Old Nichol behind and really do something with her life. She could even become a teacher herself and be

269

someone for other girls in the Old Nichol to point to and say, 'Look, she did it — and so can we'.'

'You'd help Sally do that?'

'I would — and *will* if I can find her in time.'

Arthur needed a few more moments to think over what Nessa had said before replying.

'You know where the old houses were knocked down, over by Mount Street?'

Nessa did not know and turned to Father Michael, who nodded.

Seeing the gesture, Arthur continued, 'Well, soon after they were knocked down workmen came to dig a tunnel underneath them to make a sewer, or something. They dug a shaft down a little way before starting on a tunnel, but then work was stopped and they were supposed to have filled in the shaft again, but if you climb in among the bricks and stones you can wriggle your way into what's left of the tunnel. Me and Sally made a place in there for ourselves and no one's ever found us.'

'And you think that's where she'll be?' Nessa asked eagerly.

'It's where she's always gone when something's upset her.'

'Thank you, Arthur. You may be locked up but you're still able to help Sally. We'll have a word with the gaoler and try to improve things in here for you a little, then go off and find Sally right away.'

They had turned to go when Arthur said plaintively, 'D'you think Sally could come in here and see me?'

Father Michael and Sally looked at the prison guard who had remained silent throughout their conversation with Arthur although he had heard everything that was said. Still silent, he shook his head and it was Father Michael who replied to Arthur's plea.

'I don't think this is a place to bring Sally, it would upset her far too much to see you here. We'll try to bring her to court when you are put on trial and we should be able to arrange a meeting afterwards. Until then take care of yourself as best you can.'

40

Before leaving Newgate Father Michael was able to speak to the gaoler in charge, who was surprised that anyone should show interest in such an urchin. However, after a couple of guineas had changed hands, the Old Nichol priest was assured that pending his trial Arthur would be housed in a smaller cell, among more 'select' prisoners and be supplied with adequate food.

When Nessa and Father Michael returned to the Old Nichol, the former was still affected by all she had witnessed at Newgate but the priest collected the odd-job man who worked at the ragged school and the three set off for Mount Street.

A number of sites in the street were little more than heaps of rubble, anything capable of being either burned or reused having been carried off within days of the demolition. With only the vague description of the site that Arthur had been able to give them it was an almost impossible task to locate the spot where Sally might be found, but they were fortunate enough to come across a vagrant who was known to the parish priest and he was able to point out the particular site where the aborted attempt to begin work on a sewer system had taken place.

Scrambling over the uneven piles of rubble the shallow filled-in shaft was eventually located.

Even so, it was some minutes before they found a hole between some of the stones that looked as though it *might* be the entrance to the underground tunnel, even though the odd-job man insisted it was too small for the purpose — and certainly too small for *him* to attempt to investigate the possibility.

It was frustrating, but a crowd of inquisitive young urchins had gathered to watch what was going on and Father Michael turned to them for help.

'Do any of you know whether this hole leads to an underground tunnel?'

He received no immediate reply but the knowing glances exchanged between some of the urchins did not pass unnoticed.

'Oh well, it's a pity because it could have been worth a few pennies to anyone who could tell us something about it.'

Once again there were exchanged glances, but it was a young girl of perhaps eight or nine years of age who broke the frustrating silence.

'My brother Tim's been down there.'

'Has he, indeed! When was this — and did he find a tunnel?'

'I don't know. He only went down once because a bigger boy came along and told him that if he ever went down there again he'd kill him.'

'Who was this bigger boy, do you know him?'

The young girl shook her head, but another boy whose ragged clothing was barely sufficient to preserve decency, said, 'It was Arthur Harrup.'

Nessa and Father Michael realized they had

located Arthur and Sally Harrup's secret 'home' but Nessa said, 'How are we going to find out whether Sally's in there? The hole's not large enough for a man to go through and we can't ask any of these children to risk their lives trying.'

'I don't think there's an alternative.' Addressing the young girl who had volunteered the information, Father Michael said, 'Where is this brother of yours who has been inside the hole?'

'I dunno.' The girl shrugged her thin shoulders. 'He went out fogle-hunting last week and never came back. He was probably nicked.'

If the boy had been arrested while out stealing silk handkerchiefs he would not be available to go down to the unseen tunnel again. It was a set-back, but then a skinny, frail urchin stepped forward.

'I've been down there.'

'You? When?'

'A couple of weeks ago I saw Arthur Harrup and a girl come out and I took a candle and went down there to see what they'd been doing.'

'And what *had* they been doing?'

'There were two beds, one on the floor and the other on a sort of a shelf, further along the tunnel. They'd been sleeping in there.'

'Would you go down there again now, to see if anyone's in there?'

'Not if Arthur Harrup's likely to be there.'

'He's not; we've just been talking to him in Newgate. It was him who told us about the place and wanted us to speak to his sister. One of us would go in but we're too big to pass through the entrance.'

When the urchin still appeared doubtful, Father Michael said, 'If you went in there for us I'd give you sixpence.'

'I'll do it for a shilling,' came the prompt reply.

'A shilling if you find Sally Harrup in there, sixpence if you don't.'

'All right, but I'll need to take a candle down there and that'll cost another ha'penny.'

Clutching the halfpenny the boy ran off but less than a minute later reappeared with the stub of a candle and a small pack of lucifers which he claimed had now raised the expenses to a full penny. Nessa produced the additional halfpenny and, pocketing money, candle and Lucifers, the boy squeezed his way inside the hole and disappeared from view.

Making her way gingerly over the rubble, Nessa crouched down beside the opening to await results and it was not long before she glimpsed a faint lightening of the shadows from inside the hole, indicating that the boy had reached the tunnel and put a light to the candle.

Soon afterwards she thought she could hear the sound of voices in the tunnel and this was confirmed when the candlelight became brighter and the unseen boy called, 'There is a girl in here, so I'm coming out for my shilling.'

'No you're not,' Nessa retorted, firmly. 'I want to talk to her so you'll stay in there until I tell you to come out.'

Cutting across the ensuing protest, Nessa said, 'Tell her Miss Pyne is here and wants to speak to her.'

Grumbling, the boy and his lighted candle

withdrew into the tunnel, only to return a couple of minutes later to declare, 'She says she doesn't want to talk to you and you're to go away.'

'Go back and tell her I've just come from talking to Arthur and I've a message from him.'

Grumbling, the boy said, 'You're getting more than a bob's worth from me now — and if I stay down here much longer this candle's going to burn out.'

'You'll stay until I say you can come out — but once I've got Sally up here with me I'll give you *two* shillings.'

The candlelight retreated once more, for longer this time, then the unseen boy called, 'She says she don't believe you.'

'Remind her that I've never ever lied to her — and Father Michael was with me when I spoke to Arthur. What's more, I've promised Arthur I'll take her to see him, but that's not going to happen if she doesn't come out.'

The candlelight went away for longer this time. When it reappeared, it suddenly went out and a head appeared in the hole. It was not the boy, but Sally.

Nessa reached down to help her, but Father Michael was there before her and lifted Sally clear of the hole. She was quickly followed by the boy who immediately demanded his reward.

Given the promised two shillings by Father Michael, the boy was gone before Nessa had time to thank him and ask his name.

'Have you really spoken to Arthur, or was it just a trick to get me to come out?' Sally looked desperately tired and unhappy and dirt-free streaks down her cheeks were evidence she had been crying a great deal.

'I really have spoken to him and it was Arthur who told Father Michael and me where to find you. He'll be coming before the judge in ten days' time and Father Michael is going to court to speak for him. You and I will be there too and I've promised Arthur I'll take you to speak to him afterwards.'

'Will they let him come back to the Old Nichol then?'

'I don't think so, Sally, but we'll go back to school now to get you cleaned up and have a chat about what we're going to do next.'

It was a very unhappy Sally who went with them, leaving the odd-job man behind with a small amount of money with which to pay some of the urchins to effectively block-up the entrance to the underground hideaway.

41

When they reached the ragged school Sally enjoyed the first meal she had eaten for a couple of days while Nessa and Father Michael discussed what could be done with her.

'It isn't only Arthur who is going to suffer for his transgressions,' Father Michael pointed out. 'He has left his sister totally bewildered and vulnerable, I am at a loss about what might be done for her.'

His words helped Nessa make up her mind about an idea she had been toying with since the drama began. 'She'll come back to Kensington with me after school each day.'

It was a solution that had never occurred to Father Michael. Had it done so he would most certainly have dismissed it out of hand immediately. His expression registering disbelief, he said, 'Take her to Kensington? What are you thinking about, Nessa? Your uncle would not have her inside his house.'

'Not the way she is at the moment,' Nessa agreed, 'but scrubbed and deloused, with respectable clothes, she could be made to look quite pretty.'

'I suppose she might be made to *look* pretty,' Father Michael conceded, 'but she would only need to open her mouth to dispel any illusion of respectability — and there are a great many items of value in your uncle's home which would provide a great temptation to an urchin to whom honesty is an incomprehensible concept. Then there are such things as table manners and the social graces we take for granted.'

'There *will* be problems, I fully accept that, but Sally is, without doubt, the most intelligent girl I have come across since I first began teaching at the school. If I discuss the problems with Sally beforehand I'm convinced she'll face up to them and succeed in overcoming them, but a lot will depend on what happens to her brother and whether we are able to speak to him before he's sent off somewhere to serve whatever sentence he's given. Arthur has always intended that Sally would one day escape from the Old Nichol. If he realizes the chance is there he'll persuade her to take it.'

'I think you are over-simplifying the problem, Nessa, but if you are willing to try to make it work then you have my full support.'

'Thank you, I fear I am going to need it.'

★   ★   ★

Sally's initial reaction was to oppose the idea — especially the bath and de-lousing — but Nessa convinced her with the argument that having a well turned-out sister in the courtroom to show support for her brother would impress a judge and jury far more than if she were to appear in her present state. It would also make the court authorities more inclined to allow her to visit Arthur after the court proceedings. Then, if he was given a gaol sentence, as was most likely, he would go away with the assurance that the sister he adored and had always protected, was being well cared for.

Nevertheless, it was with considerable trepidation that Nessa returned to the large house and school in Kensington accompanied by Sally, even though the clean, respectably dressed and pretty girl was unrecognizable as the young urchin who had been coaxed from a hole in the ground only that morning. Nessa was aware that if anything happened to upset Sally it was likely to provoke a stream of invective capable of shocking even the most broad-minded listener.

She had underestimated the acumen of her young ward. Sally had realized from her first day at the ragged school that her mode of speech was very different from that used by Nessa, Father Michael and the volunteer teachers. In private she had practised speaking in a similar manner allowing no one, not even Arthur to hear her.

She would never be able to pass herself off as anyone other than a Londoner but she would not immediately be identified as coming from the Old Nichol — unless someone provoked her!

Nessa was delighted when Sally practised her new skills upon meeting Cedric Couch and his wife Joan for the first time. She was also silently amused to recognize that there was a hint of Cornishness in Sally's assumed manner of speech.

Taking Nessa aside while his wife took Sally on a tour of the house's extensive gardens, Cedric Couch was dubious about having the young Old Nichol girl living in the house, especially when Nessa explained *why* she had brought Sally to his house.

'It is too much to expect a girl of her type to be suddenly thrust into such surroundings and settle down comfortably,' he said, 'quite apart from the fact that we have a great many possessions of considerable value in the house. The temptation to steal might well prove too strong for a girl who has been brought up to believe that honesty is a weakness and not a virtue.'

'I am not suggesting it's going to be easy,' Nessa admitted, 'even though I believe Sally will readily accept that she must not steal from those who are helping her and her brother. Those who live in the Old Nichol have a very strong code of behaviour when it concerns those with whom they share their surroundings. Sally is a quite exceptional girl, Uncle, but the world she knew fell to pieces when her brother was arrested. I could not simply abandon her.'

'I realize you are very fond of the child, Nessa; Father Michael commented upon it when he and I last spoke, but how long do you think of having Sally here in the house — and what of her future?'

'I really don't know,' Nessa confessed, 'but can she stay here — for a while, at least? Please?'

Cedric Couch was not at all convinced that having Sally living in his house was feasible, but he and his wife were childless and when Joan declared she found the young urchin 'utterly charming' and would be delighted to help Nessa teach Sally all she needed to know about the world beyond the Old Nichol, the Kensington teacher conceded there was no way he could win the day.

He agreed that Sally could remain in the house for an unspecified trial period, during which time she would share a room with Nessa, who would be held responsible for her behaviour for as long as she lived with them. The young orphan would accompany Nessa to the ragged school each day and receive extra lessons in deportment each evening, in order to complete the transition from urchin to respectability.

42

The outcome of Arthur's trial was never in doubt. The barrister engaged by a sympathetic Father Michael pointed out the strength of the prosecution's case and was able to persuade the young felon to plead guilty, in order that the judge might take his pleas into consideration when assessing the inconvenience he had caused, in addition to the offence for which he had been apprehended.

Sally, Nessa and Father Michael were in court for the hearing, the Old Nichol priest giving evidence on Arthur's behalf, pleading that in spite of Arthur's admitted previous minor convictions he was capable of redemption, pointing to Sally as an example of his sense of responsibility and declaring he needed only to be given the right guidance in order to bring this to the fore.

Judge Coltman appeared bored during Father Michael's impassioned plea on behalf of Arthur. Nevertheless, when the Old Nichol priest stepped down from the witness box, the judge, addressing Arthur, said, 'Arthur Harrup, you have pleaded guilty to the charge of feloniously breaking into a shop and carrying away goods from within, a crime for which only a few years ago you would have forfeited your life. Times have changed but, unfortunately, the habits of criminals like you have not. It had been my intention to sentence you to be transported for the duration of your life. However, I have listened to what Reverend Jaye has had to say about you and have taken notice of the commendable demeanour of the young sister you have seemingly cared for in the absence of either father, mother or home . . . '

He paused to shuffle the papers in front of him and Sally whispered excitedly to Nessa, 'Is he going to set Arthur free . . . ?'

Before Nessa could reply the judge began speaking again.

' . . . Rightly or wrongly I have decided to be merciful in the hope that when you have paid the penalty for your crime you will find redemption. I sentence you to be transported for a period of fourteen years . . . The next case, if you please.'

So stunned was Sally that she did not fully realize Arthur's trial was over until he was ushered down the steps behind the dock by a policeman. Dismayed, she asked, 'Where are they taking him . . . ? You said I'd be able to speak to him!'

'You will be,' Father Michael said quickly. 'We'll go out of the courtroom and down to the cells.' The severity of the sentence, at odds with the judge's declaration that he was being 'merciful' had taken him by surprise, too. He had accepted before the trial that Arthur might have been sentenced to a year, or even two, serving the sentence in a London prison where Sally would be able to visit him, but fourteen years' transportation . . . Few convicts returned from the colonies at the end of their sentences and in fourteen years time Arthur would be a very different person — and so, too, would Sally.

The Old Nichol priest had made arrangements with the court officials for a post-sentencing visit to Arthur and no problems were put in their way. However, the visit took place with Arthur being in the court's prisoners' cage and the visitors being outside.

Sally was in tears and, in spite of his attempt at bravado, Arthur came very close to breaking down, but he said, 'Don't you fret about me, Sal, I'm able to look after myself, you know that — it's you I'm worried about, although you are looking really well all dressed up like you are. I'm glad.'

'Nessa . . . Miss Pyne is looking after me and has taken me home to live with her and some of her family on the other side of London. I wish you could see the house, Arthur, it must be nearly as big as the queen's new palace!'

Neither Arthur nor Sally had ever seen the as yet incomplete Buckingham Palace, but those who had declared it to have more windows than the whole of the Old Nichol — with glass in every one!

The knowledge that he was never likely to see either Buckingham Palace, or even the old Nichol again left Arthur lost for words for some moments and Sally said unhappily, 'Will you try to get someone to write to me when you get to where you're going, Arthur? I'll be able to read it now, after being at Father Michael's school.'

'Of course I will, but I don't suppose I'll get where I'm going for a long time . . . it'll be a year, or even longer. They'll put me on a hulk first, until there's a ship to take me there, so don't expect to hear from me for a long while.'

'Where *is* it the judge has sent you to, Arthur?'

'I dunno, some says one place, others somewhere else, but it don't really matter very much, I'll get by, wherever it is.'

Sally was becoming increasingly upset and, cutting in on their conversation, Father Michael said to her, 'I spoke to the chief warden before we came down to the cells and he told me Arthur will be going to the prison hulk *Warrior*, moored at Woolwich while he's awaiting transportation to Van Diemen's Land, and he doesn't think Arthur will leave for at least a year. He also said that if Arthur behaves himself while he's on the hulk he'll be allowed a visit every three months, so it seems you haven't seen the last of each other. You'll be able to meet again and tell him how you're getting on.'

It was less than Sally had been anticipating before the trial, but it was better than nothing at all and Nessa returned to Kensington that afternoon with a less unhappy Sally than she had expected to be dealing with. The thought that she would be able to see her brother again in the foreseeable future boosted Sally's morale — albeit only briefly.

43

Despite all the hopes entertained by Sally after her brother's trial, she was destined never to see him again. Three months after Arthur's trial when she pressed Nessa to arrange for her to visit him on the *Warrior*, Nessa asked Father Michael to make the necessary arrangements.

The Old Nichol priest submitted a written request for the visit to the authorities on the prison hulk, but one morning when Nessa arrived at the ragged school with Sally to begin the day's lessons, she was greeted by a visibly shaken Father Michael.

Fearing something serious had occurred at the school in her absence, Nessa asked him what was the matter, but instead of giving her an immediate reply, he spoke to the young girl with her.

'Sally, run along and get ready for your lessons, I would like to speak privately with Miss Pyne for a few minutes.'

When Sally had gone to her classroom, Nessa asked, 'Is something wrong, Michael . . . what is it?'

'Come along to my office, Nessa. Something absolutely dreadful has happened. I just don't know what we are going to do about it . . . '

In a moment of sudden unwanted perception, Nessa asked, 'Is it do with Arthur? Is that why you sent Sally away? Is he being sent to Van

Diemen's Land sooner than was expected?'

'It's worse than that, Nessa, far worse. I had a letter this morning from the governor of the *Warrior* in response to my request for a visit to Arthur. There has been a serious outbreak of typhus on board and thirty convicts died. Arthur was one of them.'

'When did this happen, and why did no one tell us?' Nessa was horrified.

'Arthur died almost a month ago, but the governor said that although he had Sally's name as next-of-kin he had no address for her, so Arthur was buried with many of the others, on the mud flats at Woolwich.'

'This is absolutely dreadful! Sally is so excited at the thought of seeing Arthur again.' Fighting back her tears, Nessa added,' I don't know how I can break the news to her, she'll be so upset . . . '

'We'll tell her together. I'll get someone to take your class . . . '

'No!' Nessa spoke positively. 'I'd rather tell her on my own, Michael. Perhaps you could take my class and send Sally in here so I can tell her in private.'

'Are you quite certain that's the way you want to do it, Nessa?'

'Yes.'

'Very well, I'll send her to you and tell the class what has happened once she is gone.'

When the grave-faced priest told Sally to go to his office because Nessa wanted to speak to her there, she realized immediately there was something seriously wrong. 'Is it to do with Arthur? Won't they let me see him?'

'Go to speak to Miss Pyne, Sally,' Father Michael said gently, 'She'll tell you what it's about.'

Watching the young girl hurry away, he felt a deep pity for her, but could not help wondering what effect Arthur's death might have on his school. Sally's rise above the squalor and despair of the Old Nichol had brought a bright ray of hope into the lives of its children. So much now depended upon her reaction to the tragic news Nessa had to tell her.

★ ★ ★

'Come in and sit down, Sally.' Guiding the young girl across the office with an arm about her shoulders, Nessa tried very hard to conceal the distress she felt about breaking the news of Arthur's death to her protégée.

Allowing herself to be led to a chair, Sally said, 'It's about Arthur, isn't it ... something's happened?'

'I'm afraid it has, Sally ... I'm so very, very sorry.'

Now Sally realized that what Nessa had to tell her was more serious than a refused visit to her brother. 'What is it ... ? Have they already transported him?'

'No, Sally, they've had a serious outbreak of typhus on board the *Warrior* ... '

'Typhus? Arthur has typhus?'

'It spread among the convicts ... the gaolers too.'

Searching Nessa's face, Sally saw the anguish

289

there and she tried twice to speak before the broken words came out. 'Arthur . . . he's dead, ain't he?'

'I'm afraid so, Sally. More than thirty others died with him . . . I am so sorry.'

Sally sat silently rocking back and forth in her chair, gazing unseeingly down at the floor, her hands gripping each other tightly in her lap. There were no tears, but Nessa was aware of the intense grief locked inside her . . . and she knew of no way she might help her exorcise it.

Unexpectedly, Sally suddenly looked up and said, 'Where is he, can I see him?'

Nessa shook her head, 'He'll have already have been buried with the others, Sally.'

'Where?'

'Somewhere on shore with all the others, close to the hulk. Sadly, I doubt very much whether they will have marked the grave.'

'Poor Arthur . . . ' Sally was silent for a long while before saying, unexpectedly, 'Perhaps it's for the best. Arthur's used to being leader of the boys in the Old Nichol, but I knew when I saw him with the others in the cell beneath the court that they wouldn't take orders from a boy. He'd always have been bullied and in trouble . . . '

Unable to prevent a sob escaping, she added in a choked voice, 'He'd have been very unhappy.'

Nessa felt an agony of sympathy for Sally, but also a deep sense of helplessness. She wanted to take Sally into her arms and comfort her, but she had come to understand the young girl well enough to know it would be a mistake. Sadly, this was something Sally needed to work out for herself.

'I want to go for a walk around the Old Nichol for a while, Nessa — on my own.'

The thought of Sally disappearing into the Old Nichol on her own in her present state alarmed Nessa, but she said, 'If that's what you want — but you'll come back?'

Sally nodded. 'I'll come back. It's what Arthur wanted for me and what I want too.'

Nessa was relieved by her reply, she had feared Sally might be contemplating returning to a way of life she had shared with her brother, but she was apprehensive too. Sally was no longer a girl who was at one with the Old Nichol urchins.

'I don't think you should go wandering around the Old Nichol dressed the way you are now.'

Sally nodded agreement. 'Can I borrow something from the store?' Father Michael had gathered a store of old but wearable clothing at the school, some donated by a rag-and-bone man, others by sympathetic pawnbrokers. Deloused and washed, they were kept in a storeroom for the benefit of new pupils to the school.

It was a good idea but, in spite of the young girl's assurance, Nessa was apprehensive when Sally walked away from the school some minutes later, with only her cleanliness setting her apart from the many urchins of the Old Nichol. She was afraid the memories of life with Arthur all around her might prove too much for her to abandon it once and for all.

She was greatly relieved when, some hours later, Sally returned to the ragged school. She never disclosed where she had been, or what she had done, but she appeared to have come to terms with the loss of Arthur, although she would remain uncharacteristically quiet for many days to come, carrying an almost palpable air of sorrow.

Nevertheless, when she changed back into her new clothes and agreed to being taken straight back to Kensington, Nessa knew the young girl had closed the chapter of her life in the Old Nichol.

44

1840

'You're up bright and early this morning!' Goran made the comment as he entered the stables at Elworthy Farm and found Jenken feeding the two plough horses. Dawn had only just broken and it was a chilly but clear morning and on the way from the house Goran had glanced appreciatively at the trees growing nearby, their branches hidden by a cloak of leaves, proof that spring was now firmly established.

'I wanted to make a start on clearing the turnip field now the sheep have been moved out. I think the horses are going to be kept busy one way or another this year.'

Goran nodded agreement, it was likely to be an exciting year. He was now tenant of not one farm but two, Elworthy and Roach being worked as one. The change had come about at the end of what had been a severe winter during which Agnes Roach's arthritis had seriously worsened, making her a virtual invalid incapable of performing all but the simplest of household chores and making supervision of the Roach farm impossible.

Mabel Trebartha had moved in to Agnes's farmhouse for a week to take care of her, leaving Goran to eat with the ever-increasing Bolitho family. By the end of the week Mabel had secured the services of a newly widowed village woman of middle age who moved in to the Roach farmhouse to care for the needs of both Agnes and Elworthy, although Mabel would still call in at least once a day to satisfy herself the arrangement was working satisfactorily.

Then, only a few weeks after this domestic arrangement had been made, Agnes sent for Goran and offered him the tenancy of Roach Farm at a ridiculously low rent, to work with Elworthy Farm as a single holding. Her only stipulation was that she and Elworthy would remain in her farmhouse and should anything happen to render her totally incapable, physically and mentally, Goran and Mabel would take on responsibility for her brother.

Goran agreed to her terms eagerly. He would be quite content to have Elworthy working with him again. He was hard-working and could be trusted to take good care of the farm animals and carry out any of the routine tasks about the farm.

Nevertheless, Goran took on four additional farmhands to help him carry out the many plans he had for all the land now at his disposal. There would be no problems in the immediate future financing his ambitious projects. The dues from the Wheal Hope mine had exceeded all expectations, not only delighting Goran and Agnes but also the adventurers who had financed the mine and who now saw their investments reaping a rich reward.

'Have you heard about the trouble they had at the Spurre Arms, down in the village, last night?'

The question came from Jenken.

'No — but how do you know anything about it, you won't have seen anyone this morning? Were you there?'

'You won't find me wasting my money on drink,' Jenken said firmly. 'No, Pa was working very late on the mine engine and some of the men coming on night shift told him about it. The trouble was between gamekeeper Grimble and Alan Toms.'

Goran was instantly interested. 'What sort of trouble?'

'Grimble had been drinking at the inn for some time on his own and wasn't happy that so many miners were in there, even though they were apparently ignoring him. Anyway, some of the miners were talking about the news that Jacob Barlow had been transported for life for stirring up trouble among the coal miners up north. Grimble pricked up his ears when he heard the name because, of course, it was Barlow and his men who gave him such a beating. He made a loud comment to the landlord that Barlow should have been hanged, together with all those miners who supported him. Alan once being one of Barlow's men made an equally loud remark that there were some gamekeepers who deserved to be hanged too — one in particular.

'It seems Grimble took offence — as Alan no doubt intended he should — and wanted to fight him. The landlord threw Grimble out and warned Alan that he'd do the same to him if he caused any more trouble.'

Goran shook his head in disapproval. 'Alan

will need to be careful, we all know what sort of man Grimble is . . . and from all I hear he's become worse since he took to drinking heavily as a result of what happened at the last Liskeard Fair, you winning a cup while he returned home with nothing.'

Grinning happily at his memory of that day when he had been presented with a small silver cup and five guineas for coming second in a ploughing contest, Jenken said, 'I think Sir John went away even unhappier than his gamekeeper that day.'

'And with good reason, I believe,' Goran said, 'Rumour has it that Sir John gambled a lot more than he could afford on Grimble winning the shooting contest, same as he had for the last five years.'

Grimble had been favoured to win the gamekeepers' shooting contest but the prize had been taken by a newcomer who, it later transpired had served as a sharpshooter with the Spanish Legion, fighting in the Iberian Peninsular. He had shot so well that a dispirited Grimble could manage no better than fifth place. Sir John had been additionally galled because the winner's employer was a man who had made his riches from mining ventures and was regarded by the baronet landowner as an 'upstart'.

'That was the beginning of Grimble's fall from favour,' Jenken agreed, 'but after what he did to Pa I won't waste any sympathy on him. I learned only last week that his wife left him some years ago because she'd had enough of him. Ma and Annie were talking about it when Annie came down to the house a couple of evenings ago.'

'I haven't seen Annie Pyne for months. How is young Jennifer and the rest of the family?'

'The family's fine. In fact Annie came down to tell Ma that Morwenna's expecting, so I doubt whether Alan will be spending much time in the future drinking with his mates.'

'Did Annie mention Nessa? I've hardly heard anything of her since she went away and I often think of her.'

Jenken's mother had told him that Mabel had at one time thought a romance was blossoming between Goran and Nessa. The old ploughman, Horace Rundle, had also mentioned the bracelet Goran had bought for Nessa at the Liskeard Fair when the two men first met. Jenken wondered what had gone wrong for them, but thought it might be time Goran forgot about her and moved on.

'It seems she's doing well teaching up in London. Annie says her letters are full of the young vicar who's started a school for poor children. Nessa's working there with him. He's from Cornwall too and Annie says that from the way Nessa writes about the wonderful work he's doing she wouldn't be at all surprised to hear there was something going on between the two of 'em.'

Goran felt unexpectedly despondent by the news. He had always nursed a forlorn hope that one day Nessa would return to the Wheal Hope, remember the accord they once had and realize it had been more than friendship.

He believed the sole reason they had taken

different paths in life was because he had only just taken over Elworthy in those early days and had been so busy she must have believed she meant nothing to him. But he had never forgotten her and was reminded of what he had hoped the future held for them both every time he opened the drawer in his room where the box containing the bracelet he had never presented to her was kept.

Suddenly aware that Jenken was giving him a quizzical look, Goran said quickly, 'Well, we've both got a great deal to do so we'd better get on with it before there's a change in the weather, or something.'

45

'Looks as though you've got an important visitor, Cap'n, perhaps he's come to invite you to dinner at the big house!'

Looking up from his desk in the mine office at his shift-captain's words, Piran Pyne looked through the window and saw Sir John Spurre riding towards the mine office, his horse skittish because of all the noise and bustle surrounding horse and rider.

'He's more likely to be coming to complain about Alan fighting with his gamekeeper, although he usually sends one of his servants with a note when he has something on his mind. Whatever the reason, it won't be to congratulate us on how well we're doing!'

Captain Pyne was wrong. After perfunctorily shaking hands with him, Sir John waited only until the shift captain had made a judicious departure from the office before saying, 'You seem to be very busy up here, Captain Pyne — and doing well, I believe?'

'We are keeping the adventurers happy.'

'Ah yes, the all-important shareholders. Had I understood more about mining I might well have been one of them.'

'Investing in a mine is a gamble, Sir John. More adventurers lose money than make it.'

'Well, the Wheal Hope is not losing them money, by all accounts it is proving very profitable indeed for Agnes Roach and her tenant farmer.'

'Happily, yes, they have both gone out of their way to be supportive.'

Well aware he had done nothing to co-operate with Wheal Hope, Sir John ignored any implied criticism. 'It is actually mining dues I am here to speak to you about, Captain Pyne. One of the servants at Spurre Hall is friendly with one of your miners and he has told her you have discovered a very rich copper lode extending beneath the old mine which is on my land.'

'I have not carried out any work beneath your land if that is what you are suggesting, Sir John.'

Piran Pyne's reply was decidedly cool and the baronet was quick to react, 'No, no! I am not suggesting for a moment you would do such a thing without prior negotiation. In fact, the reason I am here is to say that if the information is true I will be very happy for you to pursue the lode beneath Spurre land — and I understand that if it is copper you are working the dues will be considerably higher than for tin?'

'That is so,' the mine captain confirmed.

'Have you any idea when you might begin work once we have reached agreement on the dues?' Sir John could not conceal the eagerness in his voice.

'I haven't given it a great deal of thought and before I go ahead I would need to carry out a great deal of cross-cutting in order to evaluate the lode's potential. Also — and this would need your approval — as the lode would appear to run *beneath* the old workings it might be necessary to install a pumping-engine on your land. I would need to choose the best place for such an engine.'

Doing his best to hide the disappointment he felt, Sir John said, 'Oh! So even if you did decide to work the lode it would not be in the near future.'

'I am not saying that. If this particular lode was followed we could be bringing out ore in weeks rather than months but, to be truthful, when we began working here and it was thought the mining dues would be coming to you, the percentage you demanded was so high it was quite unacceptable. In view of that I have stopped short of following the lode you are discussing. For the foreseeable future I can make a very satisfactory profit from the ore we have beneath Mrs Roach's land.'

'You must forget the dues I was asking for then, Captain Pyne.' Sir John gave the mine captain an ingratiating smile. 'That was mere 'business talk' when it was by no means certain the Wheal Hope would be successful and there was the likelihood of more disruption than profit as a result of your activities. That is no longer the case. I have no doubt we could agree dues that would be satisfactory to everyone involved.'

'Should that prove so I would be happy to follow the lode beneath your land, Sir John, but the dues question would need to be settled first.'

'Of course! As a matter of fact I am riding into Launceston today and will visit my solicitor and instruct him to call upon you to discuss the matter. If we can reach agreement when do you

301

think you will begin the work?'

'Once the legal details are settled I will begin checking the possible value of the lode immediately.'

'Splendid! If you find my solicitor is putting difficulties in your way, come and see me at Spurre Hall immediately. I am confident we will be able to overcome them man to man.'

When Sir John had left the Wheal Hope, Piran Pyne thought of all that had been discussed. It was evident the rumours about the landowner's financial state were not without foundation. Sir John's eagerness to have him extend the Wheal Hope's activities to Spurre land was that of a desperate man.

★   ★   ★

Captain Pyne's observations were confirmed when Simeon Quainton, the Spurre estate's solicitor, arrived at the mine late the following afternoon. The negotiations in respect of mining dues were settled before he returned to Launceston less than two hours later, even though the mine captain offered terms less favourable than those he was giving to Agnes Roach and Goran.

However, there were a number of factors to be considered before work would begin on the lode beneath the Spurre estate and not until two days later did Piran Pyne send two of his miners to accompany a surveyor to the piece of land beneath which mining might, or might not begin. One of the miners was Alan Toms.

The three men set out together and, with the aid of a compass and some of the surveyor's instruments, were soon satisfied they were above the unworked lode and began inspecting the terrain to examine it for signs of previous mining activity.

They had soon found a great deal to enter on the surveyor's map, but there was a strong westerly wind blowing and they decided to return to Goran's farming land and crouch in the lee of the boundary wall while the surveyor entered the information.

The second miner accompanied him to help with his instruments, leaving Alan Toms a short distance into Spurre land inspecting what he suspected might be an old capped-off mine-shaft, around which generations of rabbits had established a warren. If the hidden shaft linked up with the old mine it might prove of use to the planned Wheal Hope expansion.

He was examining the area when a voice said, 'Well now, there's nothing I enjoy more than catching a poacher red-handed — especially if it happens to be a miner!'

Startled, Alan swung around and saw Marcus Grimble advancing towards him carrying a fowling-piece, the long barrel of which was cradled in the crook of his left arm.

Recognizing Alan, the mock-humorous expression on the gamekeeper's changed to one of elation. 'It's you! Oh, this really is going to be a day to savour.'

'Don't be so bloody silly, I'm here on mine business.'

'Mine business in a rabbit warren on the Spurre estate? No court in the land would believe such a story, and neither do I.'

Alan was ill-at-ease at meeting up with the armed gamekeeper, but he was not frightened of him. 'I couldn't care less what you think, I was sent here to check out the land by Captain Pyne and that's what I've been doing. If you don't believe me go and ask him.'

'Oh, I've no doubt he'd back up your story. What is it you miners are so proud of boasting about, 'one for all and all for one'? Well, it's not going to work with me — and it won't work with the magistrate I'm taking you to.'

'You're not taking me anywhere. I came up here with a job to do and I've done it. If you want me you know where you can find me.'

With this dismissive retort, Alan turned his back on the gamekeeper and began to walk towards the boundary wall, where the sound Wheal Hope miner and the surveyor had heard the sound of voices and were peering over the wall at Alan and the gamekeeper.

He had not taken many paces when, without warning, there was the loud sound of a gunshot behind him and he felt immediate pain in his back and neck. He stumbled and fell, his head striking a large chunk of granite, excavated many years before from the now capped-off shaft — and he knew no more.

Behind him, with white smoke seeping from the barrel of the fowling-piece, gamekeeper Grimble stood looking at his victim, his emotions a confused mixture of elation and apprehension.

While he was contemplating what he should do next, there was a shout from the direction of the boundary wall where the surveyor and miner had watched horrified as the gamekeeper cold-bloodedly shot Alan in the back.

Suddenly aware of the enormity of what he had done and dismayed that there had been witnesses to the incident, Grimble turned and hurried away from the scene.

46

Alan Toms was not dead, although he would have been had Marcus Grimble's gun been firing anything heavier than birdshot. As it was there were many pellets from the gun embedded in his back, neck and scalp and one had clipped an ear.

Perhaps even more serious was the blow to his head when he fell against the granite rock. He had struck it with the side of his head, close to the forehead, and even when he regained consciousness seemed to be disorientated.

Alan's two companions helped him to Elworthy Farm, the closest place from which they believed they might be able to summon help. When they reached the farm, Goran was on hand to help them take him into the farmhouse to a spare bedroom.

Mabel was away at Agnes Roach's farm and Goran called in Harriet Bolitho to attend to Alan, while Jenken was sent off to alert Captain Pyne on all that had happened. He would then ride on to fetch the doctor from his house in the nearby village of Rilla Mill.

Jenken had no need to make the second part of his journey, the doctor being at Wheal Hope, where he was treating a young bal maiden who had managed to break a bone in her wrist wielding a cobbing hammer to separate waste from ore.

The doctor hurried to Elworthy Farm

accompanied by the Wheal Hope captain. Here, whilst the doctor examined the wounded man, Piran Pyne listened in grim silence to the story told by the shocked surveyor and miner who had witnessed the whole incident.

'Where did Grimble go after the shooting?' Piran Pyne asked.

'When he realized we must both have seen what had happened he hurried off in the direction of Spurre Hall. We didn't see exactly where he went because we were too busy rescuing Alan and getting off Spurre land in case the gamekeeper returned and shot us too,' the surveyor explained, adding, 'The man's insane!'

'Possibly,' Piran Pyne agreed, 'The chances are he was also drunk, but he'll not get away with this.' Turning to the other miner in the room, he said, 'Tell everyone on the mine to be ready to come with me and find Grimble — and they are to bring pick-handles with them. We've had quite enough of Marcus Grimble. While you're doing that I'll go to the Hall and see Sir John — then we'll go after his gamekeeper.'

Alarmed, the doctor looked up from examining Alan and pleaded, 'Let me see just how serious this young man's injuries are before you take any such drastic action. There are a great many pellets to be removed from his body, neck and head and he is quite obviously suffering concussion, but unless any of the pellets have reached his lungs or other organs he should suffer no lasting effects. Report the matter to Sir John, of course, after all he is a magistrate, but don't take the law into your own hands.'

Piran Pyne shook his head, 'Grimble wouldn't be the way he is if he hadn't been given Sir John's support for so many years. Grimble has bullied his way through life because he knew he enjoyed his employer's protection — tacit or otherwise. There are men — mostly miners — who are rotting in prison because Sir John refused to see his gamekeeper for the man he is. Alan is my son-in-law, but he is also a miner. I've had one miner crippled by Grimble and now this has happened. I'll have no more men suffer because of this unholy alliance. We'll deal with Grimble our way . . . the miners' way.'

The doctor looked at Captain Pyne in silence before shrugging his shoulders, saying, 'Well, I've told you what I think, if you choose to ignore my advice there will undoubtedly be unfortunate consequences for everyone involved. I suggest you send for your daughter before you do anything else, she might like to be with her husband while I do what needs to be done.'

★   ★   ★

Immediately after the shooting Marcus Grimble made his way to Spurre Hall where he found his employer giving his disgruntled head gardener instructions to turn the walled garden into a productive vegetable plot, sufficient not only to feed the whole household but also provide a surplus to sell in nearby mining areas, where such produce was always at a premium.

The head gardener had worked all his life at Spurre Hall and prided himself on the

308

spectacular flower beds he had so diligently nurtured in the garden that was now to be turned over to vegetables.

Sir John greeted his gamekeeper with, 'What are you doing here, Grimble? You should be out on the estate. I thought I heard the sound of a shot not long ago.'

'You did, Sir John. There was a man, a miner, poaching on the estate, up towards the moor.'

'Again? Did you catch him?'

Grimble shook his head, 'No, he ran off and, as you know, I can't run as fast as I used to before I was attacked by that miners' leader and his men. I fired after him to try to bring him to a halt but he got away.'

'Did your shot hit him?'

'It might have done but I was only carrying a fowling-piece and he had others with him, at least two of 'em and they'll have helped him get away.'

'Oh well, let's hope he needed to pick pellets out of his backside when he returned to wherever he came from. He certainly won't want to report it or he'll know where he'll end up. Well done, man.'

★ ★ ★

It was about an hour after the shooting when the Spurre Hall butler entered the study where Sir John was at his desk writing a letter. The baronet looked up irritably, but before he could complain about being interrupted, the butler said, 'I am sorry to disturb you, Sir John, but there is a

309

Captain Pyne from the Wheal Hope mine in the hall. He insists upon seeing you.'

All his irritability vanishing, Sir John said, 'Show him in immediately. It is probably something to do with mining commencing beneath the estate. That will be good news indeed!'

The landowner was on his feet to greet his visitor when he entered the room — but Piran Pyne's first words were not those of a man bearing good news. Grim-faced, he said, 'I've come here to tell you that I and my miners will be coming on the estate in search of your gamekeeper, Sir John. If he gives himself up peaceably we will take him before a magistrate in Launceston to be dealt with there, but if he puts up any resistance he will suffer the consequences as my miners will be armed with pick-handles.'

His disbelief showing, Sir John spluttered, 'You've come here to tell me you intend hunting down one of my gamekeepers on my estate? This is gross impertinence! Grimble came to tell me he'd caught a miner poaching on the estate and had fired a warning shot in an attempt to stop him from running away and persuade him to give himself up. This is what I pay him for and it is his duty to arrest poachers on Spurre land — even if it happens to be one of *your* miners. As a magistrate I demand you hand the man over to me and *I* will decide what action is to be taken — and against whom.'

'The man Grimble shot was *not* a poacher and he must have been aware of it. The miner was on your land with another of my men, and a surveyor, acting on my instructions and drawing up plans in preparation for the work you and I have discussed. Furthermore, my man was *not* running away. He was quite coldbloodedly shot in the back at close range, most probably because he and Grimble had a disagreement when they were both drinking at the village inn a few evenings ago. I have two very credible witnesses who saw what happened today. It would seem to be the culmination of a long-running feud between Grimble and miners — a feud that is seen as having your support. Miners are convinced they will receive no justice from you, which is why I intend taking Grimble before a Launceston magistrate when we catch up with him.'

'You have the audacity to question *my* integrity, Pyne? *I* will deal with Grimble, not a mob hell-bent on avenging some spurious wrongs — and if you set one foot outside the law I will deal with you too.'

'You could have dealt with Grimble a long time ago, Sir John, but have done nothing. There are a great many actions Grimble could never have taken without your support — things like laying mantraps around the estate, for instance. When evidence of these are laid before an unbiased magistrate I have no doubt he will investigate them further. In the meantime, until Grimble is tried and convicted for the shooting of my miner there will be no work carried out on any ore beneath Spurre land.'

47

Rumours circulated that immediately after Piran Pyne's visit to Spurre Hall, Marcus Grimble was summoned and told his conduct had lost his employer so much money he could no longer afford to keep him. Furthermore, because the gamekeeper's latest actions were likely to result in serious criminal proceedings, his presence on the estate had become an embarrassment.

Grimble was advised to get as far away as he could, in the shortest possible time.

Taking his long-time employer's words to heart, Marcus Grimble removed himself further away than even the titled landowner had envisaged. Returning to his lonely cottage, the world he had known for much of his life gone forever, the disgraced gamekeeper put the barrel of a loaded shotgun into his mouth and pulled the trigger.

This news was contained in a letter received by Nessa in London at breakfast time, before she left the Kensington house to go to the ragged school. Her mother's letter also told of Alan's shooting and revealed that Morwenna was expecting a baby.

It had been two-and-a-half years since Nessa had seen her family and guilt had been building up inside her for some time at not paying them a visit. Her mother's letter helped her to arrive at a decision.

Reading the pertinent sections of the letter to those having breakfast with her, she said, 'I feel I must go to Cornwall, Uncle, to see if there is anything I can do to be of help.'

'Of course.' Looking across the table at Sally who had been listening wide-eyed to the contents of Nessa's letter, he added, 'Sally has been here long enough to feel quite at home with us while you are away.'

Aware that for all Sally's apparent self-confidence, the Old Nichol girl had become extremely reliant upon her, Nessa said, 'Oh, Sally will come with me. She was telling me only the other day that she has never been outside London and has never seen cows, sheep, or live pigs. It will be a wonderful experience for her.'

The young girl's undisguised delight was evident to all those about the breakfast table, but Cedric Couch said, doubtfully, 'You have to return home at such a time, of course, but the thought of you both making such a journey without help troubles me. I will make some enquiries and see if I can learn of any responsible person who might also be travelling to Cornwall in the near future.'

*   *   *

Father Michael expressed similar concerns when Nessa informed him she would be absent from the school for some time and told him the reason — but he came up with a solution that delighted her, after asking, 'How did you travel when you first came came to London from Cornwall?'

'By ship from Falmouth.'

'A sailing-ship?'

'Yes.'

'You will find there is a much faster — and more comfortable — way to travel now. A steamer goes from here to Bristol once a week, calling at various ports along the way. You could take it as far as Plymouth then hire a carriage to carry you on to your home.'

'It sounds excellent . . . but Uncle Cedric will still insist that I wait until he has found someone to accompany us.'

'Then why don't *I* undertake the task?'

'You? Why should you do that?'

'Because I, too, have not seen my family for a number of years. My brother is vicar of a parish close to Bodmin and my father lives nearby. It is time I visited them again. Besides, I feel in need of a short rest from my work here and our other teachers can cope until my return.'

'I can't argue with any of that, Michael, and I — and Uncle Cedric I am sure — would be delighted if you came to Cornwall with Sally and me — and the steamer sounds a very exciting adventure for all of us.'

★   ★   ★

'You took your time getting back to the farm, Jenken.'

Goran made the observation when Jenken brought a horse back to the stable at Elworthy Farm after delivering piglets to miners; first at the mining community on Caradon hill, then the

314

Wheal Hope. The piglets would be kept in sties in the yards and gardens of miners' houses, fed mainly on household scraps and ultimately provide a source of meat, or sold on to swell the families' incomes.

'I was held up at Wheal Hope . . . and you'll never guess who was the cause.'

'It's been a hard day and I'm a little slow on guessing at the moment. Tell me.'

'Nessa . . . Nessa Pyne!'

His air of irritability and professed tiredness vanishing, Goran said, animatedly, 'Nessa . . . ? She's back? How long has she been here?'

Well satisfied with Goran's excited reaction to his news, Jenken replied, 'She arrived home yesterday and brought a young girl from London with her — a very pretty young girl named Sally.'

Waving Jenken's description of the young girl aside impatiently, Goran said, 'Never mind the young girl, tell me about Nessa. How is she looking? Why has she come home? Is she home for good?'

'I don't know, but I doubt it. A young vicar came with her too, Father Michael. My ma was up at the mine and I gave her and the boys a ride back here in the cart. On the way Ma said this Father Michael is the one who started the school where Nessa is teaching in a poor part of London and who Nessa's always telling Annie about in her letters.'

Perturbed by news, Goran asked, 'Why has he come to Cornwall? And when you say he's young . . . how young is he?'

'I'm not very good at telling people's ages, I

suppose he must be twenty-something. Ma seems to think Nessa's brought him home to see if Annie and Cap'n Pyne approve of him.'

'You mean Nessa's going to *marry* him?'

All the excitement Goran had felt at the news of Nessa's return disappeared and although it had frequently crossed his mind that she must be meeting men in London, he had never considered the possibility she would meet someone she really wanted to *marry*!

Watching his employer closely, Jenken belatedly remembered how Goran invariably reacted on the occasions when Nessa's name came up in conversation. He had realized long ago that Goran had probably been in love with Nessa at the time she left Cornwall and still had strong feelings for her.

'No one's said anything about it — but why else would he come all the way to Cornwall from London with her?'

Later that evening, when work was over and Goran returned to the farmhouse, he passed on the news of Nessa's return to his mother and she was delighted.

'That will make Annie happy. She's been saying lately that with Alan being laid up and Morwenna expecting, she wished Nessa was around to talk to. As she's said more than once, it seems a very long time since she saw her. Because of Morwenna's news and what's happened to Alan I expect Nessa thought she ought to be home with her family.'

'It seems she's brought a vicar with her, Ma — a *young* vicar. Jenken thinks she's probably brought him home with her to see whether Annie and Piran approve of him.'

'You mean she's getting married to a vicar! Now that's a step up in the world for a miner's daughter, even if he is a captain. But Nessa can't have said anything to Annie about marriage, or she'd have told me.'

'Well I can't think of any other reason why she should bring him all the way to Cornwall from London, can you?'

'Not at the moment — but you can be sure I'll find out.'

48

The next day, when Mabel went to Roach Farm she told Agnes news of Nessa's return to Cornwall, bringing a young vicar with her.

'What's she doing with a vicar?' Agnes demanded, 'and why has she brought him here?'

'I think he started the school where Nessa's teaching, in a poor part of London. I know she's always said a great deal about him in her letters to Annie. Young Jenken told Goran he thinks she's brought him home to get Annie and Piran's approval for her to marry him.'

'Has she, indeed? That's not going to please Goran.'

'Oh, I don't know, he hasn't said much about her lately so I expect he's got over any feelings he might have had for her.'

Agnes said nothing further on the subject but when Mabel was leaving the farmhouse later that day, she said, 'This vicar who's come to Cornwall with Nessa Pyne . . . do you think you can get word to him that I'd like to speak to him?'

Curious, Mabel asked, 'Why?'

'I'll tell you after I've spoken to him — if I think you need to know.'

When Mabel returned to Elworthy Farm she told Goran of Agnes's request and he was as puzzled as she was about the reason why she would want to see him.

'Will you go up to the mine and ask him if he'll call on Agnes?'

'Me? Wouldn't it be better if you asked Jenken, or Harriet?'

'No, you used to get on very well with Nessa and I'm sure she'd like to see you again.'

Goran was not as certain as his mother about Nessa wanting to see him, but he knew he *would* like to see her — and the man she was marrying — so that evening, after cleaning up and putting on the clothes he kept for the occasional special Sunday when he accompanied his mother to church, he set off for Wheal Hope and the home of Captain Pyne.

It was with a feeling of sadness that Mabel watched him walking away from the farmhouse. In spite of what she had said to Agnes she knew in her heart that Goran *had* felt very deeply indeed about Nessa and, although he said little about it, she believed he still did.

Annie opened the door of the house when he knocked and was very surprised to see him, but she immediately turned and called, 'Nessa . . . You have a visitor.' To Goran she said, 'Come in. Nessa and Sally are upstairs, going through one of Jennifer's books with her but Father Michael is in the sitting-room with Piran.'

Goran followed Annie into the cottage's living-room where Father Michael immediately rose from the armchair where he was seated as Annie announced the visitor.

'So you're the young man whose ingenuity and resourcefulness saved the life of her father. I was hoping I would meet you while I was here.

319

Nessa will be pleased to see you, she speaks of you often.'

Father Michael advanced towards Goran with his hand extended and a warm and apparently genuine smile of greeting on his face, but Goran's spirits sank. The priest was indeed young — and handsome. There was also a proprietary tone in his voice when he spoke about Nessa.

'It's actually you I have come to see, Father. Agnes Roach who owns the lands I farm has asked my mother to arrange a meeting with you. She can't come here herself because she's crippled with arthritis, but would like you to go to Roach Farm to see her.'

Father Michael frowned. 'I don't think I know this Agnes Roach, why does she want to see me?'

'I know no more than I've told you, but Agnes is a very special woman and will have a good reason for wanting to speak to you.'

'In that case, I will go and see her, of course. But where is this Roach Farm?'

'I'll take you there, it's just beyond Goran's farm. Hello, Goran.'

At the sound of the voice Goran had swung around and he saw Nessa standing in the doorway to the room. The sight of her left him totally lost for words for what seemed to him a long time, although it could have only been seconds.

'Nessa . . . Hello!'

All the things he had imagined he would say to her if — or when — they met again had gone. She was as he remembered her, yet she *had* changed. She was taller, certainly, and there was an air of greater self-confidence and maturity than he could remember. She was also no longer pretty . . . she was *beautiful*!

'Ma tells me you have both Elworthy and Roach Farms now and that you've made a huge success of both of them.'

'They've done well, but I can't take all the credit. The dues from Wheal Hope have allowed me to do things that wouldn't otherwise have been possible. I . . . I've also followed your advice on learning two new words from the dictionary every day . . . well, most days, anyway.'

It was a foolish, almost inconsequential thing to say, he realized, but Nessa seemed delighted. 'I wish all my pupils were as diligent! But it's lovely to see you looking so well, Goran.'

'And you too.' There was so much he knew he wanted to say, but he felt tongue-tied and, anyway, there were others in the room. This was not the right time but looking at the handsome young priest once more he thought there might *never* be a right time.

Father Michael had been watching the meeting between Goran and Nessa with great interest. A keen and experienced observer of people, he realized there was a great deal of chemistry between the two of them — perhaps far more than either of them fully knew.

Speaking to Goran, he said, 'When do you think would be a good time to call on this lady?'

'Anytime, she doesn't go anywhere these days.'

'Then I'll call on her tomorrow morning, if

321

Nessa will take me there.'

'Of course.'

Nessa made the reply to him, but her gaze had returned to Goran.

'That should be fine. Why don't you come to Elworthy on the way back? I can show you some of the things I've done there and what I plan on doing in the future.'

'That would be nice. I could also look in on Harriet Bolitho, I promised to pay her a visit some time.'

'Good, I'll see you — see you both — tomorrow.' Declining Annie's invitation to stay and have something to drink with them, Goran pleaded falsely that he still had things to do at the farm before bedtime and left.

On the way back to Elworthy Farm he tried to analyse his feelings at meeting Nessa again after so long, but stopped short of admitting the truth to himself. Instead, he looked forward to seeing her again on the following day . . . but he wished he would be meeting with her alone, without having the handsome young priest with her. But he feared that Father Michael was now very much a part of her life. A life that had left Cornwall — and him — behind.

49

When Nessa arrived at Roach Farm with Father Michael the following morning, Mabel Trebartha was also there. Goran had told her the night before that the two would be visiting Agnes that morning and she was determined not to miss them. She was curious about the reason Agnes wanted to speak to him, and also wanted to see Nessa's vicar for herself.

She met the two visitors when they arrived at the farmhouse and was able to assess Father Michael before showing them into the room where Agnes was seated by a window that looked out over the farmland, a blanket tucked about her legs.

After introductions had been made, Mabel remained in the room, but her presence did not suit Agnes.

'There's no need for you to stay here, Mabel, nor Nessa, neither. Take her off to visit Goran at Elworthy, but before you go tell the girl in the kitchen to make some tea and bring it in here with some of those saffron buns she made yesterday.' Waving a gnarled arthritic hand dismissively, she added, 'Go on, away you go — the both of you.'

When they had gone, Father Michael, who had been amused by Agnes's imperious manner towards Mabel and Nessa, said, 'I was told you wished to see me, although I can't think what it could be about, unless it's in my capacity as a priest?'

'I can't be bothered with all that nonsense! I've lived my life by Christian principles and when I meet my Maker I'll be able to look him in the eyes and declare with all honesty that I have never knowingly done anyone a bad turn.'

Father Michael thought it highly probable that Agnes would do as she said . . . but she was still talking. 'I've asked you here because I understand you started a very successful school for poor children, in London.'

'It has been more successful than I ever dared hope, yes.'

'That's the reason I want to speak to you. I'd like to do the same here, down in the village and want you to tell me what's involved; what I need to do — and to draw a plan for me of how you think the school should be built.'

Taken aback, Father Michael said, 'Opening a school is a very ambitious project, Mrs Roach, and to actually have it built for the purpose is most exciting, but such a scheme would take a great deal of money — '

He saw the imperious gesture once more, this time to silence him. 'I prefer being called Agnes, not Mrs Roach, and I am in the fortunate situation of having more money than I need for the few years I can look forward to on this earth. Goran's hard work and enterprise and Captain Pyne's mining dues have seen to that. My only family is a brother who has the mind of a child, unable to look after himself, let alone control the money I have and I can't take it with me, so I

324

would like to leave a school here as my memorial. It would give me a great deal of satisfaction. Will you help me?'

'You are a remarkable woman . . . Agnes. Yes, I will be delighted to help you in any way I can — but I think this is the tea arriving and we will have need of it, there is a great deal to discuss . . . '

★ ★ ★

Knowing nothing of what Agnes and Father Michael were planning inside the Roach farmhouse, Mabel and Nessa walked together to Elworthy Farm and, on the way, the older woman did her best to discover more of the relationship between Nessa and Father Michael, but she learned little other than of the success he was making of the ragged school in the Old Nichol.

They had almost reached the farm when they saw a girl coming down the slope of the moor from the direction of Wheal Hope and, waving to her, Nessa explained to Mabel, 'That's Sally, one of the girls who started at the ragged school at the same time I began teaching there. She is a lovely girl but has had a great deal of unhappiness in her life. An orphan, she was cared for by her brother until he died in unfortunate circumstances and left her alone in the world. I have more or less adopted her and my uncle and aunt allow her to live in their home. I told her to meet me at your farm. I didn't think Michael and I would be at Roach Farm for very long, but it

325

would seem Agnes is going to keep him there for a while so it's just as well she sent us off when she did.'

Sally met up with them before they reached the farm and when Jenken came out of the stable where he and Goran had been attending a riding-horse mare while it gave birth, he saw them approaching. Running back inside the stable he snatched up a curry-comb. As he used it to rake his hair into some semblance of order, he cried excitedly, 'Your ma's on her way here and Nessa and Sally are with her.'

'Is *that* why you're taking such a sudden interest in your hair? Well you're not doing it for Ma or Nessa, so I will need to have a look at this Sally.' As he was speaking, Goran hurriedly swilled blood from his hands in a bucket of water before trying hurriedly to bring some order to his own hair. 'They couldn't have arrived at a better time, go out and bring them in to see the foal, it's a little beauty!'

Nessa and Sally came to the stable while Mabel went on to the house to make tea for them all and the two girls agreed the foal was indeed charming. Sally in particular was utterly enamoured of it and after they had all spent time admiring it, Goran said, 'You and Sally stay here for a while, Jenken. Perhaps Sally can help you to make the mare and foal comfortable while I take Nessa into the house. When you've done that you can show Sally around the farm if she'd like to see it.'

When they were alone, Nessa said to Goran, 'That was very kind of you to suggest Jenken

326

show Sally around the farm, Goran. This is the first time she has ever left London and has never seen either live sheep or cows before. It's all new to her and she's loving every minute of it.'

'It will be no hardship for Jenken. I realized last night when he told me you were here with Sally that he was smitten by her. I think it's probably the first girl of his own age he's ever really come into contact with.'

'Wasn't that very much the same for you, when you met up with Morwenna, Jennifer and me?'

Memories of that first meeting came back to both of them and there was brief moment of embarrassment before Goran succeeded in mumbling agreement and Nessa said hastily, 'I expect you've met a great many girls since that day, after all, you must be one of the most eligible bachelors in this part of Cornwall now.'

'I haven't had time to meet girls,' Goran said honestly. 'It's only since I've taken on extra workers on the farm that I've had any time at all to myself. Before then there weren't enough hours in the day to do all that needed to be done.'

She wanted to ask him about the girl she had seen him with in the field that was being ploughed just before she left Cornwall for London, but bit back the question.

Goran also had a question. His was about her relationship with Father Michael, but he, too, said nothing, not wanting to hear what her answer might be just yet. Instead he showed her around the farm until they were joined by a flushed and happy Sally who said excitedly, 'The baby horse got to its feet and walked around! It was wobbly, but it did it, even though it had only just been born — and Jenken let me stroke it. It . . . it's *lovely!*'

Jenken stood back, beaming because he had been able to make the young London girl happy. Just then Mabel called to say there was tea and cake for them in the farmhouse.

They all chatted happily for about an hour until Harriet came into the farmhouse to join them. They were all still talking about the latest addition to the Bolitho family — another boy — when Father Michael arrived, having found his own way from Roach Farm. He reminded Nessa that she had promised to take him to a stables in a nearby large village where he hoped to hire a pony and gig, in order that he might take Nessa and Sally to Bodmin to meet with his brother and parents.

The fact that Father Michael wanted Nessa to meet the members of his family, just as he had met Nessa's, tended to confirm that his visit to Cornwall was for the couple to meet each other's families and it added to Goran's misery about the situation.

Nevertheless, he declared it would not be necessary for them to have the expense of hiring such a means of transport, they could instead borrow a pony and trap he had on the farm which he would not be using in the foreseeable future.

There was a small reward for him when Nessa squeezed his arm and said, 'Thank you, that is very kind of you, Goran. It's nice to know you haven't changed from the person you were before I went away.'

He could have told her there were a great many things about him that had not changed, particularly his feelings for her, but he realized that with marriage to the London priest seemingly imminent, it was something he could never tell her.

50

While Nessa was visiting Father Michael's parents and brother, Goran was summoned to Roach Farm by Agnes. It was not unusual for her to send for him, she liked to be kept informed of all that was happening on the combined farms. However, on this occasion she had some surprises for him.

Seated on a chair in her kitchen, facing Goran across the table, she asked, 'What do you know about the strip of Spurre land that extends into ours up on the slope to the moor?'

'Not much, gamekeeper Grimble made sure of that, it's just a nuisance having it there, that's all.'

'Is the soil any good?'

'No better and no worse than ours, I'd say — at least, it would be if they put in some work on it, but why do you want to know?'

'Because Sir John came here and offered to sell it to me.'

It was surprising news and Goran said, 'I thought he was looking to get mining dues from it!'

'He was, but after Captain Pyne's man was shot by Grimble he told Sir John he no longer intended following up the lode beneath his land — and Sir John's becoming desperate. He's decided to pass the estate over right away to the nephew who would one day inherit it anyway, but he needs money immediately.'

'How much is he asking for the land?'

'A thousand pounds. He asked for more but would settle for that.'

'It's far too much, the land isn't worth half that.'

'It would be if Captain Pyne changed his mind about working the copper lode that's beneath it — and I don't doubt that he would if *we* were to benefit from it and not Sir John. Another thing . . . there's a very nice little cottage on the land. I used to visit it a lot when I was a girl and was friends with the daughter of the gamekeeper who lived there then. This farmhouse is far too big for me now and it seems arthritis might run in the family, because it's beginning to affect Elworthy. We'd both be more comfortable in that little cottage. The garden is large enough to keep him busy and with a few chickens and a pig or two he'd be happy enough.'

'I still think you'd be paying Sir John too much, but I suppose that if the price includes mining rights and Captain Pyne *does* extend his workings in that direction it would prove a good investment, and it *would* make working Roach Farm easier.'

'Good, then I'll go ahead and when everything's settled you can take me up to the cottage and we'll see what needs doing to it to make it comfortable for Elworthy, me and a couple of live-in servants. It will leave this farmhouse free for you to move into when you decide to marry.'

'Then it's likely to stay empty for a long time.

I doubt if I'll be marrying in the foreseeable future.'

'Don't be too certain about that,' Agnes said, enigmatically. 'There's none of us can look into the future, and life has a habit of coming up with surprises.'

Deciding that the subject of his marital status had been debated for long enough, Goran said, 'Well, I suppose having the extra land would also add value to the farm in the long run.'

'As I have no intention of ever selling up that's not a consideration, but I'll let you know when everything is settled.'

Goran left Roach Farm still convinced that the price Agnes was paying Sir John for the strip of land was too high, but once he had accepted that she was going to buy it anyway, he spent the remainder of the day making plans for the addition to his two farms.

★   ★   ★

Sir John Spurre's solicitor arrived at Roach Farm a few days later, accompanied by the lawyer who managed Agnes's legal affairs and Goran was called in to act as a witness to her signature. When the legal formalities were completed, Agnes's lawyer remained behind and she asked Goran to stay too, explaining, 'If anything were to happen to me right now everything I own would go to Elworthy and there is no telling what would happen to it, so I have had a will drawn up. I would like you to read it.'

The lawyer passed a number of sheets of

parchment to Goran, each filled with neat but bold handwriting and he read them with increasing astonishment. Before he had finished reading the whole of the document he looked up and said, incredulously, to Agnes, 'You've left everything to *me* . . . *everything*! Why?'

'Who else should I leave it to? You've been the closest thing to a son I've ever had, but it doesn't come to you without conditions for taking care of Elworthy, if necessary.'

'Ma and me would care for him anyway, Agnes.'

'I know you would — and that's another reason why I'm making you my beneficiary.'

'I . . . I'm absolutely flabbergasted! I just don't know what to say!'

'Then don't say anything — to anyone. If news of it gets around you'll have every mother in the area throwing her daughter at you in anticipation. Now, I've kept you here long enough. Away you go, you have a farm to run.'

Acting on impulse, Goran did something he had never dared do before. Crossing to where Agnes was seated, he put his arms about her and kissed her. Then, standing back, he said, 'I'll never be able to thank you enough, Agnes . . . *never*, but may it be many, many years before the farm becomes mine.'

Pink with pleasurable embarrassment, Agnes said, 'Now you're being almost as foolish as Elworthy. Away with you now before I have second thoughts about it all.'

Goran had reached the door before Agnes called him back. 'Goran . . . ?'

When he turned back to her she said, 'Don't waste your kisses on old women. There's a certain young lady you ought to be charming with them before she gets away from you once again!'

Goran left Roach Farm scarcely able to believe that one day both Elworthy and Roach lands would belong to him, but he was bewildered by Agnes's parting words. She could only be talking of Nessa, but how could she possibly know of his feelings for her? Not that it made any difference to anything, she obviously did not know of Nessa's intention to marry Father Michael.

★ ★ ★

Nessa returned to the Wheal Hope the next day, having met Father Michael's family, and she immediately went on to Morwenna's house, where Alan had developed a fever which the doctor declared was probably caused by one of the pellets fired by gamekeeper Grimble having infected him.

The doctor was confident the pellet would not cause Alan long-term problems, but for now it was an anxious time for Morwenna and Nessa was giving support to her sister.

While Nessa was there Sally remained behind at the Wheal Hope but spent most of each day at Elworthy Farm where she thoroughly enjoyed working about the farm, being quite happy to take on the most menial and mucky tasks — especially if it was helping Jenken.

Watching her one morning as she was helping

Jenken clean out the stables where a number of horses were kept for work about the farm, Goran was joined by Harriet Bolitho, who said, 'Jenken is going to miss Sally when she returns to London. It's a pity she can't remain here, especially as things are going to be difficult for her there when Nessa is married and she needs to make her own way in the world.'

The thought of Nessa being married to someone else was something Goran constantly tried to push to the back of his mind and her words jolted him. 'Do you think Nessa and Father Michael *will* marry?'

He asked the question in the faint hope that Harriet might express a doubt that might give him a glimmer of hope that such a marriage would not take place. Her reply did nothing to fuel such a hope.

'Sally seems to think so. It seems Nessa got on so well with his parents that Sally thinks they might well announce a date before they leave Cornwall.'

51

Harriet's words cast a pall of gloom over Goran for the next few days, during which he tried very hard to come to terms with the thought of Nessa being married to someone else. He might have felt better about it had he been able to build up a fierce hatred for the man she was to marry, but Goran admitted to himself that not only was Father Michael a very likeable priest, he was also an exceptional one and a good man. He realized in his more honest moments that Nessa could not have chosen a better man for a husband.

His unhappiness was compounded every time he opened the drawer in his bedroom and saw the box containing the bracelet he had bought for Nessa at Liskeard Fair. He wondered what might have been had he not been so busy on the farm and had Nessa not gone to London when she did.

Nessa soon returned to the Wheal Hope because the condition of Alan Toms had improved and Morwenna was confident of being able to cope with looking after him without help. That evening Nessa came to Elworthy Farm to find Sally, who was being taught by a dairy-maid to milk a cow.

Goran took Nessa to the milking shed where Jenken was watching the proceedings with benign pride as Sally tried to master the skills required to milk a cow. She was not aware of their arrival and Nessa said quietly to Goran, 'I have never seen her so happy, she is going to miss all this when she returns to the Old Nichol.'

'Jenken is going to miss her too,' Goran replied. 'He thinks the world of her.'

'And she of him,' Nessa said, 'They make a lovely young couple.'

There was a silence between them that was beginning to last for too long when Goran asked, 'Don't you sometimes miss the countryside too, Nessa?'

After some hesitation she replied, 'There are some things I miss very much. I'd forgotten quite *how* much until I came back here . . . '

At that moment the cow being milked drew up a back leg up and kicked back at the bucket. Only swift action by Sally prevented the loss of the milk it contained and as she pulled the bucket clear the milk-maid took her place on the milking-stool, at the same time chiding the cow for its action.

Standing clear, flushed and happy, Sally announced that she was now ready to return to the Pynes' home with Nessa.

Lying in bed that night, thinking of all the events of the past few days, Goran decided upon a course of action that, while it was not what he would have wished, might help to lay the ghost of one of the matters that troubled him more than any other.

★ ★ ★

The following morning, leaving Jenken to deal with things at Elworthy Farm, Goran made his way to the Wheal Hope home of the Pynes with a heavy heart. When he arrived at his destination he knocked at the door and waited for someone to appear, trying to compose himself for what lay ahead.

The door was opened by Annie sho said immediately, 'Hello, Goran, this is a nice surprise, come inside.'

'I'd rather not, I just want to speak to Nessa briefly, is she up yet?'

Annie was inclined to insist that he come into the house but there was something in his expression that gave her pause. 'Yes, I'll call her.'

Retreating a few paces inside the house she called to Nessa, who, after a few moments appeared at the top of the stairs that led from the bedrooms. Seeing Goran, she hesitated, but before she could say anything, he said, 'Nessa, I wonder if you would come outside for a few minutes, there is something I would like you to have.'

Standing back from her daughter when she reached the foot of the stairs, Annie Pyne looked concerned, but Nessa said, 'Of course, what is it?'

At that moment, Father Michael put in an appearance from one of the downstairs rooms and, initially nonplussed, Goran gathered his wits and said, 'Perhaps Father Michael should come too . . . it really concerns you both.'

Nessa and Father Michael exchanged quizzical glances, but they both left the house and followed Goran to the gate that was the entrance to the cottage's small garden. Once there, he turned to them and from a pocket took out the small box that had been in the drawer in his bedroom for more than two years.

Proffering it to Nessa, he said, 'I'd like you to have this . . . both of you. I bought it for you Nessa, before you went to London. It was to be a 'Thank you' for the dictionary you gave me and for which you paid Morwenna with a bracelet. I should have given it to you then, but somehow the time was never quite right. It wouldn't be right now if I gave it only to you, Nessa, but as you and Father Michael are to be married I'd like you to accept it as a gift for when you have a daughter — as I'm sure you will, one day.'

Nessa exchanged yet another glance with Father Michael before accepting the gift. Opening the box she gave a gasp of delight. 'It's *beautiful*, Goran, but . . . you say you bought it for me before I went to London? Then what was the bracelet I saw you give to that girl when Jenken was having a ploughing lesson?'

Goran was puzzled, 'I don't know what you're talking about, I've never given a bracelet to anyone else. This is the only one I've ever bought.'

'But I *saw* you,' Nessa insisted. 'You gave it to her and she put it on her wrist looking very happy.'

Goran was genuinely puzzled . . . but then he remembered the incident to which she had to be referring. 'You must be thinking of when Horace Rundle came to Elworthy with his plough and horses and his niece came to see him there. She showed me the bracelet he'd bought for her birthday — from the same man I got this one from. She was very proud of it.'

Nessa was looking at Goran with increasing dismay. 'You mean . . . *you* never gave her the bracelet?'

'As I said, I've never bought a bracelet for anyone else — but I didn't see you there that day.'

'No, I didn't stay.'

Father Michael had been listening to their conversation with great interest and considerable sympathy and now he said, 'There appears to have been an unfortunate misunderstanding which — if I read it right — is probably the reason you left Cornwall and went to London, Nessa?'

She could only nod miserably and Father Michael said, 'I always felt there was some such story in your life . . . and now there has been another misunderstanding which might have resulted in very similar consequences. Fortunately, this is one that can be swiftly resolved.'

Addressing Goran, he said, 'What makes you think Nessa and I are to be married?'

Taken aback by the question, Goran sought an answer. 'Why? Well . . . everyone says so! Isn't that why you're both here in Cornwall together, so both your parents can give you their approval?'

Father Michael smiled. 'I am afraid everyone — including you — is jumping to a very wrong conclusion. There are a number of reasons why we came to Cornwall together but marriage is certainly not one of them. In fact, as Nessa has

340

always known, when I took over the parish of the Old Nichol I realized I had been set the God-given task of improving the lot of those who lived there. It's something I took so seriously I made a solemn vow of celibacy in order that I might devote the whole of my life to the task.'

Aware that Goran was not likely to have come across the word 'celibacy' among those he had learned from his dictionary, Nessa said gently, 'It means that Michael will never ever marry, although he is a wonderful friend to me and to everyone in the Old Nichol.'

Aware he had made an utter fool of himself, Goran looked from one to the other of them and then, his gaze settling on Nessa, he said, 'You've known about this all along?'

'Yes.'

'Then . . . ' Not daring to think of what the implications of Father Michael's words could be for the future, he said pessimistically, 'But you'll be going away to London again soon?'

'Now all our stupid misunderstandings have been cleared up that will depend on you, Goran. I don't know whether Agnes has said anything to you, but she intends having a school built here, in the village. She asked Michael to draw up a design for her and when the subject of teachers was mentioned, Michael suggested I would be the ideal person to teach the older children, with Sally teaching basic lessons to the very youngest.'

'And what did you say?' Goran waited in an agony of suspense for her reply, but it was Father Michael who spoke for her.

'Nessa felt she would be letting me down by

not returning with me to the Old Nichol. I have tried to convince her that thanks to the success of our ragged school I will have no difficulty finding other teachers and I truly believe there is an urgent need for her teaching skills here. Yet I feel her decision will depend very much on what *you* have to say about it, Goran.'

Despite his confusion, Goran was never in doubt about what he would say, the only difficulty being how his reply should be phrased. Eventually, he said, carefully, 'I think Sally is going to enjoy teaching here and Jenken will share her joy. As for Nessa and me . . . I just can't find words to tell you exactly how happy I feel about knowing she isn't to marry you. But, having said that . . . perhaps you'll be able to return one day — soon I hope — to marry the both of us.'

Books by E. V. Thompson
Published by The House of Ulverscroft:

THE DREAM TRADERS
CRY ONCE ALONE
BECKY
GOD'S HIGHLANDER
THE MUSIC MAKERS
CASSIE
WYCHWOOD
BLUE DRESS GIRL
THE TOLPUDDLE WOMAN
LEWIN'S MEAD
MOONTIDE
CAST NO SHADOWS
MUD HUTS AND MISSIONARIES
SOMEWHERE A BIRD IS SINGING
SEEK A NEW DAWN
WINDS OF FORTUNE
THE LOST YEARS
HERE, THERE AND YESTERDAY
PATHS OF DESTINY
TOMORROW IS FOR EVER
THE VAGRANT KING
THOUGH THE HEAVENS MAY FALL
NO LESS THAN THE JOURNEY
BEYOND THE STORM
HAWKE'S TOR

THE RETALLICK SAGA:
BEN RETALLICK
CHASE THE WIND

HARVEST OF THE SUN
SINGING SPEARS
THE STRICKEN LAND
LOTTIE TRAGO
RUDDLEMOOR
FIRES OF EVENING
BROTHERS IN WAR

THE JAGOS OF CORNWALL:
THE RESTLESS SEA
POLRUDDEN
MISTRESS OF POLRUDDEN

We do hope that you have enjoyed reading this large print book.

Did you know that all of our titles are available for purchase?

We publish a wide range of high quality large print books including:
Romances, Mysteries, Classics
General Fiction
Non Fiction and Westerns

Special interest titles available in large print are:
The Little Oxford Dictionary
Music Book
Song Book
Hymn Book
Service Book

Also available from us courtesy of Oxford University Press:
Young Readers' Dictionary
(large print edition)
Young Readers' Thesaurus
(large print edition)

For further information or a free brochure, please contact us at:
Ulverscroft Large Print Books Ltd.,
The Green, Bradgate Road, Anstey,
Leicester, LE7 7FU, England.
Tel: (00 44) 0116 236 4325
Fax: (00 44) 0116 234 0205

HAWKE'S TOR

E.V. Thompson

It's the nineteenth century. In a tiny moorland village in Cornwall, where the residents harbour dark secrets, two policemen investigate the brutal murder of a promiscuous young wife and the disappearance of her baby. Superintendent Amos Hawke and Sergeant Tom Churchyard believe the murderer will be found within the isolated and insular community, but unravelling the tangled web of lies and deceit proves frustrating. A young gypsy girl's appearance on the scene has disturbing ramifications for Tom Churchyard — but is she the answer to the mystery?